SECOND TO THE RIGHT

THE NEVERLAND CHRONICLES
VOLUME I

T.S. KINLEY

Second to the Right, by T. S. Kinley

First paperback edition April 2022
ISBN 979-8-9859074-0-7

Book design by T.S. Kinley
Editing by Elizabeth M. Danos
Cover design by Moonpress www.moonpress.co

www.TSKinleyBooks.com

The road to your dreams can be a long and arduous one. Our debut novel is that dream come true and it would not have been possible without the unwavering support from our husbands.

To Nick and Stephen, thanks for being our biggest fans and giving us the courage to keep moving forward when we thought about giving up. This book is dedicated, with our never ending love, to you.

Author's Note

Second to the Right is a why choose spicy romance. All characters in this book are above the age of eighteen. The content in this book contains sexually explicit depictions. Please be aware of the following possible trigger warnings and read at your own discretion. Lewd NSFW depictions of sexual acts, dubious consent, bondage, drug and alcohol use, anxiety and depression, violence, assault, hostage situations, cheating, terminal illness/cancer, and death. This book ends in a cliffhanger.

Before you go. Follow T.S. Kinley on social media. Let's be friends! Check out our Instagram, Facebook, Pinterest, and Tic Tok pages and get insights into the beautifully, complicated mind of not one, but two authors! Have questions? Something you are dying to know about the amazing characters we've created? Join us online, we love to engage with our readers!

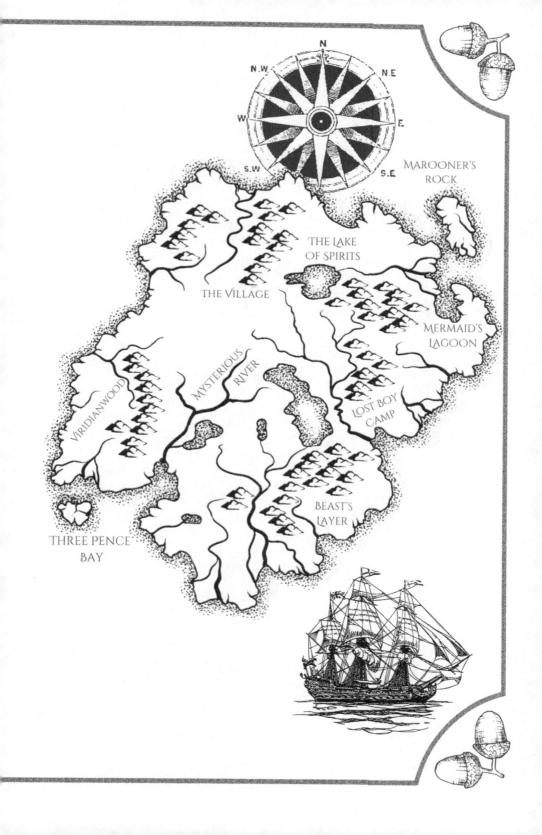

"Those who don't believe in magic
will never find it."
-Roald Dahl

PROLOGUE
-PETER-

It would be different this time. I felt it in my bones.

The past few days of watching her had made that abundantly clear. When I'd returned through the veil from Neverland, it felt as though no time had passed. Although time is funny like that, how it quietly sneaks past you. But as I sat, yet again, and watched through the window, from the outside looking in, it was obvious that everything had changed.

This time, I'd perched myself in the large oak in the backyard, which was perfectly positioned for me to see into her window. The home was the familiar old Victorian, but nothing else was the same. The gas lamps had been replaced, and the lights were much brighter than before. The furniture, the music and the girl, were all different. It had been an interesting few days as I'd watched, biding my time before I approached her. I ventured close enough at times to listen to her, waiting to see if she would tell the same stories as Wendy, but she told no stories.

She was a curious creature. I couldn't keep myself from watching her, puzzling over what she was doing and what she was saying.

Tonight, she had sat and stared at her reflection for hours, playing with her hair and putting on makeup. The outfit she had on complimented her figure in a way that had me staring at her lasciviously. Her long legs were outlined in black and the soft brown of her hair fell in waves around her face. The gentle swell of her breasts in that revealing shirt kept drawing my attention.

The way she looked had my heart racing as it does in the heat of battle and I felt a sudden urge to touch her. I broke my stare, trying to get my wayward thoughts under control as I raked my fingers through my unruly hair.

This was an entirely different experience than the last time I'd been here. This was no girl that I was watching, she was definitely a woman. I was different as well. My boyish youth, that I had clung to for so long had slowly leached away. The universe had different plans for the boy who refused to grow up. I had been forced to come to terms with the fact that absolutely nothing was permanent, no matter how much you rebelled against it. It seemed I was doomed to learn that lesson over and over again.

I wanted so badly to breeze through her window, proclaiming myself as the notorious Peter Pan and spend the night basking in her smiles as I regaled her with stories of pirates and mermaids. I got as far as springing the latch, before I thought better of it and pulled away, worried that I might scare her.

I flattened myself against the outside wall as she came to close the window. She paused there and made no move to leave. I was closer to her than I had ever been before and she was intoxicating. I could smell her, fresh and sweet, like ripe berries in summer. Her skin was creamy and smooth, her lips pouty, full and parted. She was a vision in the moonlight.

She moved away from the window as her sister called out for her. Sadly, I had noticed that her sister's health was waning, and she did not have much time left in this world. It was a shame that she had such a fleeting spirit. But this girl, this sister, was vibrant, and full of life and something altogether different.

I reached into my belt and pulled Wendy's "kiss" from the leather pouch attached there. I rolled the cool metal dome in my fingers and remembered our time together. I had been naive back then. I hadn't realized at the time, but Wendy had been a key catalyst in my life. She had changed me so completely, for both the good, and the bad. Would this girl leave her mark on me as well? Did I even want to put myself through that again? It almost broke me last time. But, the more I watched her, the more I convinced myself, that if I could only get her to come back with me, I didn't need to have all the answers right then. I had time. Against my better judgment, I was determined to bring her back with me. While she explored Neverland, I could explore her.

I was brought back to reality as I realized the two sisters were leaving the house. This was different than her normal routine that I had become accustomed to. I felt a twinge of annoyance that she would leave and deprive me of watching her. With a huff of impatience, I settled into the oak tree to wait for her to return.

I wished, briefly, that I had brought Lilleybell along to keep me company, but faeries had no room for more than one emotion at a time. Her jealousy could be all consuming and I didn't want to make the same mistakes I had made with Wendy. It would have been better if I'd gotten away with sending her off for spring cleaning, but she was a loose end that I would have to deal with later.

Alone with my thoughts, I began to get nervous, which was a relatively foreign feeling for me. If she decided not to go with me, would I stay here with her? Could I resign from my responsibilities back in Neverland? I had a vision of myself picking her up, throwing her over my shoulder, and taking her against her will to Neverland. Alas, that was something only a bastard pirate would do, those uncivilized fucks, and I wouldn't lower myself to their level.

I wondered what she would think about the Lost Boys? They had been keen to hear about the girl that I'd planned to bring back. Would they have the same feelings toward her as I did? I felt a flash of senseless jealousy at the idea of her with them. This girl was making my rational thinking go out the window.

I began to get restless just after midnight. I'm not the type to wait around for anything. I had grown tired of my tormenting thoughts, and I was spiraling down a rabbit hole of negativity. I decided it was best that I return home. Just as I was about to take my leave, and head second to the right, she returned home. I perked up instantly, thrilled at my luck. She had arrived just in time so I could continue my appreciation of her.

As they made their way into the house, I could tell something was off. Her sister was fawning over my girl, wrapping a supportive arm around her as they made their way inside. I'm not entirely sure why I thought of her as 'my girl'. I had never really considered Wendy or any one of her daughters as mine before, but my mind grabbed a hold of the notion and it just felt right with her.

The overall mood of the pair was sad and solemn. I wondered what had changed from the cheery mood they had been in when they'd left. Yet more questions surrounding this girl. She had my mind in overdrive thinking about what might've happened. I watched intently, hoping she would return to her room. The minutes ticked by like hours as I waited for her to appear.

5

She finally entered her room and walked dejectedly to the small bathroom and closed the door. I decided to get close, placing my ear to the window to see if I might hear anything that would clue me into her stark change in mood. My concern for her felt like a knot of tension in my chest and the need to make sure she was okay took over.

I could hear the sound of the shower, pouring down in her bathroom for some time. I was torn on what my next move should be. Go in to check on her or continue my wait and watch approach? My indecision was infuriating! She emerged from the bathroom in a cloud of steam. She was wearing low slung, gray sweatpants that gripped low on her hips and a short black top that exposed her flat stomach. Her skin was dewy from the steam in the air and her hair was dripping, leaving wet patches on her shirt, clinging to her chest and showing off her erect nipples.

I sucked in a deep breath as I took her in. I could no longer deny that I wanted her, to mark her and claim her as my own. A dark shadow loomed in the recesses of my mind, what consequences would I face if I followed that path? But one look at her face and my inhibitions left me. I knew that she had been crying. Her makeup was smeared, and her eyes were red and puffy. Why was she crying? The not knowing was driving me crazy.

She sat quietly at her vanity, a blank stare on her face. I looked at her reflection in the mirror, my gaze settled on her soft, caramel eyes and felt a strong desire to protect her, to take her tears away. What was going on with me? I had never felt this carnal and protective before. I was pulled from my thoughts when she swept her arm violently across the vanity, sending bottles crashing to the floor, then promptly sunk her face into her pillowed arms and started crying.

Her raw emotions spurred me into action, all my earlier hesitations forgotten. I sprung the latch in one swift flick of the wrist and landed silently on the floor behind her.

"Girl...why are you crying?"

Wendy's first words to me echoing in my head.

CHAPTER I
THE OPEN WOUND OF BETRAYAL
-GWEN-

The window was open.

Not everyone can pinpoint the moment their universe was forever altered and relate it to such a mundane thing as opening a window. But that is exactly where my life changed course, and I would never be the same.

It was the cold night air, blustering into the room that drew my attention. The engulfing chill sent an involuntary shiver up my spine. My bedroom curtains billowed in the wind that gusted through the open bay window.

How did that get open? I wondered.

I grasped my shoulders and absently rubbed my arms for warmth. The rusted hardware must have finally given out on the old window, or at least that's what I told myself. My family had owned this house since the 18th century and the logical conclusion was that it was always in some state of disrepair. I sat briefly on the window seat and paused before closing the window. It was a bitter London evening as the last vestiges of winter gave its final breath before relenting to spring. The moon was full tonight, setting a warm glow to the landscape below while the stars peppered the sky above. I smiled and took a moment to enjoy the beauty of it.

The old house groaned in protest with the wind, creating an ethereal moaning as it passed through. I felt the hairs raise on my arms and goose pimples spread across my skin. An odd sense of foreboding crept into me as the crisp air filled my lungs. It was a feeling I couldn't quite discern, something like anticipation mixed with anxiety. I felt an expectation that something was about to happen and it had me on edge.

"Gwen?" my sister, Michaela, called to me from down stairs. "Are you ready yet, birthday girl?"

Disrupting me from my reverie, I quickly pulled the window closed and managed to secure the latch, which was oddly perfect and did nothing to relieve the uneasiness I felt.

"Coming! Just need to grab my purse," I shouted down to her.

I took one final look in the tall mirror before I headed downstairs for our night on the town. I turned to check out how good my ass looked in these leather pants. It was definitely something I would never have picked out on my own, but Michaela had been right about the outfit, even though I would never admit it to her.

The fabric of my blouse clung to me in all the right places, showing off what little cleavage I could manage and the black lace of my bralette peeked out from the deep V neck of the top. Satisfied with my look, I flopped down on my bed, slipping on my favorite peep toe heels and grabbed my purse.

I found Michaela sitting at the kitchen island, staring at the little compact she was holding, intently applying her lipstick. Her face, that had once been so much like mine, now appeared thin and gaunt. Her recent treatments had taken their toll on her. Her beautiful hair had not grown back yet and tonight she sported a sleek, platinum blonde wig with a heavy bang. As children, we had often been confused for twins, but now the stark contrast between us broke my heart.

"Damn, eighteen is looking great on you!" my sister squealed as she noticed me and pulled me into a quick hug. "I wish mum and dad could be here to see you," she added softly, her eyes taking on a far away look as she remembered our late parents.

"Thanks, love," I said, a bit distantly. I was still trying to shake off the feeling I'd had at the window seat and I didn't want to add to it with thoughts of another birthday without my mum and dad.

"Everything okay?" she asked, brows instantly furrowed in concern.

"It's nothing, the bay window blew open and I guess it just creeped me out."

"It's Gram's fault for always filling our heads with her so-called fairytales about this place when we were little."

"Ugh, yes! I remember spending nights awake, petrified that someone was looking in my window because of those stories." She giggled at me as I rolled my eyes and quickly changed topics.

"Are you sure you're up for this tonight?" I asked quietly. I was hoping not to offend her but I was genuinely concerned over what a night of drinking and dancing might do to her frail health.

"Sweetie, I wouldn't miss this for the world! It's not like you turn 18 every day. It's been far too long since we've been able to act our age. So I'm taking you out and we are going to have the night of our lives." Her exuberant voice belied her weakened body.

I decided to put my worries to bed as best I could, because I selfishly wanted to spend this night with her. Not only was it my birthday, but she had just recently finished chemo and her cancer was now in remission for the second time and it was a victory worth celebrating.

"Let me text Jamie that we're leaving and he can meet us at the club."

"Are you sure you want him to come along? You're not going to have as much fun if he's there," she groaned exaggeratedly.

I gave her a chastising look, "Oh stop, can you please just give him a chance? I really like this one Mic."

"I just..." she paused, carefully considering her words. "I just think you can do better. I know you've been swooning over this guy for months now, but I don't trust him. That whole thing with his ex-girlfriend really rubbed me the wrong way."

"He explained that already, Mic! Nothing happened, she just needed closure and I think it was sweet of him not to blow her off. He told me it's over and I believe him," I rebutted in his defense. She was never going to let that go.

"My gut is telling me that something is off with him. But I've said my piece and if you trust him, then that will have to be good enough for me." Her words sounded genuinely concerned. "I can only hope, when you go away to university this fall, you'll meet some smoldering book nerd in one of your literature classes, who will make you forget all about Jamie Holder."

But Jamie Holder wasn't just some random boy. He had been the object of my affection since grade school. Albeit my affections had always been from afar, but all that had changed when he had finally noticed me in our last semester at school. I could agree that he wasn't perfect, but neither was I and I rationalized it by admitting that I couldn't hold him to impossible standards. Plus, the fact that he was hot as hell definitely hindered my better judgment when it came to him.

"Well, your intuition is wrong this time. I actually think I'm starting to fall in love with him," I admitted hesitantly, putting hopeful words into the infatuation I'd been feeling. I almost laughed at the look of shock on her face.

"Okay, this conversation is getting way too deep and it's your birthday so I'm not gonna argue with you about your lousy choice in men. We'll table this one until tomorrow."

I smiled at her and brushed it off, she had never liked any of the men I dated. She was like the boy who cried wolf. This time I wasn't about to listen to her warnings, especially not when my tall, dark and handsome crush had finally taken an interest in me. But she was right about one thing, I didn't want to argue. It was my eighteenth birthday after all.

THE CLUB WAS PACKED with half dressed people, the air thick and filled with the smell of musky sweat and stale beer. Michaela pulled me toward the VIP section at the back of the club where she had a quick exchange with the large bouncer standing guard. He pulled aside the velvet ropes and ushered us in. The swanky lounge area was filled with beautiful people on sleek white, modern couches, flirting and drinking around marble coffee tables. I spotted Jamie, staring down at his phone while he waited for me in an area marked as reserved.

"Hey babe!" he called when he saw me walk up, quickly pocketing his phone. I smiled a stupid school girl smile at him and bit my lip.

"Hey!" I said as I reached up on my tiptoes to give him a kiss. I was planning on a quick peck, but he deepened it and thrust his tongue into my mouth, tasting me briefly before pulling back and leaving me dazed.

"You are killing me in those pants. Turn around and let me see that ass."

"Nice Jamie, could've maybe started with Happy Birthday?" Michaela scoffed, her tone dripping with disapproval.

"Nice to see you too, Mickey," he responded tersely, not even bothering to look over at her, which was a good thing because she was staring daggers at him. She hated being called Mickey and he knew it. Her glare was interrupted by the sound of his phone chiming in his pocket with a new text.

"You gonna get that?" Mic asked flippantly, still holding onto her grudge. He continued to ignore her and turned to me.

"I'm putting my phone on silent so nothing can interrupt us tonight. Come on, let me buy you your first drink."

He placed his hand on the small of my back, ushering me toward the bar. Once I was in front of him, I heard a resounding *crack*, accompanied by a sharp sting on my ass as he spanked me, hard. I blushed uncontrollably. Michaela must have been mortified, but he made me feel sexy, even if it was a bit crude.

"Plenty more spankings for my birthday girl tonight," he whispered into my ear, his deep, husky voice full of innuendo.

He easily pushed through to the bar, his six foot five frame towering over almost every one. He got quick service as the female bartender catered to him right away, her voice high and flirty, her eyes lingering over him too long for my liking. He gave her a charming smile as he turned back to me with our drinks. He handed me over a shot of Jäger.

I hate Jäger.

I felt a moment of aggravation that he hadn't asked me what I wanted, but in typical girl fashion, I convince myself that it was sweet of him to get my drink.

"Thank you!" I yell to him, the loud techno drowning out our voices.

"Alright babe, down the hatch and let me get you on that dance floor." He pounded the shot and looked at me expectantly.

Like a child anticipating Gram's cough syrup, I held my breath and managed to get the nasty liquid down in one gulp. I had to continue to hold my breath to keep the drink down as my stomach rebelled. Michaela was instantly beside me, pushing a Captain and Coke into my hands. I gave her a relieved look. I took a few quick sips and finally got the taste of the Jäger out of my mouth. Jamie downed a second shot and grabbed my hand, pulling me to the dance floor.

The bass from the club pulsed through me as we danced. I was slicked in sweat, with strands of my hair plastered to my chest. I let my body sway to the music, intermittently sipping at my drink. My hand was wet and sticky as it kept spilling, but I didn't care. My glass hadn't been empty all night. I think Michaela was set on getting me sloppy drunk tonight. I was thankful that my shift at the cafe tomorrow didn't start until late in the afternoon. I had a feeling that my hangover would be brutal. I pushed the thought from my mind, I just wanted to act my age for once and not worry about my responsibilities for one night. I knew more alcohol would help with that. My inhibitions vanished with each passing drink and I began to shamelessly grind my ass against Jamie. He kept pace with me, grabbing my hips and pulling me closer.

"You are so sexy," he growled in my ear. "You have to come home with me tonight."

I giggled, peeking over my shoulder at him, giving him my best attempt at a seductive smile. I had promised to spend the night with Michaela, but I was enjoying his attention so much that I couldn't bring myself to turn him down just yet. Michaela appeared in front of me and grabbed my hand, attempting to pull me from Jamie. I was about to protest at her intrusion and being a total buzzkill to my libido when she leaned in to whisper in my ear, "I have something I need to give you. Can you please come with me?" She was insistent and continued her attempt to pull me from the dance floor. I turned back to Jamie with an apologetic look.

"I'll be right back, I promise. Mic just needs me for a minute." He shook his head at me, looking irritated at the interruption.

"Yeah, sure, whatever." His tone conveyed his irritation.

My older sister had always been overprotective when it came to boys. It was frustrating at times, but I couldn't fault her for it. I knew it came from a place of love and any boy worth his weight would understand that. I just desperately hoped that Jamie would. She pulled me to the couch that she'd reserved for us in the VIP lounge and I sat down hard. My head was spinning from all the alcohol and my gracefulness had gone out the window.

"Happy birthday baby sis," she crooned sweetly as she handed me a small box wrapped in golden paper and topped with a red bow.

I looked at her with that 'you shouldn't have' look and pulled her in for a hug before I even opened the tiny box. I pulled off the wrapping paper and opened the gift to find a familiar piece of jewelry nestled inside. I lifted out the gilded acorn locket that had been my mother's, and her mother's before that, and on and on, for more than a hundred years.

I popped the delicate clasp and looked for the inscription that I knew was inside, 'To die will be an awfully big adventure.' The quote had always seemed morbid to me and it gave me chills reading it now. I never understood why anyone would put such a quote on a prized piece of jewelry.

The heirloom locket now also included a miniature photo of Michaela and I, smiling and happy during a time before my parent's accident and her cancer had cast a gloom over everything. The words and the image affected me in my altered state so much that I felt the prick of tears come to my eyes. The drinks were making me overly sentimental.

"The quote was meant for both of us, Gwen. It's as much about living, as it is about death. Momento mori," she stated, answering the question I hadn't spoken allowed.

I stared at her in shocked awe. Her use of the Latin phrase meaning "Remember that you must die" was so profound. For the first time, the rationale for the inscription made sense to me. It was a reminder to live your life in the moment, with the knowledge that you will eventually die.

"I'm going to be okay. We both have big adventures awaiting us, just down different paths."

"I don't understand, why are you giving this to me? Mum left it to you. You're the oldest, that's how it works," I croaked out in a shaky voice, unable to say anything more or else I would break out in real tears. But I knew why she was giving it to me. I just refused to put that thought into words, but she did it for me instead.

"Gwen," she said my name gently, "this locket is meant to be handed down and I won't be here long enough to make that happen. It has to go to you. Here, let me put it on for you."

"How can you say that? You just reached remission. It's not coming back this time! I don't want the locket, it's yours." My emotional mind rationalized that if I just didn't accept it, then the tragic future she was painting wouldn't come true.

"Gwendolyn Mary Darling Carlisle, you know the odds are slim to none that the remission will last. This last treatment only bought us a little more time. So you *will* accept it because it is mine to give and I am giving it to you now. I want to give it of my own free will rather than you putting it in a box with the rest of my things when I'm gone." Her stern voice left little room for me to argue.

"If I accept it, it's not because I think you are going anywhere, and you have to agree to take it back when you have a daughter of your own to give it to."

She looked at me with pity in her eyes, pity of all things. I should be pitying her, she was the one casually talking about her early death as if it was no big deal.

"Okay, Gwen," she conceded, obviously not wanting to upset me any further. "Now turn around and let me put it on you."

I swept my sweat soaked hair to one side. Cold air ominously rushed down my exposed neck, chilling me instantly. I turned my back to her quickly, hoping she wouldn't see the fear in my eyes. The fear of what she was trying to tell me, by giving me this locket. She clasped the pendant in place and it settled beautifully between my breasts. I grasped it and the weight of it felt oddly warm and comforting in my hand.

"It looks beautiful on you, just like it did on mum," she said appraisingly. A proud smile lit up her face as she looked me over. Even her eyes seemed glassy for a brief moment before she was on her feet again and pulling me back to the bar.

"Time for another drink!" she exclaimed and weaseled her way to the front of the bar and ordered us another round.

"A toast!" she yelled as she handed me a shot of Johnnie Walker. Oh she knew me so well. "To my baby sister! Cheers to good health and a man who is sexy as fuck and will fulfill your wildest dreams!"

"Cheers!" we both yelled in unison, clinking our shot glasses together and throwing them back. I turned back to the dance floor and attempted to pull Mic with me but she pulled back.

"Go on without me, I'm gonna sit at the bar and people watch. Go find Jamie and enjoy yourself." She gave me a one-sided smile as if she could only be partially happy for me when it came to Jamie. I smiled back at her and headed off on my own to find him.

I danced my way through the packed floor, not seeing him anywhere. I'd started getting nervous, worried he was avoiding me. I desperately hoped he wouldn't be too pissed at me over Mic's mother hen routine. I was about to head to the restrooms to see if I could find him there, when a white dress caught my attention. I could make out the back of a curvy blonde in a shadowed corner of the night club. The black lights caused her dress to glow purple in the darkness. Her hair was cascading down the back of her skin tight dress and I could see that she wasn't alone.

A man's hand was cupping her ass. When she turned her head to the side, I was instantly frozen in place when I saw that the man groping her was Jamie! He pulled her hips into his like he'd just done to me on the dance floor, all the while he kissed up her neck and took her mouth. I stared in shock, completely stunned, my heart dropping at the sight of them together. I watched as the two of them made out in front of me, allowing it to go on much longer than I should. Before I knew what I was doing, I marched over to them, feeling utterly enraged, and yanked at the hand that he was still cupping her ass with.

"Jamie Fucking Holder!" I knew I was feeling more bold than usual. Normally, I would have just turned around and ran from the entire situation.

At my intrusion, the blonde turned toward me and recognition hit me. I was stuck in a moment of complete disbelief. Of course it was Bella! The girl Jamie had been dating before me. The girl he'd sworn that he no longer had any feelings for.

"Gwen, it's not... it's not what you think. Bella and I were just... talking," he stumbled over his words as he stepped toward me, his inebriated mind trying to play catch up to the situation.

"I think I know what I saw!" I shouted back at him, I could feel the disbelief dissolve and give way to anger again. I struggled to keep my temper as Bella gave me a malicious smile from her position behind him. He tried to grab my hand but I yanked it back quickly, the idea of him touching me now turning my stomach.

"Can we talk 'bout this later? You're drunk... I'm drunk... you're not thinking clearly." He tried to make me question myself and the irrational girl who was still holding onto hope was tempted to believe him. But, Bella destroyed all of my contemplating.

She stepped from behind him, pressed her chest against him and said, "I'll let you handle this with your little friend, Jamie. Text me once you've cleared things up." She planted a slow and sultry kiss on his cheek, leaving her mark of red lipstick behind. He did nothing to stop her or push her away. She sauntered off into the crowd, completely indifferent, as if she hadn't just dropped a bomb on my relationship.

"Is that who you were texting earlier?" I was fuming as I remembered him on his phone when we first arrived. I grabbed at his pocket in a flash and pulled his phone out before he had a chance to react, the alcohol making him slow.

"Gwen don't touch my... you're acting like a fucking child!" He tried to belittle me, but I needed to know the truth. The screen sprung to life, illuminating my face in the dark club, and there were the unread texts from Bella.

Hurry up and ditch her.
Take me home already! I'm not going to wait 4ever
for you 2 end things with her.

Realization hit me that I had been his side piece. That he had been sleeping with me while still carrying on a relationship with her. Our relationship was a foregone conclusion and he was simply waiting for the opportune time to dump me. Clearly my birthday was it. I thought I was going to be sick right there on the dance floor.

My fight or flight response began to kick in at this point and I chose the latter. I couldn't stand to look at him. I turned to leave, but Jamie grabbed my wrist and held me in place.

"Don't walk away from me," his words slightly slurred. I tried to pull away from him but he only tightened his grip, pain shooting up my arm.

"Stop it Jamie! You're hurting me! Let me go!" I screamed at him as I continued to struggle against his iron grip.

"Nope... not letting you go." He chuckled in my face, the smell of alcohol hot on his breath. "You're coming home with me and we're gonna... we're gonna work this out. You've been shaking your ass at me all night. I know that's what you really want. Don't be a tease and let's get out of here."

I stared at him in disgust. Was it the drinks talking, or had he always been a total dick? Had I been blind to it all this time? I began to feel panicked now, his tight grip was unrelenting and the pain only intensified the more I struggled. I needed to get away, now, but he was so much bigger than me. My mind was sluggish and there was only one thing I could think to do.

I stepped toward him as if I was giving in. He smirked at me, but the moment I got close, I kneed him in the crotch with as much force as I could muster. He grunted and doubled over in pain, releasing my wrist. I took advantage and fled through the crowd. I could hear him calling out my name behind me. My smaller frame allowed me to make my way through the throng of people and I lost him quickly as I made my way to the exit. I held it together until I burst through the doors and then the tears began to flow.

I wasn't thinking clearly. I just kept seeing the two of them together on repeat in my brain. Michaela had been right not to trust him all along. I needed to find Michaela, and we needed to leave before Jamie could find me. Mic would know what to say to calm me down, even if I knew she would be silently thinking *told you so* the whole time. I knew she wouldn't throw it in my face, at least not for a while anyway. I just wanted to go home, put on some frumpy pajamas and hibernate under my blankets until I couldn't cry anymore. I pulled my phone out of my purse and texted Mic.

I need you now, meet me outside.

Within moments, Michaela busted through the doors of the club looking wide eyed and frantic.

"What happened?" Her voice was full of empathy as she took me in her arms. I'd been constantly wiping the tears from my face with the back of my hand. I must have looked like an absolute mess with black mascara smeared across my face.

"You were right, and I don't want to talk about it. Can you please take me home?" The statement started off strong but quickly fizzled out into a sob.

"Oh Sweetie, I'm so sorry." She pulled me in for a hug, but I didn't feel like hugging, I just felt heavy. She hugged me anyway, patting the back of my hair as if I was a child. She pulled away and looked me over, landing on my wrist and gently holding it up to inspect the bruises that had already started to form there.

"Did he do this to you?" she asked, her voice coming out cold and harsh, in a way I'd never heard before.

"It's nothing. Let's just go before he finds us," I deflected.

"I'm going to kick his fucking ass!" I gave an involuntary chuckle at the preposterous idea, but she was dead serious. The open wound of the betrayal was still so fresh, that the laugh seemed inappropriate and it was gone in an instant.

"Please Mic, I just want to go home."

CHAPTER II
NOTHING LASTS FOREVER

Michaela offered just about anything she could think of to try and console me. She offered to make popcorn and watch movies, draw a bath for me to soak in, and even a full-on bitch session where we could plan out how we would cut off his dick. She even offered a simple shoulder for me to cry on too. All I wanted was to be alone so I could have a shameless pity party for myself.

"Let me know if you need *anything*!" she emphasized, "I'm just in my room okay?" I barely heard her as I walked down the hall toward my room.

"I love you!" was the last thing I heard her say as my door clicked into place.

I felt like I was on autopilot. I peeled off my clothes and got in the shower. The hot spray did nothing to relieve the tumultuous emotions I was feeling. I wavered between the pain of feeling as though I was not good enough, to fits of anger at being duped by a handsome face.

The worst part of it all was that I had allowed myself to hope, to believe that my happily ever after was just around the corner. Now it was just gone and I was alone. The only person I had left in this world was Michaela. What on earth would I do if she left me too? But should I have expected anything different? My life had gone to shit over the last several years and nothing ever seemed to end well for me, like I had some fucked up curse following me around.

I pulled on my favorite, worn sweatpants and a crop top, wincing as the fabric pressed against the tender flesh on my wrist where Jamie had grabbed me. I sat down at my vanity to remove the last remnants of my makeup. I could feel the emotions building up like a pressure cooker inside me until they exploded. I raked my arm across my vanity in one violent sweep, sending makeup and perfume bottles crashing to the floor. I buried my face into my arms as my emotions came pouring out of me in big, fat tears.

"Girl… why are you crying?"

I jumped at the sound of the unfamiliar voice, startled out of the darkness. I spun around to find a man standing in the shadows by the window behind me. I couldn't quite make out his features since he was cloaked by the darkness, but the light filtering in from the full moon highlighted his high cheekbones and chiseled jawline. I jumped up from the vanity, knocking the seat over as I plastered myself to the wall and started to sidestep toward the door. Panic began to overwhelm me at the sight of a strange man in my bedroom.

"I have some money in my purse, you...you can have it, just don't hurt me," I stammered my words as I continued to inch toward the door. He stared at me curiously, a slight smirk on his face.

"I'm not here to hurt you," he said incredulously, his voice was soft and nonthreatening, "I'm just here to get my girl." He stated this plainly as if I was somehow obtuse for not understanding that in the first place.

"Your girl?" I asked, completely confused by the whole situation.

Then it occurred to me that I must be either totally wasted, drugged, or I was having a complete mental breakdown. Had Jamie's betrayal been the last straw that my psyche could handle? Here I was starting a dialogue with an intruder who was probably here to rape me. The whole situation felt surreal, as if I'd ultimately dreamt up the entire encounter. I thought of screaming then, but if this was real the last thing I wanted to do was bring Michaela into this. I wouldn't forgive myself if something happened to her.

"You are a daughter of Wendy, are you not?" I was

derailed by his strange question.

"No, my mother's name is Mary," I replied, baffled and yet compelled to answer. I really should have been planning my next move but I felt an unnatural calmness wash over me, like the events unfolding seemed strangely familiar to me. He looked thoughtful in that moment, as if carefully considering what I'd just said, but then he was instantly animated again as if something had occurred to him.

"See I knew you were the right girl," he proclaimed. "I'm quite sure Wendy's mother was Mary too! Must be a family name," he mused to himself. He was excited by my answer and came toward me, stepping into the puddle of light that was streaming in from the open bathroom door.

Once I could see him clearly, I was struck by the oddity of his clothes. He was wearing tight, black pants, with worn holes in both knees, a sleeveless, woven tunic top in olive green that was cinched around his waist by a thick leather belt adorned with pouches and what looked like a knife, holstered on his left side. His arms were covered in tribal tattoos, accentuating his muscular shape— defined but not bulky. His face was handsome, and I was taken aback at my instant attraction to him. Yet more evidence that something was seriously wrong with me. I had an immediate, visceral attraction to a stalker that had broken into my house.

When I didn't respond, he looked at the ground as if he was thinking hard about something and ran his hand through his hair. The faint light caught on the auburn strands, leaving it looking tousled as if he'd just gotten out of bed. He looked up at me again, a cocky smile lit his face as he stepped so close to me that I could feel the heat from his body. He reached out toward me, and I froze. I couldn't seem to make myself move, it was as if I was completely entranced by him. He grasped the acorn locket and rolled it between his fingers, staring at it thoughtfully.

"If you are not a daughter of Wendy, then why do you have my kiss around your neck?" he asked, sounding rather smug in his deductions.

"Do I know you?" I whispered. The situation continued to nag at me, as if I had heard this before, but my mind was still foggy with alcohol that I couldn't seem to put two and two together.

"Of course you know who I am. It's me, Peter!"

My brain made a leap of logic then that confirmed that I was completely mad.

"Peter, as in Peter Pan?" I laughed a little at the ridiculous sound of my own words.

"See, I knew the daughters of Wendy would never forget about me! Girls are too smart for forgetting." He was still standing extraordinarily close to me, and I could feel myself blush at his playfulness. I couldn't stop staring into his eyes. They were a dark umber, rich and earthy. They were deep and inquisitive, with a flicker of mischief.

"You can't be Peter Pan. You're not a boy, and Peter Pan

never grows up." This bit of lore I knew for a fact, the stories always portrayed him as the cocky boy who refused to grow up. He scowled at this comment, apparently I had touched a nerve or poked a hole in his facade.

"Don't you know that nothing lasts forever, no matter how hard you wish it to be so?" He said this rather dejectedly as if he was still mourning his lost youth, but it only lasted for a moment before his cheeky little smile returned.

"But you could be my 'nothing' if you wanted?"

Oh my god. I couldn't believe even Peter Pan wasn't above a cheesy pick up line. Although it wasn't the worst one I'd heard, it was actually kind of endearing.

"So, are you ready, Daughter of Wendy?"

"My name is Gwen and ready for what exactly?"

"Well… to return to Neverland of course. It's time for spring cleaning."

It was the words 'spring cleaning' that brought a particular section of the faerie tales from my youth rushing back to me. We had grown up with the recounting of Peter Pan's epic adventures. But at the end of the story, Gram had said that Peter was supposed to come and take Wendy to Neverland for spring cleaning every year. But in typical Neverland fashion, Peter had soon forgotten and the visits had stopped altogether. She had always made mention that Wendy was a distant relative of ours, but I thought all grandmothers told their granddaughters that to make them feel special. I never thought that the stories were real. Who in their right mind would?

Since I had no logical explanation as to what was happening, I settled on the notion that this was a dream. I decided that if my subconscious thought I needed an escape to Neverland with a grown and gorgeous Peter Pan, then I would indulge myself to the fullest.

"I don't know how to fly, Peter. Will you teach me?" I asked coquettishly, fully embracing the lucid dream. I felt his fingers brush mine and my skin felt hot where we touched.

"It takes faith and trust. Do you believe in me, Gwen?" he asked softly. I found myself nodding even though the question seemed strange. He reached out and took my hand in his warm grasp. His touch shocked me, even my most vivid dreams had never felt this real. His hand was rough and calloused, but the gentle squeeze he gave me was reassuring.

In a flash of movement he pulled me towards him. The unexpected momentum sent me stumbling forward and I fell into him. My palms planted firmly on his chest to steady myself. His strong arms caught me effortlessly. His frame was solid beneath my hands, the warmth of him radiating into me. I looked up into his face, a little sheepishly, to find him smiling down at me. He cupped my face in his hand and rubbed a fine dust on my cheekbone, all the while holding my stare. He moved forward as if he planned to kiss me but then whispered in my ear.

"Think a happy thought, Gwen." But all I could think

about in that moment was him. With his arms still securely around me, we miraculously lifted into the air as though we were weightless. It was then that my overly stressed and still intoxicated mind threw in the towel and everything faded into darkness.

CHAPTER III
NEVERLAND'S SECRETS

I awoke to the sound of tinkling bells.

"Lill! Don't be rude."

"No! we are not going to sacrifice her!"

"Stop! Lill, don't touch her! She's just here for spring cleaning."

I opened my eyes to find a tiny, glowing, buxom… faerie? My mind told me it wasn't possible and yet she was hovering inches from my face. She wore what looked like a white lily blossom fashioned upside down and belted. The petals barely covered her ample thighs. Her platinum blonde hair styled in a high ponytail, like a luminescent pin-up with wings. Had I really just seen a faerie? Where was I? Was I lying in the grass? Did I really just fly to Neverland, with Peter fucking Pan? I was in a complete state of disbelief. Could this be, the infamous... Tinkerbell? The naughty little sprite I remembered from Gram's stories.

I slowly sat up, rubbed my hands down my face and tried to clear the confusion setting in. "Tinkerbell?" I asked.

The tiny faerie huffed and put her hands on her hips. The sound of bells became louder, more rapid, as if filled with irritation.

Peter laughed, catching my attention.

"Where am I? Is this—"

"This is Lilleybell, She's our faerie. And this," he smiled, "this is Neverland. Lill calm down, this is my girl, Gwen, Daughter of Wendy."

Her expression immediately soured at the mention of 'my girl' and I was quickly met with a death glare, when he mentioned Wendy. It would appear as though Lilleybell was as jealous and sassy as her predecessor. Clearly she wasn't thrilled to see me.

"Lovely to meet you, Lill," a touch of sarcasm in my voice.

She quickly flew to Peter's shoulder and tried to hide behind his ear. Peeking out, pretending to be coy, as she sized me up.

"She doesn't like that you called her Tinkerbell." He paused in thought. "Who is this Tinkerbell anyway?" he asked, turning his expression to Lill, who was now going off in a mad symphony of bells. "No Lill, I don't have another faerie on the side. I swear."

Lilleybell flitted out from behind Peter's ear, mocking him as he spoke. She scrunched up her face in anger, and flew off leaving a puff of sparkling dust. I tried hard not to laugh at the little outburst. A smirk forming at the corner of my mouth.

"Don't worry about her, she's just jealous. Lill likes to think she's the only faerie I've ever had. Honestly... there have been quite a lot of them, it's hard to remember them all. But she'll be fine." He shifted his focus back to me.

I got the feeling he wanted to change the subject. Either he didn't want to speak of Tink or he really did forget about her, just like the stories had suggested. I wondered what else he had forgotten over the years. Would I begin to forget, as time went on here?

"Are you okay?" he asked as he looked me over, inspecting me for injuries. His hands and eyes washed up and down my body. Nervous energy made me very aware of our unspoken chemistry.

"I'm fine. A little overwhelmed, to be honest. I did just wake up in another realm, world, dimension or whatever this place is, with a faerie hovering inches from my face. How? When?"

Breathe, Gwen.

The landscape around me started spinning. I pulled in a deep breath to center myself before continuing.

"How long have I been out?"

"You look like you're going to pass out again. Take a breath." He paused, giving me a moment. "We flew, don't you remember?" He looked at me with concern. "I was showing you how to fly and you just went limp in my arms. Are you sure you're alright? You passed out, more than once."

I smiled and nodded. My face blushed with embarrassment, but his concern was quite charming. "I'm perfectly fine Peter. I just need a minute."

He smiled, a weight lifting from his brow. "Well then, let me help you up."

It was then that I noticed I was still in my dumpy grey sweatpants. Thank god I'd chosen the crop top. I could only imagine what my hair and face looked like after the night I'd had. I must have been an utter mess. I quickly raked my fingers through my hair, pushing it back away from my face. I was still in my PJs. Clearly, that was proof that I was still dreaming. This had to be a dream. A very clear, vivid dream. I thought that maybe I should pinch myself, but I was worried that I might wake up before I had a chance to explore.

I took a moment to look around. We appeared to be in a grassy meadow. There were wild flowers in the most alluring shades of violet. When the wind blew a wave of color would shift from indigo to fuchsia. There was a brilliance to the colors here, saturated and ethereal. This place was pure magic, pure beauty. The air smelled of fresh rain fall, clean and crisp. Off in the distance, trees were all around us, shrouding the rest of the landscape, successfully keeping all of Neverland's secrets.

"Come, let me show you where we live. There is a place I'd like to take you, where you can see all of Neverland."

"We?" I questioned, confused for a moment. But then I remembered the Lost Boys! How could I forget? "You mean the Lost Boys?" I asked, trying to hide my piqued interest. Had the Lost Boys grown up too? Were they as hot as Peter? Oh my god, was I stranded on an island full of hot Lost Boys? I had so many questions.

"Well yes, I *am* Captain of the lost boys," he said with cocky arrogance. "We live just through the trees there. Come on." He waved his hand implying that I should walk with him. "You can meet the boys later. They're likely out on an adventure, probably won't be back until later" —he smirked— "it'll just be the two of us." He bit his lip as he reached for my hand.

His signals were not subtle. I had been getting little flirtations from him since the moment we met. Was I just picking up on cocky bad boy vibes, or did I leave him wanting? Maybe that's just how he was? Direct, fearless. I could learn a thing from him. I think it was Aristotle who said *'He who has overcome his fears will truly be free.'* Peter was the epitome of free. And now it was my turn to be fearless— free. What choice did I have but to follow him anyway? I was at his mercy. I took his hand and followed him blindly, into the forest. It was then that I knew I was in trouble, this boy mesmerized me.

THE CAMP WAS NESTLED amongst the treetop canopies. Sunshine poked through the leaves as they rustled in the breeze, in a dance of shadow and light. Swaying rope bridges and multi-level platforms connected the small wooden structures from tree to tree, allowing its inhabitants to remain high above the ground. I was awestruck. My mind was reeling, how was this possible? I was walking into a scene from a fairytale, holding Peter Pan's hand. Faeries were flying all around us, leaving sparkling trails of glitter behind them. If you listened carefully, just beyond the bird song, you could hear the sound of ringing bells, faerie chatter. We were completely surrounded by nature.

My mind clouded with thoughts of Mic. She would love this. I wished she were here to share in the insanity that had clearly taken me over. Bearing the weight of this reality would have been much easier with my sister at my side. At least we would both be losing our minds together. I wondered how long I'd been away. But, if I was away, that would mean this was real. Was I ready to believe that? The truth was, I was getting closer. I wanted to believe.

"Welcome to our home, Gwen." His voice brought me

back to the moment, as we approached a large oak in the center of the compound. Propped up against the massive trunk was a makeshift ladder leading up to a doorway carved into the side of the tree. Above the doorway was a weathered sign. Written in a youthful scratch were the words.

Rulez
1. Alwaze beleve in fariz
2. Pirats R bad.
3. Nevr evr grow up!!

A reminder of years past. The days of Peter's boyhood were gone. His physical form now that of a young man, and a gorgeous one at that.

I followed his lead, up the ladder and through the doorway onto the labyrinth of suspension bridges. From up here, you could see hundreds of lanterns hanging from the branches above. Signs of Mother Nature trying to reclaim her land over the years, blended beautifully with the raw construction of the wooden houses. Vines wound around the rope railings of the bridges. Moss and evergreen covered the roof tops. There was a charm to the woodland camp, a welcoming warmth.

"We have a crow's nest, you know, a look out point. From up there you can see all of the island. Trust me, It's definitely something you'll want to see."

"How far up are we going? How big is Neverland anyway?"

"Just big enough. Don't worry, you'll see. This way." He nodded to the right.

A left here, a right there, and we approached another makeshift ladder. This one climbed high into the treetops. The crow's nest looked like it was plucked off a pirate ship and placed precariously onto the tree. I wondered, could this be from the infamous Hook's Jolly Roger? Did Peter and the boys keep a souvenir after defeating the sinister pirate? The ornate railing was covered in moss suggesting it had been there for some time.

"There isn't much room up here," I said as I squeezed my way up into the small circular space.

Between the tree and the two of us, we barely had room to move. I placed my hands on his chest. He was cut. Physical activity had been kind to his physique, and he smelled amazing. Seriously, he must have been dripping in pheromones. His scent was intoxicating, warm and earthy, with a touch of cinnamon and a hint of leather. It was hard to describe, but it was doing things to my body. I wanted to bury my face in his neck and just breathe him in. I wanted to be dripping in his scent.

"What, are you afraid to be close to me? ...Gwen?" He raised his brow.

"Yes, No!" Oh god, was I just sniffing him? What was wrong with me? I looked up at him getting lost in thoughts of his lips. "No, I'm not afraid to be close to you." God help me if he bit his lip again.

"Close your eyes."

He gently turned me around, placing his hands on my hips. I realized I was about to see Neverland for the first time. I felt anxious and excited. I wasn't sure if it was the idea of seeing Neverland or if it was Peter. Either way, nervous energy surged through my body.

"Are you ready?" he asked, excitedly.

I nodded, "Mm-hmm."

"Open your eyes," he whispered into my ear.

I was speechless. The view in front of me was almost too beautiful for words. Brilliant greens from the forest canopy danced against bright blue skies. Mountain tops peeked out of the clouds, in a contrast of sharp erratic cliffs and billowing wisps. A large waterfall flowed from the mountain side into a lagoon that seemed to glisten with gemstones. The surrounding seas were a rich sapphire, the sandy floor of the shallows reflected a vibrant turquoise. The shore lines were littered with inviting beach coves and perilous cliff formations. Vast forests and meadows spread out across the landscape. Flocks of birds soared in and out of view, a reminder that this was real. Neverland was revealing more of her secrets. A little taste, and I wanted more. "It's breathtaking. Paradise."

He moved his hands from my hips and placed them on the railing, caging me in his arms and closing the gap between us. I could feel his breath on the back of my neck.

"It is beautiful isn't it?" he said, looking out at the view. I felt his lips brush against my ear, sending a shiver down my back, as he whispered, "But not as beautiful as you."

I felt my cheeks warm as a smile escaped.

He thought I was beautiful?

I felt butterflies in my stomach. He was bold, this Peter.

I giggled, "Thank you." Sincerity in my appreciation. It wasn't everyday someone called me beautiful. I turned to face him. His eyes locked on mine. He pushed a strand of hair behind my ear sending me reeling.

"Gwen, tell me. Why were you crying, back in your room?"

And just like that, my heart sank. I could feel the tears start to pool in my eyes.

"I caught my boyfriend... with another woman." Still raw from the events of the evening, I couldn't keep the tears at bay and they began to stream down my cheeks. "I thought he loved me, how could I be so foolish?" I spoke the words quietly. Ashamed at my willingness to share intimate details of my life with a man I'd just met.

"Beautiful girl, please don't cry. You are here in Neverland now. He can no longer cause you pain." He gently wiped the tears from my face. I absently touched the tender bruises on my arm, still in shock how the whole thing had ended.

Peter's gaze landed on my wrist, "Did he do that to you?" He scowled as he ran his fingers softly over the dark purple bruises that made a perfect handprint on my wrist. I couldn't speak at that moment and only nodded. "Shall I cross the veil and kill him for you?" his face was absolutely serious, "Then we can forget all about him."

I laughed at the thought of Peter's solution. "As much as I would like to see Jamie pay for what he did, killing him isn't an option. Forgetting about him sounds nice though."

"Neverland can help with that." He cupped my face and placed a gentle kiss on my forehead. "No more tears for this, Jamie." He said his name like it put a sour taste in his mouth. "We have adventures waiting and it's time for spring cleaning."

"Speaking of cleaning, is there somewhere I can wash up a bit?" I asked, breaking the tension. I needed to put some space between us. We'd only just met and I was about to shamelessly throw myself at him. "I'm kind of a hot mess. I don't assume you have a shower?"

"Yeah, we do." He paused, taking a moment to collect himself. "Come, I'll show you around camp."

We navigated our way through the bridges. Peter telling me all about how, once upon a time he had lived underground. After Wendy had taken the Lost Boys home with her, he had moved up into the tree tops to be with the faeries and he had been there ever since.

We spoke about spring cleaning. How he and the Lost Boys used this time to prepare the camp for an upcoming celebration of the changing seasons with the indigenous Neverlanders. A symbolic purifying of the camp or spring cleaning followed by decorating with flowers to usher in the summer season. As we walked he pointed out the houses of three others, Tripp, Eben, and Ryder. The Lost Boys, still shrouded in mystery, consuming my curiosity, away on an adventure.

THE 'SHOWER' was just a large tree at the edge of the camp. A simple rain barrel perched in the branches with a pull string and a basket of what looked like Hibiscus blooms hanging within arms reach. Woven towels hung carelessly about the surrounding branches drying in the sunshine. It offered very little in the way of privacy.

"This is where we wash. I'll leave you to it."

"Wait! Ummm... soap? Clean towels?"

Peter looked at me like I'd gone mad. "Do you not know how to wash? There's a basket of flowers there, just rub them on yourself. Do you need me to show you how?" He looked at me with hunger in his eyes.

"No, I don't need you to show me how to wash." Flowers for soap? How odd. When in Rome I guess. "Towel?"

"Just grab a dry one," he said as he walked away, leaving me to figure out the makeshift shower.

Just grab a dry one? This was your typical bachelor pad, not a clean towel in sight.

There wasn't much here to shield me from prying eyes. The tree was large and If I arranged a few towels from the surrounding branches I could at least make myself feel somewhat hidden. I didn't know where Peter went off to or when the Lost Boys would return. But what choice did I have? I needed a shower.

I put my insecurities away and just went with it. I stripped down reluctantly, standing under the barrel and pulled the string. A stream of water, warm from the day's sun, spilled over my body, instantly relaxing my nerves. Alone with my thoughts, memories of last night flooded my mind. Tears pricked my eyes. I decided at that moment to scrub memories of Jamie from my mind. Peter was right, the bastard didn't deserve my tears. He would no longer hold space in my thoughts. He would never hurt me again. I'd been given the gift of Neverland and I intended to enjoy it.

I grabbed a hibiscus blossom from the basket, eager to wash away the past. As I massaged the bloom through my hair it's sweet pomegranate like aroma filled my senses, bringing me back to the here and now. The petals felt velvety soft as they caressed my skin, their oils leaving me soft and scented.

I wondered if he was watching me. The thought of his eyes on my nakedness caused a rush of excitement. A warm tingling spread between my legs. I closed my eyes, imagining Peter with me, naked, showering, touching. My nipples hardened as my hands glided down my body, over my gentle curves and stopped to linger between my legs. I considered indulging my desire. My breathing became heavy as my fingers gently stroked my slickness.

What am I doing?

I'd completely forgotten that I was exposed. I regained my composure before taking one last rinse. I turned to grab a towel and that's when I saw Peter. He'd perched himself in the neighboring tree canopy staring, taking in the view.

"Peter!" I exclaimed as I quickly wrapped myself in a towel. "How long have you been watching?" Embarrassment quickly setting in. Please don't let him have seen everything.

He looked at me like he wanted to rip the towel off and ravish me right here. "Not long." A smile spread across his face. "Did you enjoy your wash?"

My cheeks instantly turned a bright crimson. "A bit of privacy please."

He hopped down from his perch. Not an ounce of remorse. "I brought you some clothes, although after what I just saw I prefer you naked." He handed me a balled up wad of clothing and turned around grumbling. "It's not like I haven't already seen everything."

"A gentleman always turns around." I was both embarrassed and excited. How could I allow myself to let go like that? What was it about Neverland that had me acting so out of character? No sense in dwelling, what's done is done. He'd obviously liked what he saw. Be happy with that and move on.

I chose a dark colored tunic top from the random selection of clothing. I should be able to make this work. If I tore the neckline just a bit, it would slide off one shoulder. Rip out the hem line for a bit of length and a raw edge, a belt to cinch the waist. This should be cute, a bit risqué, considering I had to go commando. I had washed my only pair of knickers and hung them to dry. With no mirrors around to check myself out, I had to just go with it. Seemed to be the theme here in Neverland. Just go with it.

"You can turn around now."

He walked over to me as his eyes looked me up and down. "Wow, you certainly wear that better than Eben ever has." He circled me like a wolf circles their prey "You look like a Lost Boys' wet dream." He licked his lips, "I still prefer you naked." He smiled at me with a mischievous grin.

"Well, I certainly can't walk around here naked, but thank you for the compliment."

"Oh you can, and we do." He smiled. "You'll see."

The idea of a camp full of naked men had my heart pounding, and my mind racing. It was becoming abundantly clear that I was going to like Neverland.

CHAPTER IV
THE LOST BOYS

"H ullooo!"
A bellowed greeting echoed up from the meadow where I'd first awoke. Peter responded promptly with a loud crow.

"Come on Gwen, the Lost Boys are returning. I'm sure they're anxious to meet you." Peter had been such a distraction that I had all but forgotten the Lost Boys. But at the mention of them, my earlier questions came flooding back.

"I thought the Lost Boys left Neverland to grow up with Wendy?" Peter grimaced briefly at the mention of his initial Lost Boys.

"Well the world is full of lost boys looking for a place where they belong. Neverland has always been a focal point that attracts them."

"So these are new Lost Boys?"

"Not new, they've been around awhile."

"Are they still boys or are they grown up like you?"

He looked thoughtful for a moment, "I don't know how old they are, but they do have hair on their chests so I guess you would consider them men." Lucky me. I was intrigued now.

Peter led me to the ladder and I climbed down. I glanced up as I made my way down, but Peter wasn't following.

"Down here slowpoke," Peter called to me from the ground.

"How'd you…?"

"Peter Pan and flying go hand and hand, remember?" He was so cocky when he was in his element.

"I think it might take me a while to get used to everything. It's not everyday you find out that the boy from your fairytales is real," I mumbled this half to myself. I was still trying to wrap my head around everything that had happened.

I reached the bottom and landed firmly on the ground. I'm sure Peter was overly impressed with the speed at which I descended that ladder, I thought to myself sarcastically. I must've been the most unimpressive person he'd ever met. I was still feeling vulnerable after the whole shower incident. Yet he smiled sweetly at me when I met his gaze and I smiled back reflexively. I fidgeted with the make shift dress I had fashioned out of their clothes. I was showing off more skin than I was used to and not having any knickers on, made me even more self conscious.

"Hey, hey, hey… what do we have here Pan?"

The brief connection between Peter and I was interrupted by a haughty masculine voice. Peter turned toward three guys that were strolling up to us. I could make out the glimmer of a faerie , flitting about their heads.

"Ryder, this is Gwen, the daughter of Wendy that I've been telling you about." He gestured to the one who had spoken. He came toward me and bowed theatrically.

"Milady," he said extravagantly. All I could see was a mop of unruly blonde hair as he grabbed my hand and planted a lingering kiss there with warm, full lips. He looked up then, a perfectly handsome face with indigo eyes that were a shade away from purple. His smile was so inviting and friendly. I could tell instantly that I would like him.

"Pan, have you been holding out this whole time? You never told us the daughters of Wendy were so hot!"

He winked at me and I think I actually giggled at his charming antics.

"Give her some room, Ryder. I'm sure she's had quite a

day with the trip across the veil." A tall brunette shouldered Ryder out of the way.

"Nice to meet you, Gwen. I'm Tripp."

A pair of bright, moss green eyes met mine. He was classically handsome, his hair cut short at the sides and styled back from his face. His introduction, although formal, was warm and welcoming. He offered me his hand and gave me a firm handshake, lingering just a moment too long with my hand in his, his fingertips grazing my wrist before letting go. I smiled shyly at him. "Nice to meet you, Tripp," I said, equally as cordial.

"You going to introduce yourself, Eben?" Peter asked. I could hear a little reproach in his tone. The boy lingering in the back gave Peter a 'fuck you' sort of smile.

"Gwen." Eben nodded a greeting in my direction.

He was the only boy that refused to meet my eyes, a visible stress line creased between his eyebrows. His hair was jet black and haphazardly spiked. He had a piercing in his nose and elaborate tattoos covered his exposed arms. His outward appearance screamed bad boy. What was it about bad boys that was so salaciously alluring? His brooding shyness only piqued my interest.

"Eben, right?" I asked as I stepped toward him, now it was my turn to offer a handshake. I wasn't sure if I was trying to be nice or if I just wanted to touch him.

"Yep, that's me," he said rather drolly but he took my hand anyway.

As our hands touched I was distracted by the growing

sound of tinkling bells and turned to look. I heard a quick poof, a shift in the air ruffled my hair slightly, and where a faerie had been just a moment before, stood a woman in her place. She was small, all five foot nothing, but she was stunning to look at.

"Nice of you to join us Lill, now we don't have to listen to you talk trash behind her back," Ryder said. He had now perched himself in a branch of the large tree.

"She's... Lilleybell? I'm confused."

"This is Lill in her human form. She hates it but she does it from time to time when she hangs out with us," Peter explained.

Huh? That was a new faerie trait I had never heard of. Something to add to Grams fairytales when I got home.

The faerie-sized Lilleybell had been gorgeous in all her buxom, sparkling glory. But now that she was human size, I could make her out more clearly.

Lilleybell was curvy in all the right places, her white lily dress didn't leave much room for the imagination. She had great tits with cleavage to die for. She swayed her hips when she walked in this human form, fully aware of her attractiveness. I caught myself staring at her body with envy.

"Peter, I don't know why you wasted your time bringing this one back." Her breathy voice was high pitched and sing songy. It took me a minute to realize that her beautiful voice was saying something awful about me.

"Lill, behave yourself," Peter scolded.

"I mean seriously Peter, look at how scrawny she is, she's

never gonna make it here. I can't believe you tried to send me away for this!" She said as she gestured at me as if I was some inanimate object.

"Wait, what? You tried to send Lill away for the spring cleaning?" Eben asked. Peter groaned as though he did not want to have that conversation right now.

"Lill and I worked it out, it's nothing," he said curtly. Eben looked visibly irritated at being brushed off, but didn't say anything else.

Lilleybell sauntered over to Eben as she continued to bash me. "It would have been so much better if you had just left her there. Now we're stuck babysitting her ass instead of having a good time." She made it a point to tousle Eben's hair as she leaned in against him. A clear display of her marking her territory.

"I'd appreciate it if you didn't talk about me as though I'm not here," I interjected, feeling very much the stranger in this conversation. I had no idea why she appeared to hate me so much. She had only barely met me. Was she trying to get a rise out of me? She had no modicum of politeness.

"Peter told me that he didn't even want to bring this sister back, but the other one was dying so he settled for this one." She glared at me as she spat out the words.

"Oh Lill, that was a low blow," Ryder responded in my defense.

It took a moment for her words to sink in. I could feel my face flush as angry tears threatened to leak out. I didn't have any issues ignoring petty bitches back home, but this was crossing the line.

"Don't you ever fucking talk about my sister again! Say one more goddamned thing about her and I'll make sure you regret it!" The words came out cold and sinister, with no hint of the underlying pain I was feeling.

I stood there for an awkward minute staring Lilleybell down as they all peered at me in stunned silence. Then my typical instinct to run from any uncomfortable situation kicked in and I turned and headed into the surrounding forest to get away from them.

I HAD no idea where I was going or what I would do when I got there. I stomped my way through the underbrush cursing under my breath, barely noticing the exotic forest around me. It wasn't until I reached a grove of vividly colored mushrooms that I finally came to my senses and stopped. The unique mushrooms were unlike any I'd seen before. They ranged in size with the largest ones reaching as high as my waist. The glossy caps were colored in blues and purples and speckled in white spots. The scene reminded me of something out of Alice in Wonderland.

This brought me back to reality, or at least whatever reality this was. I wasn't home and I was completely dependent on Peter. I couldn't just leave even if the situation was shit. What was I doing here in Neverland? I had finally conceded that I wasn't dreaming, and even though none of this made sense, I was physically here in Neverland, wherever the fuck that was. I really should be getting back home. My mind began to process the pros and cons. Yes, the boys were hot as fuck! And it was true that I had a special kind of chemistry with Peter that I had never felt with anyone before. I could even admit that Neverland was the most breathtaking place I'd ever seen.

But what about Mic? She was probably worried sick about me and that kind of stress wasn't good for her. Who would take care of her when she had one of her bad days? Without Mum and Dad around, it was just the two of us now. I knew exactly what she would say if she knew I was here, she would tell me to relish in this gift and enjoy every minute of my time here. She was always so selfless.

And what about my job? The cafe would probably can me if I didn't show up for my shift this afternoon. I truly hated that job, but it supplemented our dwindling inheritance and kept the bills paid. Now I'd probably have to go out and find another miserable job when I got back. Ugh, I didn't know what the right thing to do was, my conscience told me I should go but it was at war with my heart that was telling me to stay. Would Peter even bring me home if I decided to go?

I sat down on one of the spongy caps and huffed, feeling trapped and indecisive. I sat there amongst the magic of the forest and closed my eyes. I tried to clear my thoughts and I pulled in a few deep breaths, the mushrooms giving the air a slightly sweet and earthy scent. I concentrated on the sounds of the forest around me. The birds singing and chirping, insects buzzing, and some unknown beast whooped in the distance. It was so peaceful, and I could feel my anger melting away.

I opened my eyes and was immediately startled. All four boys were standing in a semicircle in front of me. I hadn't heard a single leaf rustle or branch break as they'd approached me, they had been absolutely silent. How had I not heard them? How long had they been watching me? They were all staring at me with looks of concern. Tripp knelt down in front of me until we were face to face.

"You alright, Gwen?" Tripp asked. I sighed and faked a smile.

"Yeah, I'll be fine. I don't suppose these mushrooms will make me smaller?" I asked, wishing I could hide from their curious stares after my embarrassing behavior. I heard a snort of recognition from Eben, but Tripp just cocked a brow in question. I cleared my throat. "Sorry for the outburst. I get a little touchy when it comes to Michaela."

"Don't apologize Hen, you threatening Lill was sexy as hell!" Ryder exclaimed.

"Ryder!" Peter reprimanded

"Oh come on Pan, don't act like we all didn't get a little hard when she put Lill in her place," he responded as if it was just a casual conversation. Peter shot him a look, and it was clear he was less than pleased with his lewd commentary.

"You shouldn't run off like that, you could get yourself hurt out here. This isn't fucking Wonderland!" Eben scolded, interrupting Ryder's suggestive comments with a more serious tone. I couldn't tell if he was irritated or actually concerned about my well-being. Lill had made me completely self conscious about being a burden to them. Tripp shot him a cold look but when he turned back to me, he was perfectly composed.

"What Eben *meant* to say is that pirates and wild animals roam in these woods. It's probably better if you take one of us with you next time."

"You can take me with you, Hen! I'm up for a stroll in the woods, just the two of us," Ryder added as he came and sat on the mushroom beside me, placing an arm around my shoulders like we were old friends. I stiffened for a moment at the initial touch, but then settled into his side, distracted by how firm his body was next to mine.

"Hen? Is that some kind of pet name?" I asked. I inwardly loved the thought of him coming up with a nickname for me, he made it so easy to be around him.

"It's a term of endearment," he explained slowly as if I had never heard the phrase before. "You know, like honey or sweetheart. I think it's perfect for you."

"Strolls through the woods, endearing pet names, if I didn't know any better, I'd think you liked me," I said playfully, feeding off his cheery attitude.

"I'm an open book Hen, what you see is what you get."

"So... we were thinking, since Lill ruined your morning with her shitty attitude, maybe we could make it up to you," Peter offered and he seemed excited to share what he had planned.

I felt hesitant with Peter now. I knew that Lill had been saying those things to be cruel but had there been any truth to what she said? Was I simply an afterthought when he realized Mic was too sick for the trip? Damn her for putting doubt in my head.

My inner voice was cautioning me. Don't be stupid Gwen, you just got burned by a guy because you ignored the warning signs. I could just tell him to take me home and not even bother with any of this. But he was staring at me with expectant eyes, looking hopeful. Maybe I could just see what he had planned and end my trip on a happy note, rather than leaving with Lill's bullshit ruining everything.

"Okay, sure, what do you have in mind?" Even though I was unsure about his intentions toward me, his excitement was palpable and I was curious about what fantastical thing he had in mind.

"I thought you might like to go see the mermaids at the Lagoon. What do you say, you wanna come with us?" Mermaids! He was asking if I wanted to see real life mermaids. My inner child squealed with glee.

"Of course. I'd love to!" I gushed, maybe a little too eager. Peter smiled, looking pleased with himself. Tripp offered me his hand and pulled me to my feet.

"The path is a little rough. You can hold onto me if you need to," Tripp offered, chivalrously. I looked at his muscled arms and came to the determination that if it meant I got to have his hands on me, then I would need a lot of 'assistance' on the path to the Lagoon.

CHAPTER V
BEAUTIFUL, BUT DANGEROUS

I'm not going to lie, the hike down to Mermaid's Lagoon was a lot more than 'a little rough' as Tripp had described. I never thought of myself as a clumsy person, but compared to Peter and the Lost Boys, I was an uncoordinated mess.

Tripp had been so patient with me. While the other boys went ahead of us, he stayed and never said a word about how slow I was going.

"Thanks for your help, Tripp. I'm not sure I could have made it down without you."

"It's all good. I'm enjoying the time with you without the others competing for your attention." He smiled sincerely. He had the best smile I'd ever seen— lush lips and perfectly white teeth. It lit up his whole face changing him from handsome to stunning.

"I'm sorry to hear that your sister is sick."

"Thanks, she's been sick a long time, but she's a fighter so if anyone can beat it, it's her." I felt like this was my go-to response anytime someone asked about Mic, and I can't remember how many times I'd repeated it. People would always ask, but their concern was never really genuine. They were simply ticking off a box on their social etiquette checklist when in reality, they didn't give a shit. But I reminded myself that he was trying to be polite. He nodded at my response, but didn't push any further.

"What about you? What's your story? How long have you been in Neverland?" I asked a barrage of questions, wanting to change the topic of conversation from me to him. After all, their stories seemed so much more exciting than the sad, mundaneness of mine.

He laughed a little. "It's a long story and the details are spotty at best after being in Neverland for so long. But the short version is that I had a shit dad." He paused there and I worried that was all I was going to get out of him, but he continued, "He abandoned us, leaving my mum with nothing and I couldn't stand to see her working so hard to support me. I figured she'd be better off without me. So I left." He told the story as if he was telling it about someone else, not a hint of emotion from a childhood that must have been awful.

"How did you end up in Neverland?"

"I was living on the streets for a while. Back then, life was tough for a kid living rough like that. But then Peter found me, and offered me a different choice. I've been here ever since." When he mentioned Peter in his story, he sounded sort of reverent. It was obvious that he felt he owed a lot to Peter. I wonder what he had meant when he said 'back then'.

"How long have you been here with Peter?" I couldn't quell my curiosity.

"Time is a funny thing, even more so here in Neverland." His non-answer was vague and riddle-like, and only sparked more questions. I was still curious about how time in Neverland could affect one's memories. The idea of forgetting my life back home seemed selfishly alluring, but then again, I could never forget my sister. I didn't push for more of the story. I felt like I had gotten a few pieces to the puzzle that was the Lost Boys and I made a mental note to find out more along the way.

We fell into a companionable silence. It was as though we were old friends. It was comfortable, just being together, no pressure to carry on a conversation.

As we made our way down to the Lagoon, I watched curiously as one by one, they disappeared over the lip of a cliff that abruptly ended the path we'd been following. I hesitantly approached the edge and peeked over to find more than a ten foot drop, with a continuation of the path at the bottom. The boys had all managed the cliff without any issues and looked back up at us, expectantly.

"How do we get down?" I asked, hoping that there was another option for me besides jumping.

"We jump. It's really not as bad as it looks. We do it all the time," Tripp said casually. I grasped at Tripp's hand, my palm going sweaty with the idea of jumping down from the ledge. Was it too much to ask for a gently sloping, perfectly paved road down to the Lagoon?

"Can't we just fly down?" I asked Tripp, reminded of Peter, skipping the ladder and floating to the ground at the camp earlier. I couldn't believe I was recommending flying, as if it was something that I did on a daily basis, but it seemed like a much better option than jumping.

"Well seeing that you've completely pissed off Lill. I doubt she'll be coming back any time soon to replenish our faerie dust, so we've got to keep what we have for emergencies."

Ugh, was there no end to Lilleybell's intrusion into my perfect Neverland experience?

"I'm sorry. I haven't even been here a full day and I'm causing issues," I said apologetically. The last thing I wanted was to be a nuisance to them.

"Don't worry about it, we've managed before without

faerie dust when Pan's been on her shit list," he assured me. "Come on then. I'll go first and then I'll catch you. It'll be fine, trust me." He then headed toward the cliff's ledge, as if this was all no big deal.

After everything I'd been through, most recently with Jamie, I had some serious trust issues. But wasn't I working toward being fearless and free while I was here in Neverland? I could just think of it like a trust fall exercise. It wasn't *that* far down and I knew I was being ridiculous. I'd been thrust into adulthood at such a young age, and it was clear that I'd forgotten how to let loose and live a little. But even as I tried to convince myself, I could feel my anxiety begin to bloom, regardless of my positive thinking. I just needed to swallow my fears and go with it. I nodded at Tripp and he jumped from the edge, landing gracefully in a crouch at the bottom. He made it look so easy.

"Alright Gwen, now you go," he called up to me. "You can do it, just sit down on the ledge and slide off." I realized my hesitancy must have been obvious on my face.

All the boys called up to me with encouraging words, all except Eben, who was waiting further down the path, looking utterly bored. I didn't let myself contemplate it any further. My runaway thoughts could be my own worst enemy, and I felt this odd need to prove to Eben that I could manage it. I followed exactly what Tripp said. Sitting on the graveled ledge, I closed my eyes and pushed off, letting go and allowing myself to trust him wholeheartedly.

I could feel myself falling through the air for a moment, my heart racing in panic. What if Tripp didn't catch me? What if I made a fool of myself? What if I flashed them a view of my nether regions, seeing that I still didn't have any damn knickers on? But then Tripp's arms were around me, catching me. One of his hands, sliding up my thigh underneath my makeshift dress as I landed in his arms. He maneuvered me, effortlessly, until I was cradled in his arms and he was staring at me, smiling.

"Told you I'd catch you." He was teasing and haughty. I could only huff in response and he laughed.

"You don't ever have to be scared when I'm around. I promise I'll always keep you safe." This time he was completely serious and sincere. I felt almost overwhelmed. He couldn't have fully grasped the impact that his statement had on me. I had been taking care of Mic by myself, shouldering the weight of everything for so long. I felt a sense of relief, a weight lifted off my shoulders to finally have someone who was looking out for me.

He set me on the ground then and placed his hands around my waist to steady me. His big hands wrapped almost entirely around my middle. I could still feel the places where his hands had slid up my bare thigh, the tingling sensation lingering long after he'd stopped touching me.

By the time we reached the water's edge I was covered in sweat. I had scrapes on my knees from a few falls and I was clinging to Tripp's arm for dear life. After a moment of catching my breath, I was drawn in by the beauty of the Lagoon. I was standing on a small crescent beach nestled on the edge of the forest. The sand was pure white and silky smooth beneath my feet. Craggy rocks capped the edges of the beach and extended into peaked ridges covered in deep green foliage. The little cove was completely protected from the elements, yet a soft breeze rustled my hair and cooled my overheated skin.

The water in the Lagoon was a saturated shade of turquoise. The surface of the water shimmered like the sun reflecting off the facets of a gemstone. The spray from the surf breaking over the rocks misted the air with a salty scent of the ocean and rainbows reflected off the mist. It was one of the most serene places I had ever seen.

Peter came up behind me, and leaned in to talk in my ear. "You see them Gwen? Look over there at Marooner's Rock."

I looked out to where he pointed.

A large rock jutted from the water, with a portion of it being perfectly flat. I could see three mermaids perched there, bathing in the sun. Two of them were sitting with their tails tucked up under them while they brushed the tangles out of their hair. Another was laying on her stomach, playing with seaweed in a tide pool.

Their damp hair hung long and covered the swell of their bare breasts. They had petite faces with high cheekbones and small, slightly upturned noses. Their skin was so pale that you could even make out delicate blue veining underneath. Their tails varied in color from their hips to the wispy tips of their fins like a Betta fish.

"They are so beautiful!" I sighed as I admired them, fascinated to actually see a mermaid in the flesh.

"Beautiful, yes, but most definitely dangerous. Beautiful things in Neverland aren't always what they seem," Tripp warned. Peter stepped in front of me and crowed a greeting to them. They all perked up and looked at Peter, waving excitedly at him.

"Hello, Peter!" all three of them called in unison. Their voices were the most beautiful sound I had ever heard, like a siren's call.

They noticed me standing behind Peter and their gleeful welcome faded abruptly, giving way to hateful scowls. I think I may have even heard a hiss. They promptly returned to the water with an exaggerated splash, their brightly colored tails slapping the water in evident irritation. Was there no end to Peter's effect on any female creature?

"You wanna go swimming, Hen?" Ryder looked at me with a mischievous look on his face. Before I could even answer he pulled his top over his head and started undoing his pants. His chest was defined with a six pack and those sexy V cut lines at his waist. I had to remind myself to close my mouth once my jaw had dropped at the sight of him. I looked at the other boys and realized they were all stripping their clothes off as well.

"I... uhh... I don't have a bathing suit," I stumbled through my response. My face blushed furiously as Ryder kicked off the rest of his clothes and stood naked in front of me.

"You don't need a bathing suit, haven't you ever been skinny dipping before?" I tried, and failed miserably, to keep my eyes off his body. He was a golden Adonis standing there, and the size of his cock, made my eyes widen. Ryder had the biggest shit-eating grin on his face. He raised his eyebrows at me suggestively, that cheeky bastard.

"Stop staring at her like a piece of meat, Ryder," Peter interrupted, copping a pissy attitude.

"Here, you can wear my shirt if you want." Tripp, ever the gentleman, handed me his shirt. My manners kept my eyes only on his face, even though my peripheral vision could tell that he was completely naked too, and I burned with curiosity to drink in the sight of him.

"But is it safe to swim with the mermaids? I don't think they were too happy to see me."

"Like I said, you don't have to worry about anything when we're around," Tripp confirmed, and at that point I felt as though I was out of excuses.

"First one to the water gets a kiss from Gwen!" Ryder

winked at me and all four boys darted for the water, sand flying up in their wakes. I had the most amazing view of their tight asses as they ran. Neverland was bringing to life every fantasy a girl could conceive of.

I took a moment to compose myself and while they were distracted with their mad dash to win a kiss, I slipped out of my makeshift outfit and put Tripp's shirt on. It was sleeveless and came to my mid thigh. It was better than nothing, but much to my chagrin, the shirt was white. Tripp had been more devious than I'd expected with his offering. I rolled my eyes and gave myself a little pep talk.

You can do this!

Once I was below the surface of the water, they wouldn't be able to see anything, I assured myself.

"Come on, Gwen. The water is perfect, and no one ever looked so stunning in my shirt," Tripp called to me.

I made my way to the water's edge slowly. It was exactly the right temperature, not too cold but still refreshing. I waded in and I could feel the shirt cling to every inch of my body. What was I doing? Mic would never believe I went swimming in a mermaid cove with four gorgeously naked men. I was having a hard time believing it was happening myself.

"So who won the bet?" I asked, trying to make casual conversation so I could distract myself.

"Eben!" Ryder groaned. "I should have known, that fucker is too fast and he had some serious incentive."

I hadn't expected Eben to win the bet. He seemed so

aloof. The other boys had been so attentive while he held back. Why would he have pushed to win the bet? I recalled his rebuke when I had stalked off from the camp. I couldn't put a finger on what his intentions were towards me.

"You don't have to, I wasn't expecting anything from you. I just couldn't let Ryder win or we'd have to listen to him gloat non stop." It was the most I'd heard Eben speak and he seemed flustered in his response. Even though we'd just met, his quick dismissal of me hurt more than I cared to admit. Was he just trying to be nice, I thought hopefully, or was he really not interested in a kiss from me?

"Don't be a dick!" Ryder retorted and he splashed at Eben. In a flash, he grabbed Ryder in a headlock and the two went end over end, spraying the rest of us as they wrestled in the water.

"Don't worry, it's all in good fun," Peter offered. Apparently the look of concern on my face was more obvious than I realized.

"They'll come around once they've blown off some steam. You've created quite a stir in the short time you've been here."

"Me? What did I do?"

"Let's just say that we don't often spend time with beautiful girls from our own realm, so it might take us a while to get our animal instincts under control."

I blushed. It felt like I was in a perpetual state of blushing around these boys. Everything about them created a carnal, sexual tension that left me reeling and my libido demanding to be sated.

Just as Peter predicted, the two came swimming back to us, both of them laughing and bantering over who had won the "fight".

CHAPTER VI
A BET'S A BET

We spent the rest of the afternoon swimming and splashing each other, looking for a glimpse of the elusive mermaids. I was feeling so at ease. I couldn't remember the last time I had really been myself, happy and content with nothing looming over my head. I had actually forgotten about my responsibilities back home for a short time. As I relaxed, I felt something brush against my leg. Tripp was beside me instantly, placing an arm around my waist and pulling me behind him, slapping at the surface of the water.

"Don't think I don't know your tricks. We won't make the same mistakes this time!" he called out to the water, but no one was there.

I watched the scene, confused by what was happening, when a beautiful face popped out of the water a few feet from us. Her eyes turned to slits as she glared at Tripp, and this time I really did hear a hiss before she plunged back into the water, slapping the surface with her tail and deliberately splashing Tripp and I.

"See, I told you, nothing to worry about." Tripp seemed at ease, but I couldn't help but wonder what would have happened if he hadn't been there, and it sent a shiver up my spine. I thought I knew what I was getting into when I arrived in Neverland— an epic adventure. But I realized that I was completely naive about so many things, which made me a vulnerable target and I didn't like it. I would have to start educating myself on the reality that was Neverland.

"Hey, Gwen," Peter called to me, "I have something I want to show you. You want to come with me?" I was reminded of the last time he'd wanted to show me something and our moment in the crow's nest flashed into my mind.

"Of course, what is it?"

"Come on, I'll show you. It's over by the cliffs."

We walked out of the water and I was keenly aware that Tripp's borrowed shirt was completely see through and plastered to me. My nipples pebbled as the breeze chilled my wet skin. I pulled the top from my body quickly when I noticed all the boys had stopped to stare at me. I awkwardly clutched the wet fabric in my fists, trying to regain some modesty. I couldn't do much about my back side but I opted to give them a glance of my heart shaped ass rather than my small chest.

Thankfully, Peter stopped and pulled on his pants. At least now I wouldn't be completely distracted by his delicious nakedness. But of course he had left them loose at the top so that I could just see the soft patch of curls that beckoned my gaze downward.

I could hear one of them whistle at me as Peter and I walked toward the cliffs. I turned and squinted my eyes at Ryder in mocking reproach, knowing it had been him.

When we reached the cliffs, Peter grabbed my hand and led me into a dark opening in the cliff wall.

"Watch your step, the rocks can be a little slick," Peter cautioned as he led me into the darkness of the cave.

The tight passage gave way to a large cavern in the rock. A small opening in the ceiling filtered light onto a turquoise pool below. The walls around the pool stretched a soaring twenty feet up. The cavern ceiling was covered in crystalline stalactites creating the look of a sparkling night sky above.

"This place is amazing!" I stared around in wonder. Neverland was full of extraordinary places.

"I'm glad you like it." Peter's voice was soft and sultry, his eyes fixated on me as I walked around the grotto. "I come here a lot when I need a place to think and clear my head."

As much as I wanted to avoid it, this was the perfect opportunity to talk about Lilleybell's comments before I began to fall any harder for him.

"Peter, can I ask you something?"

"What do you want to know?"

"When Lill said you planned to bring Michaela back to Neverland, was that true?" I was anxious to hear the answer, but I needed to know and I hoped he would be honest with me.

"Gwen, you know she was just trying to upset you, right?"

"But was there any truth to what she said?" I was a little more firm this time.

"No," Peter said definitively. "I've been watching you for some time and I always planned to bring you back with me."

He had been watching me? That was something I hadn't known and I found it oddly exciting.

"You were watching me?" I asked curiously as I looked down at my fidgeting hands.

"If you haven't noticed, I can't seem to stop watching you." His voice was husky now.

"But what Lill said about Mic dying... was that true?"

The question came out almost pleadingly. Peter took a deep sigh and ran his hands through his damp hair. He wouldn't meet my gaze as he thought about what to say. I'm not sure why I was nervous about his answer, it's not like he was a fucking doctor or anything. Why the hell should I care what his opinion of Mic's health was? Yet if I was completely honest with myself, I cared more than I should.

"It's complicated Gwen, I can't be sure of anything," he stalled.

"But you must have come to some conclusion. You obviously told Lill something." I could feel my temper rising.

"I... I could tell she was sick, that's all."

I could tell that he was being as vague as possible. Now it was my turn to run my hands through my hair in frustration.

"Does it matter what Lill said about your sister? If I told you she was dying would you even believe anything I said?" he asked softly.

"No," I admitted. "I believe we make our own fate. No one can know for certain what will happen and I choose to believe that Michaela will live a long, happy life." I said it with as much conviction as I could muster. Peter smiled and stepped closer to me. He pushed a loose strand of my hair back from my face and tucked it behind my ear.

"That's why I chose you Gwen, your optimism for the future is something I've never had."

He was so close I could feel his warm breath on my lips. His cinnamon and leather scent filled my senses, intoxicating me. My heart was pounding in my chest. It felt like every nerve ending was electrified. He placed his hands on either side of my face, holding me still while he stared at me, heavy lidded. He leaned in and brushed his lips ever so softly on mine, as if asking permission to go further.

My mind was conflicted, swimming with need, but I had only just met him yesterday. Did it really matter, though? I was in Neverland with boys I would never see again. I was always doing 'the right thing' and how good had that worked out for me? No, I wanted this. Correction— I needed this.

Once my mind was made up, I pressed hard against his lips, claiming them. He followed my lead, turning his head so he could deepen the kiss while he grasped the nape of my neck to pull me in closer. His tongue parted my lips and was soft as it caressed mine. As quickly as it began, it was over. He pulled away abruptly as if I'd burned him, cutting off the kiss, leaving me wanting. He pressed his forehead against mine and shook his head while he pulled in a few ragged breaths.

"I'm sorry, Gwen. I shouldn't have done that. I can't do this."

He pulled away from me completely then, leaving me chilled in the space he vacated. What had I done wrong? He had seemed so into me only a moment before. What the hell was wrong with me? First Jamie and now Peter. I felt flayed open, completely vulnerable, and yet the aching need between my legs, annoyingly, wouldn't go away regardless of the rejection, which only made it worse.

"Why?" was the only thing I could think to ask.

"It's not you. My life here in Neverland is… unusual, at least for a normal girl like you and I—"

"You're really using the 'it's not you it's me' line? You think my life is normal, that I'm just like every other girl? Well you're wrong, you don't know anything about me!" I tried to keep the emotion out of my voice. After all, we'd only just met. Why the hell were my emotions going haywire over this guy?

Peter reached for me, a pained look on his face. "Gwen, I—"

"Pan, Hen, you guys decent?" Ryder called from the cave's entrance, effectively interrupting what Peter had been about to say.

"What is it, Ryder?" Peter sounded frustrated.

He walked into the grotto then, his usual happy go lucky mood was gone. "Pan you gotta come out and see this."

"See what?" Peter yelled. He was short with Ryder and it was a side of Peter I hadn't seen yet. Ryder didn't respond, just nodded his head toward the beach and headed back out. Peter huffed a deep sigh and followed after him, leaving me behind to pick my way through the path myself.

When we reached the beach, the bright blue skies had shifted and were now turning gray with dark thunder clouds rolling in from the sea. The wind had picked up too, whipping my hair across my face. We met up with the rest of the Lost Boys who were all deep in discussion.

"What's going on?" Peter barked, still irritable.

"We spotted the Jolly Roger coming up the northern

route, toward fae territory," Tripp explained and then pointed out toward the sea.

We all turned to look and I could make out the massive white sails coming through mists that had rolled in with the impending storm. The wind had whipped a black flag ragged, but I thought I could make out a skull and crossbones. The ship moved slowly across the horizon. This was not like any modern ship I'd ever seen. It was a ship straight from my history books with wooden planks and cannon ports.

"What the fuck are they doing on this side of the island?" Peter asked through gritted teeth.

"Same thing we were wondering," Tripp said. "You wanna go check it out?"

"Yeah, we better see if we can figure out what old Jas is up too." Peter paused for a moment before I could see his irritation flare, "Damn it, we're going to have to split up. Ryder, you and Eben take Gwen back to the camp and keep an eye on her. Tripp and I will follow the Jolly Roger and meet you back there later." Peter rattled off his orders quickly and aside from a scowl from Eben, no one protested. He and Tripp turned to go without even saying goodbye.

"Peter!" I called to him and he turned to face me, his normally cheeky expression replaced with a brooding one. His eyes were dark and his soft lips were set in a harsh line. The weather around us continued to deteriorate and I could hear rolling thunder come in off the water. I didn't have any idea what I was going to say. I wanted some answers to what had happened in the grotto, but now didn't seem like the time for that conversation. Had that one kiss changed everything between us?

"Be safe… with the storm, I mean." I knew it sounded ridiculous as I said it. He gave me a half smile and snorted before he and Tripp took to the air and headed off after the Jolly Roger. It began to rain and it poured down, chilling me to the bone. Ryder was at my side and led me to a rock outcropping to keep me out of the rain.

"Hen, can you wait here for a minute with Eben? I'm going to scout ahead and just make sure everything is clear before we head back."

"Should we just wait here a bit and see if the storm passes?" I suggested.

"Oh this ain't gonna let up, not with the mood Pan's in," he said, then turned and ran into the surrounding forest.

Peter's mood? What did he mean by that? This was so frustrating. I couldn't make sense of anything when it came to Peter. Should I even care? I had three other Lost Boys around me, each was insanely gorgeous in their own way. Maybe it was for the best that I didn't get involved with him. He had made it abundantly clear that he didn't want me in the grotto. Fuck it. I wasn't going to waste my time or feelings on a boy who was playing games. Well, at least I could pretend not to care— fake it until you make it, right? I felt motivated to prove it to myself as my eyes landed on Eben.

He was standing in the rain, his black shirt and pants

saturated and clinging to him. His normally spiked hair was plastered to his head and rain dripped from his straight nose. He wasn't paying me any attention at all. His dark eyes were scanning the landscape. He hadn't seemed pleased with the idea of 'babysitting' me, but he at least appeared to be taking the job seriously. He was tantalizingly sexy in that moment, and before I could stop myself, I ran through the rain to him.

"What are you doing out here? You should wait under the outcrop so you can stay dry." He had his typical lecturing tone about him, but I wasn't going to let that stop me and I had the perfect excuse to get what I wanted.

"Well… a bet's a bet," I said without hesitation.

I ran my hand along his jawline, grasped the back of his neck and pulled him to me until my lips found his. His body resisted briefly, but I didn't let up. I flicked my tongue along his lips and bit his lower lip softly. The bite set him off and his body reacted almost violently. As one hand cupped my face and grabbed a fist full of my hair, the other palmed my ass and pulled me into him, molding my body to his. I could feel his arousal, growing hard against my body. His tongue entered my mouth, exploring, soft as it slid across my tongue, almost desperate with need. His hand shifted from my ass to my thigh and hitched my leg up.

My whole body was on fire and the cool rain coursing over us did nothing to calm it. When our lips parted we were both breathless in the aftermath. My mind was spinning with the intensity of the kiss. I don't think I'd ever been kissed with such fierce passion before. I wanted more.

"I guess Eben decided to cash in on his bet after all." Ryder's presence interrupted my foggy brain that had shut out everything but Eben.

I stepped back, embarrassed that we had been caught. When I looked up at Ryder, he looked… disappointed? I felt instant shame. Ryder had been so sweet to me and he had been the most straightforward in his intentions, yet I had kissed his two friends instead.

I felt like shit. I didn't want to hurt him because I absolutely adored him, but my feelings were all over the place. I liked them all. I couldn't even deny my attraction to Peter, even after he'd rejected me. Would they be willing to share? That sounded so ridiculous, but honestly, I wanted to experience what each of them had to offer.

"Ryder, I'm sorry, I…"

"It's fine, just remember that I'm your favorite Lost Boy the next time you're looking for a make out session," he said as he reverted back to his typical, flirty self.

My heart warmed and I felt relieved that he didn't seem too upset at my kiss with Eben. I looked back at Eben, not wanting him to be upset either. He was looking at me with lust in his eyes and he licked his lips as if savoring the last taste of me.

CHAPTER VII
YOUR ENDING IS A BIT OFF

The trip back to camp was arduous. The boys kept close to me and took turns holding my hand and helping me navigate the trail. The rain came down so hard that it drowned everything else out, the white noise only interrupted by the occasional rumble of thunder. Eben was quiet the entire trek back. His mood was somber and he looked lost in thought, so much so that he had a pained expression on his face. Had I been too forward with my kiss? Maybe I misread his signals. There was a tension between us that was palpable. I couldn't deny the attraction I felt, and I thought he felt it too.

We finally reached the camp as the last remnants of light had disappeared and the dark of night had enveloped Neverland. We were soaked through and caked in mud. Eben turned toward his place, and my heart sank when he didn't even offer so much as a goodbye. I watched his back as he walked away, but then he paused and stopped in his tracks. He turned and walked back to us, purpose in his step as if he'd forgotten something.

Instead of going up to Ryder, he walked straight to me. He grabbed my hand and planted a brief, chaste kiss on my cheek. "Goodnight, Gwen. Dream of me," he whispered before he disappeared into the maze of suspension bridges. My heart fluttered and I smiled to myself. Maybe I had left an impression after all. I decided that tomorrow I would try harder to crack his tough exterior.

Ryder turned me toward one of the houses nestled in the treetops. He went around the tiny room and lit an array of candles in varying shapes and sizes, providing a warm glow to the space. It was a small, rustic room with open windows, and minimal furnishings. Soft cushions were strewn around the floor and a hammock was strategically placed to optimize the view out of the window. It felt amazing to be out of the rain.

"Let me draw you a bath so you can clean up," Ryder offered. I melted at the mention of a hot bath. The rain barrel shower I'd had earlier wasn't really feasible now.

Furthermore, why didn't Peter tell me there was another option than the overly public 'shower?' That cheeky bastard!

"That's so sweet of you Ryder, thank you. A bath would be amazing." I masked my irritation at Peter with an overly grateful response. "When do you think they will be back?" I asked, seemingly unable to get Peter out of my head.

He brought me here and tried to seduce me with his flirty charm. Then dropped me cold as soon as I'd shown any interest and proceeded to leave me here with his lackeys! Well, the Lost Boys weren't lackeys really. In all honesty, I was crushing on each of them.

"Wish I could tell you, Hen, but Pan does whatever Pan does and there ain't no one that can pin him down," he explained matter-of-factly. Of course this only further inflamed my irritation with him.

I was stewing inwardly as Ryder went to work quickly. He started a fire in the center of the room and then left briefly, only to return with a large wooden tub. It looked almost like a wine barrel cut in half. I found myself intrigued and pulled from my exasperated thoughts, as he set to the task of preparing the bath.

He went to a small pantry that was lined with shelves and a countertop that had a sink fashioned out of a clay bowl, with an old fashioned water pump. Ryder pulled a bucket off one of the shelves and proceeded to fill the tub, one bucket full at a time.

Once the tub was filled, he used tongs to fish some hot stones out of the fire he'd made and plopped them into the tub— the water hissing with the addition of the hot stones. The water began to steam slightly as it heated.

The storm continued to rage outside, the dark night interrupted by flashes of lightning, followed by the ominous rumble of thunder.

"I think it's ready. I'll let you get cleaned up and get some rest. You've had a long day." Ryder turned and started toward the door.

"Wait," I called. "Don't go. Would you stay with me? I don't really want to be alone right now."

I had never really cared for thunderstorms and I didn't want to be alone in an unfamiliar place. Ryder sighed contentedly, "If that's what you want, Hen. I don't have anywhere else to be."

"Thank you." I sighed in relief. "Now can you turn around for a second while I get in the bath?"

"Aww really, you're not even going to give me a quick peek?" I slapped his shoulder and laughed.

"You are unbelievable, Ryder."

"Well you can't fault me for trying." He winked and turned around then, not wanting to push his luck.

I stripped the wet clothes off, covering my breasts, not putting it past him to sneak a peek. When I stepped into the tub it was heavenly. I could feel my whole body relax in the warm water. The tub was small, so I pulled my knees up and rested my arms along the barrel's edges. I leaned my head back and let out a little moan of pleasure.

"I knew I'd get you moaning before the day was done!"

Ryder teased. I laughed out loud. His flirty banter was so refreshing.

"Well, I'm glad I didn't disappoint you." I opened my eyes and looked over at him, he had situated himself on one of the floor cushions and he stared at me, biting his lower lip. Damn, his lips looked so inviting.

"Ryder" —I sighed as I luxuriated in the warm bath— "tell me a story."

"According to Pan, it's the daughters of Wendy that come to tell us the stories and not the other way around," he quipped.

He stood up and moved his cushion behind the tub and positioned himself at my back so I couldn't see him. I felt his fingertips caress along my shoulders and down my arms to my elbows and then back up across my collar bones. His strong hands then started to work out the knots of tension in my shoulders and I groaned again.

"That feels amazing! You have very talented fingers." I sighed. I couldn't remember the last time I had been taken care of like this.

"If you only knew how talented my fingers could be," he insinuated. "If you keep making noises like that, I'll tell you whatever story you want. What kind of stories do you like?"

"Hmm... maybe one about pirates?"

"Well you're in luck because I've got a lot of stories about pirates."

"Maybe you could tell me how the Jolly Roger is still

traipsing around Neverland after Peter defeated Hook in the epic battle to save Wendy?"

"That's a good story, but your ending is a bit off. Pan did win that battle but the war still rages on," he corrected.

I turned around to look at him in surprise. "But all the stories I've heard ended with the crocodile swallowing Hook, and the pirates being driven out of Neverland by a victorious Peter Pan?" I remembered it clearly because it was Gram's favorite part of the story.

"I like the happy ending to your fairytale Hen, but that's not how it went down." He seemed adamant and now I really wanted to hear the story —the real story.

"Then what happened to Hook?"

"Good old Captain James Hook is like a cat with nine lives," he started.

"More like a cat than a codfish huh?" I laughed at my own joke and Ryder looked at me confused with his eyebrows drawn in. I cleared my throat. "I guess you never heard that part of the story before," I mumbled and he continued.

"A lot of this happened before I got here so this isn't a first hand account. So the story goes that Hook, that slimy bastard, somehow managed to escape the crocodile and made his way back to the mainland.

He was laid low, licking his wounds, plotting and planning his revenge, growing his numbers, training his pirate crew and rebuilding the Jolly Roger. Laying in wait to make his triumphant return as Pan's arch nemesis."

Ryder was animated as he went on, a natural storyteller. "Pan, who was completely unaware that Hook had survived the ordeal, left his whole Lost Boy crew with Wendy and returned to Neverland, all alone and melancholy."

The mention of Peter, abandoned by his Lost Boys, made my heart ache for him.

"Neverland was in a bad way. You see Pan and Neverland are connected somehow. Don't ask me how because I have no fucking idea, but when Pan's in a mood, nothing in Neverland is right. Good old Jas stalked the unwitting Pan and waited until he was at his lowest point before he pounced.

At the time, Pan was dejected and had no spirit left to fight. Thankfully, Tiger Lily and the rest of the Neverland Council had been watching Pan closely and were able to swoop in and save his sorry ass from certain death. Took awhile to knock some sense into him, but eventually he came around and went in search of new Lost Boys to help protect the island from pirates and restore the balance to Neverland.

And that's my queue to enter the scene. Well, technically Tripp came first. But nobody gives a shit about Tripp," he said mockingly. "And we've been pushing the pirates back ever since. It hasn't been easy, especially now that Hooks tamed that damned beastly crocodile to do his bidding. The fucker is more ruthless than ever. We've had many victories and some tragic defeats, but I think I'll save the rest for another time. If I leave you hanging then we can do this again sometime soon."

I was stunned at the continuation of my childhood fairytale. The once happily ever after had taken a turn for the worst and gone down a dark path. That was what Ryder had meant earlier about Peter and the storm. Things were starting to make more sense and yet, I had more questions.

"Ryder, how did you end up in Neverland?" I asked cautiously, wondering if he would be as open with his own story as he was with Peter's.

He ruffled his blonde mop of hair and bit his lip, looking uncomfortable. "You don't have to tell me, I get it, I don't like telling my story either," I conceded.

"Really Hen, it's not my favorite story to tell and honestly it's gotten a little muddled over the years. Not that I mind telling you, I just had great parents and the story brings back memories I'd rather not think about."

He sighed and paused as if collecting his thoughts. "My dad was a prominent lawyer, and his dad before that. Every son followed in their father's footsteps, taking over the family firm. My family was prestigious within the community. They had everything… except the perfect son."

His whole demeanor fell as he told the story. "I was by far the cutest baby and my parents doted on me," he bragged. "Everything was perfect until I started school. I… uhh… I wasn't able to read," he admitted, looking embarrassed.

"No matter how hard I tried, the words just reversed themselves and I could never make any sense of it. It broke my parent's hearts. After a while, I just couldn't let them down anymore. I would never be the man they expected me to be. I left so they could try for another son that wouldn't disappoint them. Pan offered me the opportunity to actually do something useful." He concluded his story and he glanced over at me, his face weary, as if looking for my approval or something.

"That's awful, Ryder. I'm so sorry. You know... I could teach you to read, if you wanted me too," I asked quietly, not wanting to offend him. I'd tutored on occasion at school and I knew teaching techniques for dyslexia had come a long way over the years. It made me even more curious about how long he'd been in Neverland.

"You'd do that for me? I mean, I think I'm probably a lost cause, but if it means I get to snuggle up with you and a book, I'm game."

I laughed at his eagerness. "Yeah, I'd love to teach you. It's one of my favorite pastimes. Reading helped me get through losing my parents and my sister's illness. I'm not sure what I would have done if I hadn't had a way to escape. Books gave me that escape."

I don't know why I shared that with him. He hadn't pressed for more details, but he looked genuinely interested as I opened up to him a little. I squirmed, feeling momentarily uncomfortable as he looked at me, waiting to see what more I would say. "You must miss them— your parents, I mean. I miss mine too," I admitted, trying to change the focus from me to him.

"What happened to your folks?"

"There was an accident when I was fifteen. They both died. I understand completely when you said it brings back memories you'd rather not think of."

What I couldn't tell him was just how angry I was with them. Angry that they up and left us right after Michaela's diagnosis, for a so-called 'business trip.' I think they were just looking for an escape from the despair of Mic's prognosis, but parents don't get to run away. I know that plane crash hadn't been their fault, that they hadn't wanted to die, but damn it, they never should have left us. I'm not sure I'd ever forgive them, and that cast a dark shadow over the amazing parents they had always been.

"I'm sorry, Hen. Life's a bitch. But one thing about Neverland— it takes care of those memories that you'd rather not think of. Dulls the sharpness of them anyway."

We both sat for a moment in silent contemplation before a yawn escaped my lips. I realized then, that the bath water was starting to get cold. I couldn't believe it had only been one day, so much had happened. I couldn't explain the ease and comfort I felt around the boys after such a short time. I'm sure if you'd told me yesterday that I'd be lazily enjoying a bath in front of a man I'd just met, I would have laughed at the notion. And yet here I was with Ryder, perfectly content with his company.

"I'm exhausted. You guys wore me out today," I told him. "Would you be a love and get me a towel?"

He grabbed a towel for me from a pile of linens that were stacked haphazardly in the corner. He held the edges out for me and closed his eyes.

"Come on, Hen. I won't peek." I took his word and stood up, the cool air felt good on my warmed skin. I stepped out of the tub and toward Ryder. When he felt me close, he wrapped me in the towel and pulled me into him. I rested my head on his chest and let him hold me.

"I could really get used to this. I never knew what I was missing before."

"Would you maybe want to spend the night with me?" I asked, still not wanting to be alone and not ready to end our time together.

"We just met and you want me to sleep with you!" he feigned outrage. I giggled at his antics and then nodded.

"I guess I could indulge you, since you asked so sweetly and I can't say no to a naked girl in my arms." We both laughed.

Once I had slipped into one of Ryders shirts, we arranged the cushions into a pallet on the floor. Ryder crawled in behind me and spooned me in his big body. His arms pulled me in tight against him and I could feel him nuzzling the back of my neck. Even though I was spent, sleep eluded me with him so close.

Even his smell was stimulating— citrus, mixed with fresh

cut cedar, and hints of his underlying musk. It felt like he put all of my senses in overdrive as his hand came up and caressed the swell of my hip, light fingers dragged along the dip of my waist and moved up to softly trace the curve of my breast.

"You have the most beautiful body, Hen." His voice was harsh with need and I could feel him, hard, against my back. He kissed the back of my neck and nipped at my ear lobe and then he sighed contentedly.

"Try to get some sleep, my sweet Hen."

I finally began to drift off to sleep with the lulling patter of rain and the repetitive caress of his hand along my body. As I slipped into the clouded haze of sleep, I thought I heard Ryder's soft voice whisper, "We have time. I won't rush things with you. I plan to draw this out. Savor every step along the way... then maybe you'll stay."

CHAPTER VIII
FORGIVE ME

I was extremely warm when I woke up. I opened my eyes to find my limbs entangled with a still sleeping Ryder. His face was only inches from mine and looked peaceful and serene. The corners of his mouth turned up slightly at the edges in the barest hint of a smile. The morning sun was filtering in, creating light shadows that danced along his face as the wind blew through the leaves outside.

The prior day came flooding back to me. I was grateful that Ryder had been a gentleman and I hadn't given in to my hormonal urges. If we'd had sex, it would've made everything seriously complicated, not only with Ryder, but with the other boys, too… with Peter. I heaved a small sigh of relief. Maybe I needed to find some private time so I could finish what I'd started in the shower yesterday. Maybe then I could think clearly around these boys.

My thoughts quickly shifted to Peter. I wondered if he and Tripp had returned to the camp yet, and I began to get worried. What if something had happened to them? I knew the concern was ridiculous. Peter had survived countless years in Neverland without anyone worrying over his every move, but I couldn't help the unease I felt. I needed to find them and see for myself that they were okay.

I unraveled myself ever so carefully from Ryder's sleeping grip, not wanting to wake him. I sat up slowly and rubbed the sleep from my eyes and pulled my fingers through my sleep mussed hair.

"Did you sleep well?"

I jumped at the unexpected voice and let out a little mew of panic. Peter was perched in the window, glaring at me. Ryder thrashed in the bed beside me, sitting up abruptly, reaching for his belt and deftly pulling a knife to battle my would-be attacker.

"What the fuck?" Ryder gasped, looking disheveled and wide eyed.

"Stand down, Ryder. It's only me," Peter said dismissively.

"Peter! Oh my god, you scared me!" I declared, holding my hand to my chest as my heart pounded.

"Well shit, Pan! You interrupted a damn good dream," Ryder scolded.

"The real thing wasn't good enough for you?" Peter insinuated.

"Well what the fuck is that supposed to mean?" Ryder barked, the two now standing and staring each other down.

"Ryder," I said softly, standing between the two of them. I placed my hand on Ryder's chest. "Could you give Peter and I a moment?" I asked sweetly. He broke his stand off with Peter and looked down at me.

"Of course, Hen. Whatever makes you happy." He leaned down and kissed my cheek before leaving me alone with Peter.

"So did everything go alright last night? Any news on the Jolly Roger?" I asked, trying to ease the tension, not completely sure why he was so pissed off.

"Did you fuck him?" Peter spat the words at me and I pulled away from him in shock.

"First of all, it is none of your goddamn business who I fuck!" The words tumbled out in a heated torrent. "But just to set your little mind at ease, no, we didn't fuck." I was steaming and I could feel my face heat in irritation. He sighed and looked relieved, but it lasted only for a moment.

"Well you kissed me, and now I find you in bed with Ryder! What am I supposed to think?" He was still angry, but the edge to his voice was gone.

"I asked him to spend the night with me because you left me! You brought me to Neverland and *you* kissed me. And then you got all weird and left me alone, in a strange place, on my first night here!"

Apparently, I was more upset with him for leaving than I'd realized. We hadn't had the chance to discuss what had happened in the grotto and I had the feeling he'd been running away to avoid me. He looked totally deflated after I called him out, absently pulling his hands through his unruly hair.

"It wasn't my intention to leave you, but I have responsibilities. I am Neverland's protector."

"I guess it was just a perfectly convenient excuse to avoid me after you snubbed me in the grotto."

Why was I so irritated? Maybe it was because his actions were so damn confusing. If he wasn't interested in me, why was he so angry at the thought of Ryder and I together? I couldn't figure out what he wanted, but the idea of him not wanting me hurt.

"It's complicated Gwen," he started.

"I'm getting sick of 'it's complicated.' You keep saying that. Do you think I'm incapable of understanding? I'm not expecting anything from you. All I ask is that you're honest with me, and I will do the same for you."

"I'm sorry. I know, I'm a total ass. This is all just... new for me. And there is more at stake here than you and me," he grumbled. Well what the hell did that mean?

"I might fuck up," he continued, "but if you can just put me in my place and forgive me when I do stupid shit." Peter's words came out almost pleadingly. He came up to me and grasped my shoulders, staring into my eyes, mesmerizing me again. Fuck! Did he know just how much that affected me?

"Do you forgive me?" he asked quietly, still holding my stare.

"Yes, I forgive you. But... I'll let you make it up to me today." I gave him a sly smile. He narrowed his eyes at me briefly, but it quickly melted into one of his cheeky smiles.

"Okay, so what is it that Gwen wants to do today?"

"Anything I want, right?"

"Sure, if it means that I'm forgiven then I'm at your beck and call."

"Perfect! Then I'd love to see some pirates!" I threw it out there, hoping he wouldn't change his mind.

"No...no way."

"But Peter, you promised." I sounded like a pleading child, but I didn't care. Ryder had stirred a deep curiosity with his story and I was craving more answers.

"If you think I'm going to expose you to those lecherous bastards then you are seriously mistaken. I won't put you in danger like that." He was stern, a scowl replacing his cheeky smile. "There is no need for you to get wrapped up in the feuds between us and the pirates. That's not what I brought you here for." He sounded resolved in his decision.

"Well what the hell did you bring me here for?" I shot back at him.

He stared at me, his jaw clenched in frustration. "Gwen, I don't want to argue with you."

"I'm not asking you to walk me down and introduce me to them. But maybe we could watch them at a distance, and you can add to the interesting story that Ryder was telling me last night. I can assure you, it is not the same story that Wendy passed down. So either she lied to us or you never told her what really happened after she left Neverland."

He spun away from me. "Fucking Ryder can't keep his damn mouth shut," he mumbled, completely exasperated. He stood there for a moment, his back turned to me, letting out a deep sigh.

"If you want to see pirates, then we are going to have to make nice with Lill and get her to give us more faerie dust." He sounded defeated, but I felt thrilled at my triumph. He turned back to me and I lunged into his arms, startling him as I wrapped my arms around him in a bear hug.

"Thank you. I promise, I won't be a bother."

"You're not a bother. I just don't think you have any idea what you're getting into when it comes to pirates. You are mine to protect and I wouldn't forgive myself if I let anything happen to you." His concern was stark on his face.

I got caught up in the word 'mine'. The idea of Peter Pan claiming me as his own sent a wave of elation coursing through me, causing me to blush. It was that sense of belonging, of being cared for and protected, that I was so desperate to feel.

Maybe it was losing my parents at a pivotal age, when I'd needed their protection the most, that had left me scarred. Their deaths had pulled the metaphorical safety net out from underneath me and I'd felt as though I'd been falling ever since, expecting to hit the ground at any moment.

I'd had to make every decision without any guidance, taking the full responsibility of my actions squarely on my own shoulders. Planning my parent's funerals, handling their estates, submitting my own guardianship papers when Michaela was too sick to do it, so I could keep the two of us together. It had been such a lonely existence that I almost felt like I could cry at the relief his simple statement gave me.

CHAPTER IX
FAERIE DUST

We found the other boys outside, sitting around an old tree stump that had been fashioned into a tabletop. On the table was a spread of fruits, nuts and seeds. I could see some foods that were familiar and some that were quite unique, exotic and beautiful.

"Good morning, Gwen." Tripp got to his feet when he saw me and proceeded to kiss both of my cheeks in greeting.

"Glad to see you made it home okay," I said warmly, genuinely happy to see him safe and sound.

"Oh, it was nothing. Come on over and have some

breakfast with us. We've gone all out to get you the best the island has to offer."

"It looks amazing! Thank you."

The scent of the fruit was mouthwatering. I took a seat between Eben and Ryder and started to fill the small wooden plate set in front of me.

Eben leaned in toward me and whispered in my ear so only I could hear, "You look delicious this morning." His breath was warm on my neck, sending a shiver through me.

"Good morning to you too," I said and I felt my cheeks flush, a reaction the boys must be getting used to.

"So what's on the agenda today, Pan?" Ryder asked, no hint of irritation from their earlier confrontation.

"Gwen wants to go see some pirates today. So first up, Eben, I need you to come see if you can help me sweet talk Lill into giving us some faerie dust, seeing as you're her favorite."

Eben rolled his eyes at this. "I don't know what you expect me to do."

"Take off your shirt and play with your nipple rings, that ought to do it!" Ryder teased and everyone at the table laughed, except for Eben, who attempted to scowl, but cracked a smile instead.

"You have nipple rings? How did I miss that yesterday?" My own thoughts came out before I realized it.

"Well that's easy, you were too busy looking at his cock to notice them!" Ryder howled a laugh and now it was Eben's turn to blush.

"Don't worry Gwen, I'll be sure to show them to you later," Eben said as he tossed a grape at Ryder's head. I loved to see Eben relaxed and joking, it was a nice contrast to his typical brooding that I'd gotten used to yesterday.

"Yeah, Pan, count me in. As long as Gwen comes with us," Eben countered with a sly smirk on his face.

Peter scowled at him. "Do you really think that's a good idea?"

"If I'm in hell, then we all should be. Plus, I think if Gwen's around, I can use it to my advantage and get Lill to play nice."

"It's up to Gwen." Peter looked at me, waiting for my decision before agreeing to Eben's plan.

"Well, since I'm the reason you're having issues with Lill, it's the least I can do. She can't be that bad, can she?" I asked. The boys all stared at me for a long moment without saying a word.

"So where are you planning to take her to actually get a glimpse of them?" Tripp asked quickly, trying to change the subject.

"I was thinking we could take the Mysterious River to Three Pence Bay. We tracked the Jolly Roger up into the Native lands, but Tiger Lily was already planning to intercept them once we alerted them to their presence. I expect they would have been run off and returned to the bay to make berth."

"Gwen, you are such a badass! Second day in Neverland

and you want to tangle with pirates," Ryder exclaimed as he gave me a wink.

"There will be no 'tangling' going on today. We are taking Gwen to look from a safe distance and that's it. We don't draw attention, we don't engage. Everyone got that?" Peter was stern and everyone was quiet. Ryder cleared his throat, but said nothing.

"So what's the plan if shit goes sideways?" Tripp inquired.

"First sign of trouble and we split up. I'll take Gwen and leave you three to handle things and we'll meet back here."

"You're going to take Gwen and leave all the fun of fighting pirates to us?" Eben sounded incredulous at Peter's plan.

"I'm not going to leave her side when pirates are involved. The moment they know she's with us she'll be a target."

I started to feel a little concerned at the seriousness of their planning. I guess when I heard the fairytales as a child, I never gave much credence to the real danger they posed. I almost felt bad for cornering Peter into bringing me to see them, but I had full faith in the boys to keep me safe.

PETER AND EBEN led me along the bridge ways to a tree at the edge of the encampment. The tree was filled with ornate lanterns, each one, a house for one of the many faeries that shared the Lost Boys home. We stopped in front of a large, white lantern, about the size of a birdcage. It had stained glass windows and vines of flowering jasmine that grew around the edges.

"Lill, can we talk?" Peter called. I could just make out a slight tinkling of bells behind the lantern glass.

"No, I haven't taken her back yet. It's still spring cleaning."

Peter seemed exasperated and rolled his eyes as a tirade of bells came from the lantern. "Come on. Be reasonable, Lill!"

"Could you at least come out and speak to me face to face? I've brought Eben with me," Peter offered, obviously hoping to butter her up with Eben's presence. After a moment of silence, I could hear the rusted hinges of the lantern squeak as the door swung open slowly and her perfect, petite face peeked out. The moment she saw Eben, it looked as though her whole body flushed and she permeated a pink glow as she smiled coyly at him.

"Nice to see you too, Lill," Eben responded to her chimed greeting. She flitted up to him and he opened his palm for her to land in.

"You know you're my favorite, too."

"No, Gwen doesn't interest me in the least." Eben

looked at me with a half smirk and winked so quickly that Lill didn't even notice.

"You could do us a solid though and set us up with some more faerie dust."

Lill glared at him for a moment before she answered.

"No it's not for Gwen! Really Lill, I think you're getting a bit carried away. Didn't Peter tell you that we spotted the Jolly Roger on this side of the island yesterday?"

Lill's face looked stunned for a moment before it turned to a scowl. Her whole body glowed red this time as she stomped around Eben's palm, pulling off one of her dainty shoes and throwing it hard against his hand in a flurry of sparkles, all the while tinkling off what I assumed were a line of obscenities. Both Peter and Eben laughed at her overly exaggerated tantrum.

"Don't yell at me!" Peter rebutted. "We only found out yesterday and if you hadn't stormed off in such a tizzy over Gwen, then you would have known."

"Yes, fine, alright. I'll talk to the Pixie Elders. But will you help us out with the faerie dust?"

"What do you mean, 'what's in it for you?' I thought me talking to the Pixie Elders would be enough?" Peter looked like he was on his last nerve with her.

"Lill, how about I promise to bring you back one of those shiny gold doubloon's you like so much? Just think how great it will look with your Tiddlywinks chandelier," Eben offered.

She perked up quickly with a ravishing smile, shaking her head vigorously. Obviously a bargain had been struck.

"Alright, alright... *and* I will take you to the May Day festival too," he agreed in a huff. Lill flew up to his cheek and planted a tiny kiss before flying back to Peter and landing on his shoulder.

"I've got to go update the Pixie Elders. Eben, can you keep Gwen company for a bit?" Peter asked. Eben didn't answer right away and Lill began to chime in on his shoulder.

"Lill, enough already! I need someone to keep Gwen company since you've insisted that I update the Elders," Peter responded, annoyed with whatever her comment had been. She obviously did not want me anywhere near Eben, much less let the two of us spend the morning together. She glared at Peter from her perch on his shoulder and crossed her arms over her chest in a huff.

"I can get Ryder and Tripp to keep her company if you have something else you'd rather be doing." Peter's words seemed more of a challenge than a choice.

"No, I've got it Pan. Do what you've gotta do." I could detect a hint of irritation in his voice.

"Gwen, does that work for you? I don't want to leave you if you need me," Peter asked, giving me his full attention as he waited for my answer.

He really had listened to me earlier. He knew I'd been upset that he'd left me alone last night, and now he was running it by me before he left again. And I expected that he would stay with me if I asked him to. Against my better judgment, I fall, just a little harder, for this boy. Damn my uncontrollable emotions, what trouble would they get me into?

"I'm good with Eben. You go, I know you have responsibilities you need to tend to." He gave me a knowing smile and planted a barely there kiss on my lips before he turned and left me alone with Eben.

CHAPTER X
TARGET PRACTICE

E ben looked visibly uncomfortable and unsure of what to do with me. We stood there, in stark silence that seemed to drag on forever. Eben, not able to make eye contact with me, ran his hands through his haphazard hair, looking deep in thought.

"So, did you have any plans this morning?" I asked casually, trying to start some sort of conversation. I knew I wanted to find a way to get to know him better, crack his tough exterior so to speak, but that was easier said than done.

"Well this is Neverland, so there's never really much in the way of plans. But I've been meaning to go to the practice fields and work on my aim with this new hatchet that I've got. Of course that's really nothing a lady wants to do, so I don't know. Do you have any ideas?" I could tell he was rambling a bit and I found it adorable.

"Did you just refer to me as a lady?"

"Well... I... uh," he stumbled some more and I laughed.

"I'm as much a lady as you are a gentleman." He looked at me with a peculiar look on his face, as if I had taken him off guard with my comments.

"Why don't you take me to the practice field with you? That sounds interesting."

"Really? Are you sure? I could take you to the Never Cliffs or something? What is it that you like to do for fun?"

"Hmm, fun... I haven't had a whole lot of that recently. I work, go to school and take care of my sister. There isn't room in my life for much else." Damn, did my life sound absolutely pathetic as I contemplated my own words. I decided it might be better to leave out the mundane details of my own life and focus on him. "The Never Cliffs do sound enticing, and I definitely expect you to take me there on our next date, but this time, I'd love for you to take me to the practice fields."

"Date?"

"Yes! Now come on. I want to see what mad skills you have with that hatchet," I said playfully, as I tucked my hand in the crook of his arm.

THE PRACTICE FIELD was more of a clearing in the woods just outside of the main encampment. The meadow was beautiful. Tall, seeded grasses blew in the wind in varying shades of green and gold.

"That's the sparring ring over there." Eben pointed out a dirt square carved out of the grass at one end, "And over here" —he motioned to the other end of the meadow— "is where we do target practice."

A line of trees painted with targets were opposite the sparring ring. Eben led me to a circle of seven tree stumps in the center of the clearing. He pulled up on one of the stumps and revealed a hatch that had been hidden below.

He motioned me over. "This is the old Lost Boys home. It was repurposed into an arms cellar after Peter moved into the trees with the faeries."

I peeked down to find a dark hole under the hatch door Eben had lifted.

"So you want me to go down there?" I asked, a bit skeptical.

"I'll go first and you can follow." And before I could ask any more questions, he stepped into the hole and disappeared from view.

"Come on, Gwen. Just slide down. I have something I want to show you," Eben's voice echoed back up to me. I had to remind myself that I'd agreed to this excursion, and stepped into the small, black hole and slipped down an underground slide. I landed on my ass inside a large cavern. Eben was lighting wall sconces with a flame, bringing a glow to the room and illuminating rows of shelves, filled with all the medieval weapons you could think of. Swords, daggers, staffs, antique style pistols, bows and arrows. Even crossbows lined the shelves. I walked slowly around the room, looking over all the weapons.

"So this is where Peter and Wendy lived with the Lost Boys," I stated in awe. It seemed surreal to be here, even more so, knowing that Wendy was my several times great grandmother. I came across an old carving on the wall, P.P + W.D. and I ran my fingers along the worn lines.

"According to Pan, it had been one of the best times of his life," Eben said. "There was something about Wendy that changed him."

Could one be jealous of their own ancestors, especially ones that had died many years before? I wished the initials were P.P. + G.C., and I felt utterly childish at the thought.

"I wonder if I'm anything like her?" I thought aloud. Eben glanced over his shoulder at me, looking me up and down.

"Well, I never met her. I've also never seen Pan act this way before, so I guess there's that."

"And what way is that?" I asked, curiosity getting the better of me.

"I don't really know how to explain it, just different.

Protective maybe, and… scared?" The inflection on the last part of the statement made it sound like more of a question than an observation, as if he lacked full confidence in his assumption. "I've never seen Pan scared before so I can't be positive, but something about you makes him an overprotective asshole, so I can only assume he's scared about something."

I was surprised that he had been so observant. He typically seemed disinterested, but I was starting to wonder if that was only a facade that he put on for everyone else.

"Come check these out, Gwen."

Eben motioned me over to a table at the center of the room. He laid a cloth down and unrolled it to reveal four dainty knives. Each one was the size of my palm, tapered to a wicked point. The blades were etched in elaborate scrollwork that had a veining that seemed to sparkle in the glow of the torches. The handles tapered into a ring at the bottom that was inlaid with an opalescent stone. They were vicious and beautiful at the same time.

"These are throwing knives that have a vein of faerie dust at their core. They fly farther and truer than a regular blade. I thought they might be good for you, you know, just in case you need them. I can show you how to use them if you want."

I ran my fingers along the cool metal of the blades, "These are so beautiful. Yes, I would love it if you'd teach me to use them." I smiled at him, grateful for his offer.

"Not that I think you'll ever need them. I mean, when

you're around us, we're all the protection you need, but if there is ever a time you're not with us..." he trailed off as his dark eyes met mine, not finishing his sentence. Did the idea of me leaving Neverland— of me leaving them, bother him?

His eyes were black in the darkened room, and I could see the reflection of the flames dancing in them. It was as if his eyes were seeing straight into me, taking in more than just my outward appearance. It was both intense and unnerving and I found myself pulling away and staring back at the daggers for a distraction.

"Well, I'm used to surviving on my own, so that's nothing new. I get the feeling that surviving in my world is a bit different from surviving in yours. But I'm happy to add a new skill set. Anything helps."

My mind drifted to Jamie and how out of hand things had gotten in the club. I wondered how far he would have taken things if we had been alone and I shivered. I guess I really did need to find a way to protect myself and I felt a renewed wave of gratitude that Eben had agreed to teach me.

"You don't have a man to protect you in your world?"

"No." The word came out more forcefully than I intended. I looked down and traced the slight hint of bruising that remained on my wrist from where Jamie had grabbed me. Oddly, it had only been one day since the encounter and the bruises that had been a deep purple yesterday, were almost completely faded now.

"No, I don't have anyone. It's just me, and my sister. But she's so frail, she needs me to protect her too," I admitted.

I hated talking about my own problems. Putting into words how horribly things had been for the last several years only made me feel more out of control of my own situation. Not to mention the fact that I didn't want anyone's pity, or was it the fact that opening up to them only made me more vulnerable? But, somehow Eben was the one getting me to open up today and not the other way around. Eben only nodded and I was happy he didn't push. My mind was a rollercoaster of emotions at the moment, and I wasn't ready to share those feelings with any of the boys just yet.

Eben led me up a ladder that had been carved into one of the tree stumps and brought me over to the target lanes. He put a knife in my hand and positioned himself right behind me. I could feel his body pressed against my back.

He placed his foot between mine and pushed them apart. "Keep your legs at about hips distance, with your left leg forward. We're at a good distance, so hold it by the handle. But in close proximity, hold it by the blade since you don't need as much rotation." His words were soft and patient as he explained.

But he was so close, with his warm breath on my neck, that I was finding it difficult to concentrate. His fingers grazed down my arm and gently grasped my wrist in his hand, bringing my arm up over my head, making my heart race and a warm flush spread across my cheeks.

"When you bring your arm forward, let the blade go just

before you straighten out your elbow." His voice was low and husky, and I was acutely aware of every place our bodies were touching. Who knew target practice could be so… sexual.

His hand let go of my wrist then, his fingers dragging down my arm and coming to rest on my hip.

"Okay, now think of where you want the blade to go and give it a toss."

I had to take a deep breath to clear my head, but it only made things worse. His earthy, leather scent had a hint of vanilla and it titillated my senses.

I took another breath, this time through my mouth, trying my best to tame my wayward thoughts. I shook my head trying to clear my mind and attempted to concentrate on the target ahead of us, visualizing the blade hitting the bullseye as I threw it. I was rewarded with a resounding twang as the knife hit its target. Not only did it hit the tree, but it was exactly where I had envisioned it in the center of the bullseye.

"I can't believe I made that shot!" I gasped, astonished, unable to keep the excitement from my voice.

"You're a natural. I guess these were a good choice for you." I turned back to find Eben grinning from ear to ear. "You can keep them."

"No, I can't keep them. They're too nice for me to keep."

"I want you to have them. Consider it my gift to you." He stared at me again, his eyes deep and searching, as if he could figure out my secrets just by looking into my eyes, into my soul.

"Why did you kiss me yesterday?" he asked, his question catching me completely off guard.

"I... I don't know," I admitted, sputtering through my words. "I'm sorry. I'm not sure what I was thinking. Neverland has me acting a little out of character. You were just there, in the rain, and you looked so... good, and well I..." my words trailed off.

I couldn't admit to him that my initial reasoning was to ease the disappointment I'd felt after Peter's rejection in the grotto. Not that I wasn't interested in Eben. The more I was around him, the stronger my attraction was. And that kiss, that kiss had only strengthened my feelings for him. The way he kissed me so passionately made me hungry for more, and I felt incredibly insecure in that moment. I knew I couldn't handle another rejection and a nervous unease hit my stomach. I had no clue how he felt about the kiss.

"Neverland has a way of doing that." He sounded a little disappointed as he looked down and shuffled his feet.

"I don't regret it, if that's what you're wondering," I added quickly. I didn't want him to think I hadn't enjoyed it.

"Did you tell Pan?"

"No." I sighed. "I haven't found the right moment to bring it up."

"Remember how I said that Pan was overprotective when it comes to you?"

I nodded.

"I'm not sure if he will be willing to share you."

Share me? I'm not sure why, but the idea of them sharing me enthralled me in a way I'd never expected and my heart did a little stutter.

"Well, Peter doesn't get to choose who I'm with. It doesn't really matter anyway, he's not interested in me."

He cocked an eyebrow at me and chuckled. "If that's what you really think. But you should tell him about the kiss. Things like that have a way of coming up at the worst time if you try to keep it hidden."

I scowled a little, thinking of Peter's reaction to Ryder and I this morning. I wasn't eager to tell him about the kiss with Eben.

"How did you meet Peter anyway?" I asked. Somehow, Eben had completely derailed me from my attempts to find out more about him and I took the opportunity to get back on track.

"Well, unlike the others I went looking for Pan. I'd heard the stories and I wanted to escape to Neverland."

His story seemed odd to me. It was Peter who went out looking for the Lost Boys he wanted to bring back to Neverland. I'd never heard of anyone seeking him out before. Even Wendy had been beholden to Peter's whim to return to Neverland for the spring cleaning.

"I didn't even realize that was possible. How did you find him?"

"Didn't Pan tell you? It takes faith and trust." He was

smiling at me then, and it was obvious that he was being a bit facetious and I couldn't help but roll my eyes at him. Did he have to be so cryptic in his answers?

"So why did you go looking for him?" I asked, redirecting my question. But he remained silent, his eyes were heavy lidded as he took his time appraising me. I couldn't tell if he was pondering my question or deciding how much of an answer to give me.

"I think you know, just as much as the rest of us, that your world can be a cruel one. Have you figured it out yet?"

"Figured out what?"

"What you're looking for in Neverland." He had a seamless way of turning my own questions around on me, and somehow I felt compelled to answer.

"I'm not sure. A break from reality maybe... but whatever it is, hopefully I'll know it when I find it." I sighed. "Have you found what you were looking for in Neverland?"

"Maybe." He smiled at me as his one word answer had my mind contemplating exactly what he'd meant.

THE MORNING PASSED QUICKLY. Eben helped me work on my form and technique with the throwing knives. I also thoroughly enjoyed watching him display his skills with his own weapons. He even took his shirt off as the day began to warm. The tattoos that had been visible on his arms continued up and covered his chest and back. A grayscale rams skull, with large horns that curved just above his pierced nipples, was the centerpiece on his chest. I had never seen tattoos so detailed and elaborate. They were beautiful, but in a masculine, sexy as hell, sort of way.

He wielded his weapons with deadly precision. His skills were impressive and utterly lethal. He had been right when he'd said that I had nothing to worry about when I was with him and the other boys— at least nothing physical. But I was starting to think I needed to start worrying about my emotions when I was around them.

"There you are, Hen! I've been missing that beautiful face of yours." Ryder and Tripp came into the practice field and I couldn't help but smile. I couldn't hide the fact that I was thrilled to see them. I guess I had missed them, too.

"Eben's been showing me how to use these throwing knives," I said, showing Ryder one of the blades Eben had given me.

"Really? Well let me see what you got," Ryder encouraged.

I was a little more self conscious around the others than I had been around Eben, but I didn't want to disappoint my teacher. If I couldn't perform in front of my boys, then how would I be able to use them when it really mattered? My boys... that was the first time I'd thought of them as 'my boys.' Damn, I really was falling down the rabbit hole that was Neverland.

I took up my stance remembering everything Eben had taught me, and I let them fly one after another. They didn't all hit the bullseye, but they all landed solidly within the target. I turned, smiling, to see Ryder with his hand over his heart.

"Damn, that was so hot! Like you threw a knife right into my heart. I think I just fell in love with you a little more!"

I laughed his comment off. He was just joking with me, wasn't he?

"Gwen, we came to find you and let you know that Pan's been delayed a bit. His meeting with the Pixie Elders is taking longer than he anticipated, and he wanted us to keep you updated," Tripp said.

I felt my mood fall just a little. Peter was in such high demand, and he'd been pulled away from our time together more than I liked. I knew I couldn't be selfish. Just because I was here didn't mean he could escape from his responsibilities. I wondered then just how long I had here in Neverland. I had a sudden sense of urgency to get in as much time as possible with each of them. Nothing like knowing you had limited time to motivate you to live in the moment and treasure every minute together.

Is this how my sister felt all the time? My sister, my sister... What was her name? Oh my god! I had to stop and really search my thoughts.

Michaela!

How could I forget that? I shook my head, as if trying to clear it. It must be that I was so consumed by this experience, by these boys, that I'd had a momentary lapse. That had to be it. I grasped the acorn locket she'd given me and squeezed it tight in my fist, enjoying the slight prick of pain it caused, as if that's what I needed to bring me back to reality.

An immense wave of guilt washed over me. I was here in the paradise of Neverland being wooed and seduced by the most amazingly gorgeous men, who say all the right things, all the while Mic was probably worried sick about where I'd disappeared to. If only I could call or text her, to let her know I was alright, then maybe I wouldn't feel so bad.

I hated these warring emotions, I just wanted to ignore them and live for myself, in the here and now. Well fuck me if that didn't sound like the most selfish thing I'd ever thought. I didn't want to think of tomorrow and what that might bring or how I might feel when I got there. Just give yourself this one thing, I thought. Once I was done with Neverland I'd go back to the depressing purgatory that was my life, clinging to the hope that Michaela wouldn't leave me too. And I'd do it without any complaints, if I could just have this.

I popped the clasp and opened the small locket, running my finger gently over the miniature photograph of the two of us. The inscription caught my eye, '*To die will be an awfully big adventure.'* I smiled and chuckled to myself. It was like her words were coming across the veil to give me the message I needed to hear.

"Everything Okay, Gwen?" Tripp asked. I had a bad habit of showing my emotions all over my face.

"I'm fine, really. Maybe I just need to take a break," I confirmed as I rubbed at my temples for a minute.

"You want to watch us in the sparring ring for a bit?" Ryder offered. "I think I need to kick Eben's ass for stealing your attention all day! What do you say, Eben? Are you game?" Ryder taunted with that sly smirk on his face.

"You are all talk my brother, but I'm in."

Tripp and I settled on a patch of grass beside the sparring ring. Ryder quickly joined Eben in removing his shirt. As if the sight of their toned, half naked bodies wasn't enough, once they started fighting, they glistened in a sheen of sweat. I felt a nagging throbbing in my core that was now screaming to be sated. Neither boy held back. This wasn't just practice, they were throwing real punches and kicks. I could hear them grunting with the strain. I even noticed a bit of blood on Ryder's lips after Eben landed a particularly good blow. But Ryder only smiled wickedly before wiping the blood on his fists and then renewed his efforts. Why was that so sexy?

"Have you been enjoying your time here so far?" Tripp asked, distracting me from the performance the other two were putting on.

His nearness did nothing but fuel the desire that

continued to burn inside me. He was so attractive, a small lock of his dark brown hair had fallen down onto his forehead and his hair looked perfectly tousled and sexy. His olive tone skin was a deep bronze from days spent in the sun. When my gaze settled on his full lips, I bit my own as my mind drifted to thoughts of how soft and warm they would feel on mine. I had to beat down the urge to kiss him just then. Did Neverland mess with your hormones, too? Not sure if that was possible, but I'd never felt so needy before.

"Yes, I think I'm enjoying it more than I should."

"Don't you deserve to enjoy yourself?" The question was blunt and it felt a little personal, which instantly got my guard up.

"Well, I just mean that it seems... unfair, maybe, that I'm here, enjoying everything Neverland has to offer, while ignoring my responsibilities back home."

"By responsibilities, do you mean, taking care of your sister?" He asked so casually, as if he wasn't posing prying questions.

I wasn't used to people taking the time to get to know me— like really get to know me. It was both refreshing and intimidating at the same time. Would he still be interested in me when he realized that I'd been reduced to an old nurse maid, taking care of my sister and keeping up the household? My maturity level had gone from sassy teenager to that of an old lady in the few years since my parents had died.

"Yes," I admitted. "I'm all she has left and her illness takes its toll. She needs me." He nodded as if agreeing with me.

"That's noble of you, just be sure you don't lose yourself in the process. I would bet that your sister wouldn't want that, and I've gotten far too attached to you to see that happen."

I was speechless. I wasn't sure where to begin with his statement. The part where he pegged Mic so accurately or the part where he plainly stated that he was attached to me? It had my mind reeling and my heart doing a little stutter at the thought. These boys had been so straightforward. It seemed like everything they said was exactly what I needed to hear, when I needed to hear it.

Could I really trust the things they were saying? It was so easy to be around them. They made me feel special, wanted. But did they really mean what they said? Could they just be typical players, saying whatever they thought I wanted to hear to get into my knickers? Or in my current circumstance, under my makeshift dress— seeing that I had been going without any damn knickers since I'd arrived here.

I heaved a deep sigh. I had spent so much time trying to analyze the intentions of the men in my life and I was tired of it. I came back to my original thoughts that I would only have these boys for a limited time, and it would be reduced to nothing more than a fond memory when I returned home. So what really was the harm in indulging myself, regardless of what their end game was? I knew that it was a dangerous game to play. If I allowed myself to feel something for them, what price would I pay when it was finally time to leave?

CHAPTER XI
TRUST OR FAITH

When we finally returned to the camp, the sun had begun to sink into the horizon. It was clear that the time for spying on pirates had passed. Peter was waiting for us, a look of disappointment clear on his face. He was staring down at his hands where he held a wrapped package.

"Hi, Peter!" I called to him. I hated to see such a somber look on his face. I wondered if anything had happened with the Pixie Elders to disrupt his typical cocksure demeanor.

"Gwen, I'm so sorry about today. I really had planned

for us to go see pirates. Pixies can be so damn tedious," he said this with a deep scowl on his face.

"It's okay, really. I had a wonderful day with Eben and the boys. How did everything go with the Pixie Elders?" I asked. Peter gave the others a momentary glare. Was he jealous that they were able to spend the day with me, while he'd been pulled away by his responsibilities?

"News of the Jolly Roger's breach into fae territory only lasted a short time. Then I was roped into the May Day celebration planning. I should have known that Lill had ulterior motives to keep us apart." Peter looked tired and exasperated. Was he also feeling like our time together was quickly slipping through our fingers?

"Here, I brought you something to make up for today," he said as he presented me with the wrapped package. I pulled the twine strings holding it closed and opened the gift to find a neatly folded outfit inside.

"I thought you could use something of your own to wear. Not that I mind seeing you in my clothes, but I figured this might be more functional if we are going to see pirates tomorrow."

I looked up at him, surprised. I had figured that he would have pushed aside the idea of taking me to see pirates now that the opportunity had passed us by. He had been so against it in the first place.

"Don't look so surprised." He chuckled and I was delighted to see his cockiness begin to return. "I told you that I'd take you and I never go back on my word."

"Thank you, Peter. That was so thoughtful," I beamed as I began to pull out each piece to look it over. The outfit consisted of fine linens, with green and gold brocade fabrics, and even included a pair of knee high leather boots.

"These are beautiful. Where did you get them?" I asked.

"There are gnomes in Neverland that are mostly tailors. I asked them to put something together for you," he stated simply. Hmm... gnomes and pixies. I was beginning to think there was no limit to the fantastical nature of Neverland.

"Are you about done groveling so we can get some food and begin tonight's festivities?" Ryder asked.

THE BOYS HAD BUILT a large bonfire in the center of the camp. Apparently fire was considered a purifier and a healer. It was also an integral part of the spring cleaning festivities, and, according to the boys, would be a nightly occurrence until the May Day celebration. We all settled in after a long day and found ourselves in companionable conversation.

"Pan, you should have seen Gwen with those throwing knives— she's a natural. Not to mention it may be one of the hottest things I've ever seen." Ryder winked at me and I couldn't help but notice Peter's downcast expression, still irritated at missing out on our time in the practice fields.

"Well, I owe it all to Eben's expertise," I said as I nodded at Eben, giving him a warm smile.

"Anyone up for a game of Trust or Faith?" Ryder suggested, barely hiding his anticipation.

"Trust or Faith?" I asked, a perplexed expression on my face.

"You've never played Trust or Faith before?" Ryder asked, surprised.

"Can't say that I have, can you explain how it goes?"

"You start with trust, where you have to answer a question, and we trust that you will tell the truth. If you refuse to answer your trust question, then you're required to take a faith challenge, where you have to have faith that we will give you a challenge you can complete," Ryder explained.

"You mean, like Truth or Dare?" I asked, and all the boys stared at me as if I was speaking a different language. "I guess that Trust or Faith is Neverland's version of our Truth or Dare, but I get the concept."

"So, would you like to play?" Tripp asked, always making sure I was comfortable in whatever situation presented itself.

I thought for a moment. I wasn't keen on opening up about my problems, but what the hell, if they wanted to know the real me, I couldn't hide it forever.

Not like I had to worry about running into them at a pub someday, or finding out they were attending the same university as I was. It was actually a double edged sword.

One day soon I'd have to leave these amazing guys behind, knowing I'd probably never see the likes of them in my world. But also, I could confide in them, anything I wanted to and leave knowing that Neverland would keep all my flaws, fears and secrets. Not to mention the fact that I had some burning questions of my own, and now I had a perfect excuse to ask them.

"Okay, I'm game. Ryder, are you going first since you suggested it?" I asked.

"Nope, guests and ladies first, of course. We may be Lost Boys but we still have our manners," he assured me.

"Alright, Peter, my question is for you," I said quickly, eager now to get the game going. This was going to be interesting. Peter perked up at the sound of his name. He'd been wallowing across the bonfire from me since we'd returned from our day. He blinked a couple times as he took a moment to comprehend what I'd just said.

"Why didn't you tell Wendy about Hook's return after she left with your Lost Boys?"

I was going out on a limb here. I wasn't one hundred percent sure that's what happened. Wendy could have recreated the story to make it more like a fairytale in order to pass it on to her children. Peter glared at me and I could tell that I was on the right track. I felt bad and momentarily considered giving him another question, but I waited, to see if he would answer or opt out for the faith. He pressed his lips into a thin line, his brow furrowed.

"Because," he grumbled, "they would have insisted on coming back."

"So you didn't want them to come back?" His answer only spurred more questions.

"You only get to ask one question, Gwen." Peter smirked, happy with his half answer and now I was glowering, only feeling more confused than before.

Now it was Peter's turn to ask a trust question and he turned to Ryder.

"Why didn't you have sex with Gwen last night, like you do with all the other fae girls?"

Peter added that little detail about Ryder's promiscuity as an obvious dig. All eyes turned to Ryder for a response, but what the hell? As if I didn't have any say in whether or not we'd had sex. Ryder gave Peter a menacing look that only lasted for a moment. I really don't think that boy could stay mad at anyone.

"Don't get me wrong, I wanted to. The way her sweet ass rubbed against my cock had me rock hard." He stopped and sighed, a far off look in his eyes as if he was recalling our night together. "But Gwen's different. She's not just a quick fuck for a good time. *If* she decides to have sex with me, I want it to mean something for both of us."

Ryder looked at me, a sweet expression on his face and I melted. My romantic mind was swooning over his words and my libido was already agreeing to the aforementioned sex. Peter snorted at the response, but the game moved on.

"Gwen!" Ryder called to me for the next trust question

and I froze. I knew it was coming but I was instantly anxious over what his question might be.

"Which one of us do you like the best?" he asked. I knew it was an impossible question to answer.

"I can't answer that. Honestly, I like all of you the same."

"Aww that's a non answer! You've gotta take the faith challenge if that's what you're going with."

I looked around at the other boys and they all nodded in agreement with Ryder. He'd asked me a trick question— one he knew I couldn't answer, in an effort to force me into a faith challenge. That cheeky bastard!

"Okay, then what's my faith challenge?" I asked, rather snarky. Honestly I was glad he hadn't asked something personal.

"Kiss all the Lost Boys that you haven't kissed yet."

He really was a cheeky bastard. He obviously knew that he would be included in the remaining two Lost Boys that I hadn't kissed. But I now had to reveal to Peter that I had kissed Eben before I'd had the chance to tell him myself, privately. Of course Eben had to be right about these things coming up at the most inopportune time.

I looked at Eben briefly and he was staring at me, his chin resting on his steepled fingers, his brow slightly raised like he was just waiting for the shit show to begin.

"What kind of kiss are you talking about, like a peck or does it need to include tongue?" I asked, trying to stall.

"The same way you kissed Eben," Ryder said. Peter's

eyes shot up to mine with a look of shock on his face and his mouth slightly a gape. He looked between Eben and I a few times.

"Peter, I was going to tell you, we just haven't had a moment to talk." I don't know why I was explaining myself to him, I knew I didn't owe him anything, but for some odd reason, I felt as though I had cheated.

"Eben, huh?" Peter just shook his head, but didn't say anything else. He stared off into the fire, his jaw working and tense.

"Go on, Gwen. Time to complete your faith," Peter said coldly. I got to my feet. I wasn't about to let Peter ruin this for me. Peter had been clear that he didn't want anything with me, and if he was still torn over that decision then that was on him. I wouldn't reject the other boys. I couldn't deny that I was developing feelings for each of them. I wanted to kiss them; I wanted all of them.

I walked over to where Ryder sat on the other side of the fire. It had been his challenge, so I guessed that would be the best place to start. I felt terrible that he had resorted to a game in order to kiss me. All he'd had to do was make a move and I would have eagerly obliged.

I reached my hand to him, and when he grabbed my hand, I pulled to encourage him to stand. He straightened to his full height, towering over me, making me feel small as he placed his warm hands around my waist.

"Ryder," I said quietly as I placed my hands on either

side of his handsome face. "I would have kissed you without the faith."

I pulled him toward me and ever so softly, I started the kiss. His lips were warm and soft. I felt a tingling sensation race down my body, all the way to my fingertips and toes. His hand slid up my back, fisting in my hair and crushing me to him. I angled my head slightly to deepen the kiss. I slipped my tongue into his mouth and he moaned softly as we explored each other. I could hear my racing heartbeat pounding in my ears. It felt like the whole world fell away and it was only the two of us.

I finally came back to reality when I heard one of the other boys clearing their throat and I pulled away. When I opened my eyes, I found Ryder, still breathless with a stunned look on his face, as if I had just rocked his world. I loved that I'd put that look there.

"Damn, Hen, that was..." Ryder didn't finish his sentence, but pulled a hand through his hair and I laughed at his bemused state.

"Well shit, Ry, how am I going to compete with that?" Tripp interrupted. I looked up then to find Tripp striding over to me, his long legs closing the distance between us. He wasn't waiting for me to come to him, oh no, he was coming to get me. Before I knew what was happening, he'd hoisted me up, his hands cupping my ass as my legs wrapped around his waist, my arms encircling his neck. It was my turn to be a little muddled. My normally reserved and polite Tripp, had completely surprised me with his forwardness.

"You've been biting that lip all day and now it's my turn for a taste," he said, his voice husky.

His lips were on mine, hard. It felt passionate and needy. He wasted no time before his tongue found mine and we kissed as if we'd been starved for each other. He grasped me tight with one arm and then he was laying me down on my back beside the fire. He positioned himself on top of me, never breaking the kiss. His leg pressed against my core and I shamelessly rubbed my throbbing sex against him, moaning into his mouth. His hand came up and traced along my jaw softly, before he pulled away.

We were both panting in the aftermath. My mind was scrambled. Two mind blowing kisses back to back had me reeling. I didn't think I could remember my own name at that point. He smiled down at me and chuckled a little.

"How was that?" He asked, flashing me one of his beautiful smiles.

I smiled, what I could only assume was a ridiculous smile in return.

"That was… that was…" I stumbled and Tripp laughed again.

"I'll take your speechlessness as a good sign."

All I could do was nod, my mind still clouded with the rush of hormones.

After I took a moment to compose myself, I sat up and looked at Peter, expecting him to be angry, but instead he looked… aroused. I looked around at the other boys and they all had similar expressions on their faces. I felt like prey, surrounded by a pack of hungry wolves. I wasn't sure how much longer I could stave off this pent up desire. I needed a release and I wanted nothing more than my boys to give it to me.

"It's your turn," Tripp reminded me.

I had to shake my head to clear it. I was having a hard time thinking of what to ask, even though I knew I'd had questions when we'd started playing. But for the life of me, I couldn't remember them. So I asked the first question that popped into my head.

"Eben, why are you Lilleybell's favorite?" I wasn't sure why I asked that. It had nagged at me when Peter had originally mentioned it. She had seemed to stake her claim on him the very first time we'd met. What was it about him that she was so possessive of? The thought of her possessing him brought on an unexpected surge of anger. If anyone would possess him, it would be me.

I had never been one to be jealous, but Lillybell provoked a side of me that I'd never known existed. Ugh, Neverland took every emotion I had and amplified it. Eben looked momentarily surprised by my question.

"Oooh ain't that a bitch of a question, Eben!" Ryder said with a little laugh. Eben remained quiet for longer than I anticipated. I had expected it to be an easy question.

"You gonna hide the truth from her Eben?" Peter challenged, he was still raw from finding out that we'd kissed. Eben sighed then and I fully expected him to take the faith rather than answer. But with all the build up, I was definitely curious to what the answer was.

"The reason that I'm Lill's favorite is because," he paused again, giving careful consideration to his answer and I began to get nervous. "Because we have a casual relationship, and out of all the Lost Boys she's slept with, she knows I fuck her the best."

I had to actually remind myself to close my mouth after my jaw had dropped open when I heard his response. He had seemed hesitant to tell me, but when he had said 'I fuck her the best,' he'd said it with such conviction, as if it was something he was proud of.

There was so much to digest here. The Lost Boys had sex with Lill? I hadn't even thought that was possible! And yet I was reminded of how stunning she had been in her human form and I can't believe the idea hadn't even occurred to me— she was a faerie for fucks sake. But she was so beautiful, and I was so mediocre. How could I compete with a blonde bombshell with wings?

I remembered Peter calling out Ryder for sleeping with fae girls earlier and it hadn't bothered me then. I wasn't a virgin and I didn't expect them to be either. But the idea of him with Lill had me seeing red. She had been nothing but a bitch to me since I'd arrived. I guess that made sense now seeing as how she'd obviously had them first. But, damn it, they were my boys now, and I didn't want to share them.

"Pan," Eben started, aiming his trust question at Peter and effectively distracting my racing mind over his admission about Lill. "If Gwen would have us, are you willing to share her with the rest of us?" Eben asked and the mood at the camp changed. No one spoke and the only noise was the crackle and pop of the fire.

I looked around at all the boys and they were staring, expectantly, at Peter. The contrast of the glowing firelight and shadowed darkness gave their features an ominous look. I could feel the tension in the air and it made me uncomfortable. Why had Eben asked such an odd question? And why was it up to Peter which Lost Boy I could be with?

But as I looked at the boys, it occurred to me that their dynamic was unlike anything I'd seen before. They were more than just friends, they were brothers, they were family. Not just the common concept of a modern day family either. These boys had each other's back through life and death situations on a daily basis. I guess I hadn't given much thought as to how strong their bonds must be. Of course they bickered like any brothers would, but I guessed the possibility of a girl, of me, coming between them all, was something that needed to be addressed.

"Of course you had to go and fucking ask that!" Peter's words were cold and harsh and his brow was furrowed. "I didn't bring her here for you all to fuck her. She's a daughter of Wendy. You know what that means to me! She's better than that, and you don't deserve her!"

A loud crack of thunder boomed from out of nowhere. I startled at the sound, the evening had been perfectly peaceful until this moment and now things seemed to be getting out of hand. Even Neverland was responding to Peter's anger.

"And you think you deserve her?" Eben shot back, not backing down from Peter at all.

Now both of them were on their feet, fists clenched, in a standoff. I wasn't sure what to do and I looked frantically at Tripp and Ryder for reassurance. Neither of them were looking at me. Their attention focused on the two boys about to clash. Peter grimaced at Eben's question.

"The difference between you and I, is that I know I'm not good enough for her. I won't lead her on, just for my own selfish pleasure."

"Oh, so now you're better than me? Isn't that how it always is with you Peter? You think you're better than all of us."

"Well at least I don't go around sticking my cock into every hot piece of ass that walks by. She'd be just another notch on your belt, and then you'd be more than happy to send her back, without a second thought."

"That's a fucking lie Pan and you know it!"

"So what, one day with her and now you think you have feelings for her? You don't care about anyone but yourself, Eben!" Peter hissed the words out and before I knew what was happening, Eben lashed out and landed a solid right hook to Peter's jaw. The sound was sickening, and I think I let out a little yelp. Tripp was beside me instantly, slipping his arm around my waist as we watched the spectacle.

Peter regained his composure and the two were now

trading punch for punch, their bodies circling each other, taught and poised. Peter with a bloody lip, Eben with a bloody nose. I couldn't take it, I hated to see them hurting each other over me. I had to stop this.

"STOP IT!" I screamed at them, my own voice sounded foreign to me— raw with emotion. I hadn't realized before, but tears leaked from the corner of my eyes. Was I really crying? I didn't know what emotion I felt in that moment.

The boys both stopped in their tracks and looked at me. The irritation drained from their faces as they stared at me. Their fisted arms dropped to their sides, and everything was quiet again, save for the panting breaths of the boys.

"You guys can't fight over me! I am not this virtuous lady that you are making me out to be." Now I was panting as my emotions poured out. "And I sure as hell am not Wendy!" I glared at Peter as I said this and his face fell as his gaze shifted to his feet. He couldn't even look at me.

"I get to choose! I choose who I want, how I feel, and, yes, I choose who I fuck. I don't belong on this pedestal that you're trying to put me on."

I grabbed Tripp's hand and started walking away from the bonfire. I needed a moment alone, but I was reminded of Tripp's warning that I shouldn't be wandering the Neverland by myself, especially now that it was nighttime. Tripp came along without saying a word.

"Can you just give me a moment, and watch over me from a distance?" I asked, despondently.

"Of course, Gwen. Look, I'm sorry about what

happened back there. It's usually just us guys, and we don't always act properly. When things get heated, it's not uncommon for us to settle it with our fists. I'm not trying to make excuses… or maybe I am, but I just wanted to at least try and explain." Tripp was so genuine. I loved that he was always trying to do or say the right thing.

"I know. I just hate the idea that I've intruded on your lives here and pitted brother against brother. That wasn't my intention. I truly care about you all, and I just don't want to be the reason you are fighting. I'm really not worth it."

Tripp grunted at this. "You really don't see yourself clearly, Gwen. I hope that's something I can change before you leave." He said this as he tucked a loose strand of hair behind my ear and traced his fingers along my jaw before dropping his hand.

I wanted him to kiss me then. To clear my mind of all these confusing emotions and replace it with lusty desire. At least that I knew how to handle. But he left me then, giving me the space I had asked for and a sudden emptiness washed over me. I'd been around the boys so much that their absence was palpable and I felt desperately lonely.

CHAPTER XII
INTENTIONS

When Tripp and I returned to the fire only Ryder remained. He'd been drinking mead while conversing with pixies and his eyes had taken on a glassy look. I smiled at the sight of him. He'd had a few too many, and it looked like he had a good buzz going on.

"Hen! Milady! I'm so glad you came back and you didn't let those fuckers run you off altogether!" He held up a cup and his drink splashed over his hand as he got to his feet, and I giggled at him.

"Can I interest you in some mead? It's quite good actually, it's one of the fae's special spring cleaning brews."

"That sounds absolutely perfect right now."

He handed me a cup of the mead and I accepted eagerly looking forward to the reprieve the alcohol might give me. A spicy tang hit my dry throat with the first swallow, and turned to a small ball of fire at the pit of my stomach. The sweet aftertaste of honey was delightful in my mouth and I felt a bit light headed after several gulps.

"Mmmm. This is exactly what I needed! Thanks Ryder."

We sat around the fire, just the three of us, and the occasional pixie that came by for a taste of the mead. I helped myself to several glasses before the earlier events of the evening began to fade.

"We should probably be getting to bed. We'll be up early, in search of pirates in the morning." Tripp yawned and stretched.

"Would you like a sleeping companion again tonight?" Ryder asked. I looked at him a moment and he quickly put his hands up, "Just sleeping Hen, I swear. Cross my heart, hope to die! Because Pan really will kill me if I try anything." He winked at me and his words were a little slurred, which made it extra cute, and I giggled. I knew I'd had too much to drink myself, because everything was making me giggle.

"But what about Tripp? I can't leave him to sleep all alone," I said, feeling rather bold because of the alcohol.

"Alright Tripp, I get her right and you can have her left," Ryder agreed. "But no fucking! You heard Pan, he'll have your balls!" We all laughed at the joke, breaking the tension about the earlier events.

"Okay Gwen, I couldn't leave your left side to get all cold. What kind of gentleman would I be if I allowed that to happen?"

The three of us laughed ridiculously as we made our way to the treehouses, trying our best to navigate the the darkened rope bridges in our altered state. As we walked along one of the balconies, something grabbed at my hand and pulled me into the shadows. I was about to scream when I realized it was Peter.

"Shh, Gwen, don't scream, I just wanted to talk to you for a minute," Peter said in hushed tones.

I looked back toward Ryder and Tripp. They were waiting for me, just out of hearing distance. Apparently, they had been fully aware that Peter had been waiting for me in the shadows. Peter pulled me into an alcove that was lit with flaming sconces. When I saw his face in the light, I noticed a bruise on his jaw and a split in his bottom lip.

"Oh Peter, look at your face! Are you okay?" I asked as I gently touched my fingers to his marred face. He closed his eyes and leaned his cheek into my hand. He let out a deep sigh and looked at me, with that disarming stare of his, and all of my frustrations from the earlier confrontation melted away.

"I'm so sorry about earlier. I didn't mean for it to go that far in front of you."

"It's okay, really," I said dismissively.

"No, wait. Let me say something." There was a sense of urgency in his tone. "I didn't want to leave you alone yet again, tonight." He stopped then, looking away from me and fisted his hand in his hair for a moment in obvious frustration. "I keep fucking this up. You do something to me that I can't explain. I'm not myself around you. I haven't felt anything remotely like this since... well, since Wendy. But I needed you to know that I don't think you are Wendy. You are so much more."

"If you care for me, then why are you trying to put this distance between us? I don't understand?"

"I just can't... I can't. It's what's best for both of us." He tried to sound stern and all I could do was look up at him, dewy eyed. My mind started running through all the reasons why I wasn't good enough for him. I wasn't some flawless fae— I had no fantastic powers. In his eyes, I was just a simple girl, completely naive to the world he'd been a part of for countless years. I wasn't Wendy. I had to swallow the lump that was forming in my throat. Would I reduce myself to begging for his affection? A part of me thought about it, but my pride wouldn't let me beg.

"Don't look at me like that... shit! I want you to enjoy your time here and I'll do everything I can to make that happen, whatever you need. I just can't give you... that."

By 'that', he meant I could have whatever I wanted,

except him. His words were yet another rejection, but his body language said otherwise. He stood too close, he'd backed me up against the wall and caged me in with his hands planted on either side of my head, his eyes looked hungry.

"Okay Peter, if that's what you want."

"It's not what I want, damn it! It's what's best," he snarled as he punched his fist into the wall behind me, making it shudder with the impact. He was at war with himself and I couldn't figure out his volatile moods.

"Peter, I'm tired and spent from today. I'm going to bed. Unless you care to explain why it has to be this way? Why we can't just enjoy each other in the time we have and let that be enough?" I asked, knowing it was a long shot for him to answer me. And just as expected, he pressed his lips together and looked away from me.

"Okay, I get it. We'll try the friend thing. I'll see you in the morning, Peter." He glared at me, but he didn't say anything and he didn't try to stop me either.

I rejoined Ryder and Tripp, leaving Peter in the shadows. My heart broke a little, knowing that he'd put a stop to any relationship we might have had. Even if it was fleeting, I'd wanted it desperately, maybe too desperately. But I wouldn't allow myself to mourn for what could have been, even if that was easier said than done. I tried to focus my attention on Tripp and Ryder, the two boys who were true and genuine, and not afraid of their feelings for me.

We headed to a different house than the one I'd slept in

last night. This one had a large loft bed made from thick branches with a rustic ladder. Under the loft was a brightly colored hammock swing.

"This is my place," Tripp informed me, but I think I could have figured that out on my own anyway. The place was perfectly neat and tidy, nothing out of place and not a hint of dust or dirt anywhere.

"His bed's bigger and more comfortable," Ryder conceded as he pulled his shirt off over his head and ambled up the ladder, landing in a huff on the loft bed. I crawled up behind him and nestled into the bed. It enveloped me, the smell of clean, line dried linens, filled my senses and the warmth of Ryder beside me was so comforting.

Tripp came up next, the bed dipping with his weight. He positioned himself beside me, his arm draped over my belly, his face buried in my cascade of hair. I sighed deeply, completely content and safe between these two boys.

"I'm not sure how I'll ever sleep without you, Hen." Ryder breathed softly, and in the next second I could hear a soft snore coming from him and I smiled.

"I'm not sure how he can sleep while you're this close. You're so warm and soft, and you smell so good." He inhaled deeply and I let out a small laugh.

I reached over and ran my fingers through his hair, it felt soft and sleek as I raked my fingers through its thickness. He let out a soft moan as I gently massaged the back of his neck, before running my fingers through his hair again. I lost my train of thought with the repetitive motion of stroking his hair, focusing on the feel of him under my hand. The nearness of both boys and the calm, relaxation washing over my body was cathartic and blissful in that quiet moment before sleep.

I WAS on my back and my arms and legs were being caressed. It was dark and everything had a soft glow of a flickering fire. I looked to my right and I saw Ryder. The blue of his irises are piercing, standing out against the black mask painted around his eyes. He was kissing, languidly, up my arm. It was soft and tickling, leaving wet patches as he worked his way up my arm. I looked to my left and there was Tripp, his green eyes too, were outlined in a black mask, while he planted lazy kisses up my left side. His big hand reached for my nipple, tweaking it and rolling it between his thumb and forefinger.

I looked down to my leg to find Eben, his face painted in a similar fashion. He was holding my left ankle in his hand and he planted sultry kisses to my instep and bit my baby toe, sending a shock of pleasure directly to my core and I moaned. I looked to my right to find Peter. He was kissing up my inner thigh, dragging his tongue along my sensitive skin as he worked his way up, nipping at me here and there.

The graze of his teeth pushed my pleasure further and another moan escaped my lips.

"Can you handle this, Hen?" Ryder asked, his voice monotone and bereft of his normal wittiness.

I nodded.

"Do you want this, Gwen?" My gaze is pulled to Tripp, his voice in that same monotone, but his eyes are expressive. I wasn't able to answer him. I could only nod.

"Are we enough for you, Gwen?" Eben asked. I looked down to him and he was still caressing and kissing my leg, one hand sliding up to cup my ass.

I nodded at him as well.

"Do you want us to satisfy you, Gwen?" Peter's voice was a whisper. "All you have to do is ask." He was no longer kissing me. All of them had stopped and were staring at me, waiting for my response.

"Please!" I begged, the word came out in a moan.

Then they were all kissing me at once and a rush of sensation raced across my body, making me tremble. Oh god, my body was on fire with the onslaught of kisses, licks and nips from all four of my boys. I looked down to see Peter, reaching his hand up to my sex, palming my clit as he slowly slid his finger into the slick wetness of my folds. I raised my hips, grinding against his hand, asking for more. He slipped a finger deep inside me and I let out a cry.

Fuck, it felt amazing! I needed more. I opened my eyes again and Eben's hand joined Peter's and then he, too, slipped a finger deep inside me. Their paired fingers stretched me sweetly, caressing my G-spot and sending a shock wave of pleasure through my body. Then they were working me in conjunction, both of their fingers moving in unison, slowly stroking me in and out, in and out. I could feel my pleasure building.

Tripp and Ryder took each one of my nipples into their mouths. Tripp sucked on my left, while Ryder nibbled on my right. The overload of sensation makes me come undone and tips me over the edge to my climax. I was drowning in pleasure— my orgasm tearing me apart at the seams. I let out a loud moan and I startled.... awake.

I woke up with my heart pounding, my breath coming in pants and an obvious wetness between my thighs. Did I just cum in my sleep? I repeated the dream in my mind and my core clenched again. Damn, I was so sexually frustrated! Aargh... I needed to get laid— and soon.

I rubbed my eyes, trying to clear not only the sleep, but also the tormenting need that pulsated deep inside me. I looked over and found both boys sleeping soundly beside me in the pre-dawn light of morning. They looked so peaceful, and I enjoyed the opportune moment to stare, unabashedly, at them.

My mind strayed to Eben. I hadn't seen him last night after his fight with Peter. I hoped he was alright. I worried that this might change things between us. I'd finally felt like I'd made some headway with him yesterday. I needed to see him. I needed some time, just the two of us so we could talk things over.

I wondered about some of the things he'd mentioned in his fight with Peter. Did he actually have feelings for me? Or did he just want to have a casual relationship with me, like he did with Lill? After Peter's negative reaction, I wondered if he would even talk to me again. What if he'd determined I wasn't worth all the drama?

I needed to find him and clear the air between us, especially before we went adventuring to find pirates. Peter had pointed out his house to me when I first arrived. Maybe I could get lucky and find him without incident. I at least had to try. The first step was getting out of this bed without waking Tripp and Ryder.

They seemed deep in sleep, their faces relaxed, not a single worry line visible. Ever so slowly, I inched my way toward the ladder, trying hard not to touch them or make any sudden movements. Ryder groaned and I froze. He rolled over, mumbling something incoherent, but I was able to catch the word 'Hen' at the end of his rambling and I smiled, knowing he was even thinking of me in his sleep.

I reached the ladder without incident, but when I stepped on the first rung, the wood creaked with the addition of my weight. I paused, holding my breath, watching them closely, but neither moved and I said a little 'thank you' to the universe when I reached the bottom without waking either of them.

I found the neatly wrapped package that Peter had given me yesterday and pulled out the new outfit. It was a bit more complex than my clothes back home and it took me several minutes to figure out how to even put it on and I was glad no one was around to watch me fumble. I wished desperately that I had a mirror to see how it looked on me.

The outfit consisted of a blousy, white peasant shirt that hung off my shoulders and it was held in place with a corseted top made of thick, woven fabric. It was sleeveless and pressed my small breasts together, giving me more cleavage than I'd ever had. The fabric was black and was decorated in a green and gold threaded design. The skirts had pointed hems, like a star, with the longest points falling just below my knee. Peter had also provided me with black, thigh high stockings, held in place with garter straps. I finished off the outfit with a pair of tan, knee high leather boots with laces all the way to the top.

From what I could see of myself, the outfit was incredibly flattering. The corset cinched in my waist and the flaring skirts accentuated my hips, giving me an hourglass figure. Everything fit perfectly and I wondered how Peter knew exactly what size I needed. That cheeky bastard had probably spent more time than I'd realized looking me over when I'd been naked in the shower. Regardless, I was grateful to finally have some clothes of my own, rather than one of the boy's hand-me-downs. I still didn't have any knickers though. Was this another little joke of Peter's or was underwear really not a thing in Neverland?

Feeling sexy and confident in my new outfit, I set out looking for Eben's place. The night was just starting to give way to morning and the sky was turning from black to purple. The camp was eerily quiet and no one was up yet. A hint of smoke swirling up from the remnants of last night's fire was the only movement in the camp.

I walked along the rope bridges, racking my brain to remember where Peter had pointed out Eben's house. I peeked into a few windows with no luck. I was about to give up, completely frustrated because everything looked so different in the shadowed light. But I decided I'd check one last home toward the edge of the camp. I figured if Eben would be anywhere, it would be in the most isolated house in the camp, as far away from everyone else as possible.

I peeked into one of the small windows and I was thrilled to find him, lying sound asleep in his bed. I decided to let myself in, without knocking. I didn't want him to turn me away without even seeing me, plus I wanted desperately to see him up close while he slept. He always seemed so deep in thought and distracted. I wanted to see him, peaceful, in the abyss of sleep.

Thankfully, the door didn't squeak when I swung it open and closed it softly behind me. I took in the small room. He had a chair positioned in the corner next to a large trunk, and a small oil lamp was still lit and turned down low. He had shelves on the walls filled with books and I was tempted to peruse his collection to see what he'd been reading, but his sleeping form captured my attention and I was drawn to him, like a moth to flame. I know it's so cliche, but that's exactly how I felt.

He was laid out on his side in a small daybed, curled

into himself. He was shirtless and his normally spiked hair was a disheveled mess on his pillow— his black hair in stark contrast to the white of his bed linens. His face was relaxed, his mouth parted. It was a wonder to look at him without those dark eyes of his piercing through me, calculating everything I was doing. He looked younger while he slept, not like the man who always appeared to have the world on his shoulders.

I noticed that he, too, hadn't gotten out of the fight with Peter unscathed. He had a hint of a bruise under his eye and along his cheekbone. His knuckles were bruised. Old, dried blood still lingered there, but the cuts had already scabbed over. I got lost in the moment and reached down to run my fingers along his cheek.

The instant my hand touched his skin, his eyes popped open and he was a blur of motion. Before I could say anything, Eben had spun me around, crushing my back to his chest, his one arm grasped both of my wrists in a vice grip as he held a knife firmly against my neck.

It happened so quickly that I didn't have time to process what was happening. I could hear his breathing, ragged against my ear, and my body trembled involuntarily. What had I been thinking? I knew how lethal he was and I'd just snuck up on him unannounced, while he slept.

"Eben." My voice was quiet and shaky, but it was the best I could manage in my instant panic. I felt his body relax as recognition hit him.

"Fucking Christ, Gwen! What the fuck are you doing in my room? I could have killed you just then!"

He lowered the knife from my throat and I felt a burning sting where the blade had left a small abrasion on the delicate skin of my neck. He let go of my wrists and spun me around, grabbing my shoulders forcefully and staring at me with his dark, brooding eyes, his brow pulled down in a deep furrow. I couldn't speak in that moment.

"What are you doing here, Gwen?" he asked again, this time more stern and he shook my shoulders.

"I needed to see you after the fight last night. I wanted to make sure you were okay— make sure that *we* were okay," I stammered. Eben let out a deep sigh and hung his head.

"Well, damn, you could have picked a better time to come and find me." He sounded frustrated, but I could also detect a hint of amusement too.

"I wanted to see you, alone, and I wasn't sure you would even agree to see me again. I figured this would be the only way I could get you to talk to me," I admitted quietly, now feeling reckless in my decision to come and find him.

"Why would you think I wouldn't want to see you again?"

"I just… I seem to be causing all sorts of problems since I arrived. With Lill, with you and Peter. I guess I wouldn't blame you if you didn't want to bother with me anymore."

Eben reached up to where he'd held his knife against my throat and ran his thumb along the slight nick in my skin. I felt a hint of pain along with the rush of pleasure at having his warm hand on me. When he pulled his hand away, I noticed a smear of blood on his thumb. He held it up to his mouth and sucked the blood, *my blood*, from his thumb and it was oddly erotic. My breath hitched in my throat. He was staring intently at me and it was unnerving.

Eben smirked at me then. "Gwen, a simple disagreement with Pan isn't enough to keep me from what I want." His voice was firm and alluring. I felt butterflies in my stomach. Hell I felt butterflies everywhere.

"You were right, you know— about telling Peter about our kiss. I knew I should have told him, but I didn't want him to overreact, not that he should be overreacting seeing that he wants nothing to do with me—"

"Gwen, it's okay." He cut me off mid rant.

"I'm rambling, aren't I? I'm sorry, I just… sometimes you make me nervous," I admitted as I looked down at my fidgeting hands.

He raised his eyebrows at my admission. He moved closer to me then, invading my personal space, continuing to stare at me with his fathomless eyes.

"This makes you nervous?" he asked as he raised his hand to tuck a strand of hair behind my ear and then dragged his fingers slowly along my jaw.

I couldn't answer him, I could only nod. I blinked a few times and shook my head, coming back to my senses for a moment and pulled away. I couldn't have any kind of rational discussion with him while he was mesmerizing me and stroking my neglected libido.

I placed my hand on his chest and pushed him back. Only then, did it feel like I could take a full breath.

"What are your actual intentions toward me, Eben?"

"Intentions? What exactly are you expecting, Gwen?"

"I don't know, Eben! I just want to know what's going through your head," I exclaimed, the frustration in my voice was clear as day.

"Well, let's look at this logically," he said, as he laid back on his bed, his hand coming to his chin and rubbing the stubble that was beginning to show there. "You will be here, in Neverland, for a finite amount of time. You have four men, all vying for your attention. Your plan is to spend time with us all, culminating in the May Day celebration, which is only a short time from now. Then you plan to return home, to your own little world, and leave all of us behind. What is it you expect to accomplish in that time? I think I should be the one to question what your intentions are."

Well damn, when he put it like that, all the anticipation I'd been feeling shattered into a myriad of pieces at my feet. In reality, I knew I only had time for a short tryst with all of my boys. What was I expecting? To get them all to fall for me and then turn around and leave? Why was I ignoring the fact that I would have to leave them soon?

I hated that Eben was calling me out, but I had to face the fact that he was speaking the truth. I hated it so much because, deep down, I didn't want to leave them. I wanted to explore just how far this would go, with all of my boys, with no expiration date looming over my head. I knew it was wrong to ignore the obvious, to toy with their feelings, but I couldn't help it. I couldn't be sure if I would ever feel this way again.

"Everything," I whispered slowly. "I want everything, because when I finally leave and return to my destitute life, watch my beautiful sister shrivel and die, nothing will be left of me. I will be a shell of my former self and I will never be able to feel this way again. I will never be able to feel anything at all, ever again."

It was the most honest I'd ever been, with anyone. My darkest fears poured out of me. Eben seemed to have a way of eliciting the truth from me. The look on his face was one I'd never seen before. He looked utterly shocked by my words. Shocked, sad, and awed all at the same time.

"Stop staring at me like that!" I scolded, feeling incredibly self conscious in that moment. "Now will you answer my question?" I asked, hopeful that my truth would inspire an honest response from him.

"Gwen, I didn't realize... you know you could stay here with us in Neverland for as long as you'd like." His words sounded more like a plea, than an offer.

"I can't. I have to go back. She needs me." I'd forgotten her name again, my sister, and I was too overwhelmed to try and fish it from my waning memories.

"You want to know what my intentions are? I'm not really sure I can answer that just yet..." he sighed. "But, I'll admit that I can't explain what it is that I feel for you. I enjoy your company more than I should. I look forward to seeing you when you're not with me. Actually, you fill my every thought when you're not with me. You're beautiful and sexy. I can't stop thinking about that kiss, and every way I want to take you, every way I want to make you scream my name. It's infuriating and exciting all at the same time."

His words meant everything to me in that moment. I'd been honest with him and he'd, in turn given the gift back to me, validating my feelings with his own.

"So we're good then?" I asked, looking up at him, still feeling vulnerable.

"Mostly. I just need to revisit one thing." Then he reached for me as he slipped his hand to the nape of my neck and leaned into me, brushing his lips softly against mine.

This time he bit my lower lip, raking it between his teeth and then sealed his mouth to mine. This kiss was slow and exploratory, his tongue finding mine, moving in and out in time with mine. He pushed me back on his bed, his big body landing between my thighs with his bare chest pressed against me. His hands held my face in place as he continued. There was no rush this time, no one to interrupt us. When I started to reach down for his pants, he stopped and pulled away from me, stopping the natural progression of the kiss.

"It's not everything, but it's a start." He breathed softly, still resting on top of me. I didn't want him to move, loving the weight of him on top of me.

"I'd say that was a pretty good start. Did this kiss live up to the first?" I asked coyly.

"Oh yes. I think maybe we should continue this later." He smiled a wicked, bad boy grin at me and I melted.

Why later? I'm ready and wanting now! But he was already getting up and putting a shirt on. My libido was pouting.

"Think you're ready for pirates today?" he asked as he got himself ready, attaching a belt to his waist and filling it with weapons. A dagger to his right, his hatchet to his left. He even hid a small pistol in his boot.

"As ready as I'll ever be, I guess. I grew up hearing stories about Captain Hook. I'm looking forward to putting a face to the infamous pirate."

"God help us if we run into Hook. Trust me, he's not someone you want to cross paths with. But with that in mind, I made this for you," he said as he threw a small leather belt my way.

"What's this?" I asked as I unwrapped the leather.

"It's for your throwing knives. Here let me show you," he said as he came and kneeled in front of me. He grabbed the leather belt from my hands and pushed up my skirt, exposing my thigh. A cool gust chilled my exposed parts and I shivered. He deftly belted the leather holder to my upper thigh, pulling the buckle tight against my skin. He pulled out the bundled knives that he'd kept for me, and slowly slid all four blades into place.

"There. Now you're ready for pirates," he said, still kneeling before me. He planted a slow kiss on my inner thigh and I let out a low moan at the feel of his soft lips on my sensitive skin. He stood and began walking around me, taking me in. I felt hot all over and my cheeks— flushed as usual.

"Gwen!"

I was distracted from Eben's appraising eyes when I heard my name being called.

"Gwen!"

There it was again, this time a bit more desperate. Shit! I'd forgotten about Tripp and Ryder. I had left them sleeping without so much as a note to let them know where I'd gone.

I rushed out of Eben's place, anxious to find the other boys and reassure them that I was fine. I saw Peter first, stalking along one of the bridges and I called out to him.

"Gwen! Damn, there you are! Are you okay? We've been looking all over the camp for you." He looked relieved to find me but his words still sounded frantic.

"I'm okay, I'm fine. I just went to talk to Eben. I should have told Ryder and Tripp so they didn't worry. I'm sorry."

I felt awful for causing them to worry. Peter had said that he was the one who was constantly fucking things up and yet, I was starting to wonder if it was really me that was the problem.

Peter held me at arms length and the last vestiges of tension melted from his features as he looked me over. His eyes raked over me appreciatively in my new outfit, a hungry look in his eyes.

"Wow, Gwen. You look—"

"Hen! Oh my god, there you are. You had me worried sick," Ryder interrupted. As soon as he reached me, he threw his arms around me, squeezing me tight to him. His concern was so endearing, and his hug was an added bonus. Tripp joined us next and his face transformed from relief to irritation.

"Tripp, I'm so sorry. I should have said something. Please don't be angry with me," I pleaded. I didn't want to start the day off on the wrong foot. Tripp came in and pulled me to him.

"It's not you I'm angry with," he huffed, "I should never have let my guard down. What if someone had come to take you, and I slept right through it? I'm sorry Gwen, it won't happen again."

He pulled me away and looked at me with an imploring look. Was he looking for my forgiveness? Tripp was like my white knight, sweet and chivalrous. He was taking all the blame on himself because I'd slipped past him.

"Don't be too hard on yourself," Ryder consoled. "It was your first night sleeping with Hen. You couldn't have known how good you'd sleep or that you wouldn't want to wake up from the amazing dreams she brings on!" Ryder laughed as he punched Tripp's arm. He was such a joy to be around, the perpetual optimist. He made light of every situation and I smiled at him adoringly.

Tripp smirked a half smile. "Pan, are we all set to head out then?" And just like that, we'd moved on with our day, no drama, and it was a welcome relief.

Peter had taken a step back as the other boys had rushed in to check on me and he looked almost pained as he watched them fawn over me. It took him a moment to realize that Tripp had asked him a question.

"We are just waiting for…" Peter hesitated in his answer, and just then, a glowing Lilleybell joined our group.

"What is she doing here?" I demanded. I'd had my fill of Lilleybell and I wanted nothing to do with her for the rest of my stay in Neverland.

"She insisted on coming along, as another condition for supplying the faerie dust." Peter seemed tense as he explained, like he was waiting for me to protest.

Well, I'll show him, I thought and scowled. I bit my lip and crossed my arms over my chest, determined not to make this an issue. I wanted to continue with a drama free morning as much as possible.

"Well, I guess we're ready then." Peter exhaled the breath he'd been holding. "Let's head out, I want to get this over as quickly as possible. Remember, we do not engage. Stay hidden, this is just a simple recon and then back here." All the Lost Boys agreed and then we were off.

CHAPTER XIII
NOTHING BUT A STAND IN

I was giddy with the idea of pirates. They were the overly romanticized, misunderstood bad boys that still had women swooning even in the 21st century. I knew the stereotype was nothing like reality, but I couldn't help my anticipation for our adventure.

We made our way along the Mysterious River throughout the morning. It was beautiful, like everything else in Neverland. The river was crystal clear, with varying shades of blue and green as it meandered around rock outcroppings. Exotic birds, in rainbow colors, flew in and out of the lush, green canopies surrounding the riverbanks. The river itself was filled with colorful fish, and we even caught sight of pink dolphins as they breached the water's surface.

I tried to focus on the beauty of everything around me rather than focus on the deteriorating mood that was washing over the group. We all remained fairly silent, except for the tinkling coming from Lill. The boy's moods had started off fun and excited, but quickly began to change to somber and irritable as she tinkled on, and I could only assume that she was going off about me.

"Lill, can you just shut the fuck up already, we get that you don't like her. No need to keep carrying on about it," Ryder finally snapped.

Lill stopped and glared at him, her whole body glowing red in her irritation, but her silence only lasted a moment before she started chiming in again.

Tripp leaned in toward me. "She said that you…"

"No, I don't want to know what she said! I'm perfectly happy not knowing what she is saying. I would prefer to continue to ignore her," I stated plainly, trying not to let my frustrations get the better of me.

Lill was always trying to sabotage my time with the boys and it was irritating as fuck. Then I heard the soft poof, followed by a slight gust of wind as Lill transformed into her human body. I stared at her perfect form and my jaw dropped a little. I had known she was beautiful, but I saw her differently now, knowing she had been with all of my boys. She knew them all, intimately, in a way that I didn't. They had taken their pleasures from her, and she from them. I felt that irrational jealousy swell up inside me and I could feel my hands fisting at my sides.

"Try and ignore me now, Gwen." She exaggerated my name as she said her snarky come back.

"That's enough, Lill. Let's just keep moving. We've got a lot of ground to cover," Peter interjected, a scowl on his face as he glared at her.

Lill remained in her human form as we pressed on, and she was quiet— for a little while anyway. I thought maybe Peter's rebuke had worked to shut her up, but she just couldn't help herself.

"Have you guys been wondering why she wants to see pirates so badly?" No one answered her, but she didn't need them to answer for her to continue. "You know, now that I think about it, this demure little act of hers seems like just the right kind of girl to suit Hook's... particular tastes," she mused.

"Jas will never get his grimy hook on Gwen, Lill. So your point is moot," Eben retorted. I wondered what she meant? What kind of 'particular tastes' did Hook have?

"No, you're right. She's probably too prude for that. Hook would break her for sure."

"Prude? I doubt the boys would agree with you. Not after last night." I couldn't help myself. I knew I should be trying to be the bigger woman here, but I couldn't resist the chance to throw it in her face that I had kissed them all. Her face paled and she stared at me in surprise. This was something she hadn't been expecting and I reveled in it, a devious smirk on my face.

"Really, Eben, you lowered yourself to her level? I mean, I guess I can understand the rest... Tripp is a lost puppy looking for love, Ryder will fuck anything female and Peter is distracted by her lineage, but you? Really?"

Lill stared at Eben, her preference for him obvious in her statement. I had no idea how the others put up with her shit. I could see that she was gorgeous, but her personality turned her into the ugliest person I'd ever met. Didn't the boys have any standards, or did their basic human urges supersede everything else?

"Lill, I don't think you want to get into this with me right now. I know you can't see past your jealousy, and I get that, but, need I remind you, that our relationship isn't exclusive? I don't care how, or with whom, you indulge your needs with and I expect you to stay the fuck out of my business."

Eben was cold in his response to her. She stared at him, with hurt and longing in her eyes. She looked like she might even start to cry. For a moment I felt bad for Lill. I wouldn't want to be on the other side of Eben's wrath. But that only lasted for a moment— a very short moment.

"I know they haven't taken you to bed yet, Gwen." She leered at me as I tried to ignore her. "And I know why. Do you want to know why? Who are we kidding, of course you want to know why they've slept with half the fae girls in

Neverland, but they still haven't fucked you yet." Lill laughed, but it wasn't a pretty laugh. She was obviously getting off on tormenting me. "Because you are nothing but a stand-in for a long dead Wendy. And you just don't match up to her, in Peter's eyes. You'll never be her. You'll never mean to Peter what Wendy meant to him. We'll all be happier when you're gone. Then none of us will have to pretend anymore."

My eyes widened as I clutched my locket. Wendy's locket. Peter's kiss…to Wendy.

"Shut up, Lill!"

"Low blow, Lill."

"What the fuck, Lill?!"

All the boys yelled at her in unison. Her attacks on me were only getting more ruthless. She was like the worst part of your psyche, spewing out all of your deepest, darkest insecurities for everyone to hear.

"Lill, that's it! You're done, get the fuck out of here. I don't need you and I don't need your faerie dust!" Peter yelled at her and her face fell instantly, her jaw dropping open.

"But Peter, you know I'm right!" she retorted.

"You don't know a fucking thing about it! Now get the hell out of here. I don't want to see you until after spring cleaning is over." Peter glared at her, daring her to challenge him.

"Don't send me away, Peter. You know you'll regret it later," she pleaded with him.

"I can't take it anymore, Lill. I was right when I tried to send you away for spring cleaning. It'll be best for all of us if you just go." Peter seemed resolved and determined to send her away.

"Fine, I'll go, but Eben promised to take me to the May Day celebration. He can't back out of our agreement." She stood her ground, standing as tall as she could manage with a mask over her emotions and her nose turned up in the air.

Peter sighed heavily and shot Eben a menacing look. "That's between you and Eben. I won't stand in the way of your agreement, but if you say one more thing about Gwen I will banish you from the festivities altogether."

Lill's lip trembled just the slightest before she could hide it behind her stoic mask.

"Fuck you, Peter." She spat at him and then morphed into her pixie form, her twinkling light disappearing into the vast forest.

Peter ran his hand through his hair, leaving it looking disheveled. He was obviously frustrated by the whole situation and of course I felt instantly guilty for all the trouble I'd caused.

"I'm sorry, Peter," I said softly as I walked over to his side and placed my hand on his forearm.

"It's not your fault, Gwen. It's not even Lill's fault really. You know pixies are single minded creatures, she can't see past her jealousy whenever you're around. It's my fault. I knew I should've sent her away right in the beginning."

"Don't let it bother you, Gwen. Just think, we're almost

at Three Pence Bay and you can watch us run through some pirates. I know fighting always leaves me horny as hell, maybe watching will do the same for you." Ryder winked at me and I laughed in shock over his words.

"No, Ryder! Fuck, I said no fighting today," Peter scolded.

"Shit, Pan. Sorry I forgot."

As we neared the end, where the river emptied into the bay, Peter veered off the path we'd been following all morning and headed toward one of the surrounding cliffs. I was thankful I had new boots as we climbed higher and higher up the rugged terrain until the trees began to get sparse.

Peter stopped the entire group just before we broke the tree line and I was relieved. I was completely out of breath and trying my best to hide it. The boys all appeared cool and calm as if taking a nice morning stroll. I hated it and I told myself I needed to get in better shape.

"Gwen, do you remember how to fly?" Peter asked.

"A happy thought? I don't remember much from my first time flying," I admitted.

"That's the gist of it. Faerie dust, a happy thought and no passing out this time. Can you handle that?" he teased as I narrowed my eyes at him.

"Maybe I'd rather have Tripp teach me to fly this time," I countered, irritably.

He shot me one of his cocky smiles. "You know I'm just teasing, right? Having you in my arms made it one of the best trips I've ever taken across the veil. I got to stare at that beautiful face the whole way here." I melted at his words and I couldn't help but smile back at him. "Now come over here and take my hand. Maneuvering takes a bit of practice and we don't have time for that. There is a rock outcropping on the summit. We should be able to get a good view of the Jolly Roger from there."

Peter's eyes met mine, like he was looking for my approval of his plan, but I momentarily got lost in the depths of his brown eyes, still reveling in his admission about our trip across the veil.

"Gwen?"

"Umm... yes. Let's go," I stumbled. Why was he always mesmerizing me? You'd think I'd be use to him by now.

"Alright, boys. Line up for your dust. Remember, this is an information finding mission only. Ryder, I'm looking at you. No showing off for Gwen's sake."

"I don't need to show off for Gwen, she already knows I'm the shit," Ryder teased. He was so cocky. All the boys were cocky, but Ryder was the most vocal about it, and I found his confidence sexy.

Tripp, Ryder and Eben all surrounded Peter, forming a circle and Peter doled out the last rations of faerie dust. He dipped his thumb into the pouch at his belt and dragged a line of dust across both cheekbones of one Lost Boy after the other. When he was finished, they all nodded, closed their eyes for a moment as they found their happy thoughts. I wondered, idly what their happy thoughts were. Would they ever let me in enough to tell me? They all lifted into the air and headed in opposite directions, leaving me and Peter alone.

"Are you ready?" he asked.

"As I'll ever be." I sighed. I felt nervous angst begin to bloom in my chest and my heart rate accelerated to a frenzied pace even though we hadn't moved yet.

Peter spread faerie dust across my cheekbones, just like he had done the night we first met— at least that much I remembered. With Peter's hand firmly in mine, I thought of a particular memory of my sister and I, at a lake where my parents had brought us for holiday when we were little. I felt myself begin to lift off the ground. It was one of the happiest memories I had, and I desperately missed my sister in that moment. The more I thought of how much I missed her, the more I strayed from the happy memory and I found myself promptly back on the ground.

"You're trying too hard," Peter said.

"I can't help it. Pretty much all of my happy memories are tainted with sadness. I can't think of the happy memories without them being overshadowed by the bad ones."

I felt like an utter failure. I knew I'd done it before, I had to have some happy thoughts. I shook my head, trying to clear it. I needed something untainted with grief that I could hold on to. I closed my eyes and without a conscious effort, my mind began to flash images of me and my boys over the last few days. As I moved from memory to memory,

I felt my mood lift and then my whole body lifted into the air. Peter still holding tight to my hand.

"That's it, Gwen. You're doing great! Just keep your happy thoughts, okay? It shouldn't take us long to get there."

I flashed him a brilliant smile. The feeling of flying was so exhilarating, especially now that I wasn't completely intoxicated.

"Oh Peter! This is incredible!" I said in awe as we picked up speed, heading for the cliff top. Peter smiled back at me, he was definitely in his element. His expression was vibrant and carefree and his eyes were electric with excitement.

"Watch this, Gwen!" Peter called out to me.

Instead of slowing as we reached the summit, Peter pulled me along faster, leaving the cliff tops behind. I felt the temperature change from the heat of the day to cool and damp as Peter flew us directly into the center of a cloud. We were enveloped in wispy mist, surrounded by the silver lining that blocked everything else out. It felt like we had left Neverland altogether, and only the two of us existed in this whole other plane.

We slowed to a hover and Peter pulled me up to him so we were face to face. He wrapped my arms around his neck and slid his hands to my waist, wrapping around to the small of my back. We began to float in circles. We were dancing! In the clouds!

How could this man be so absolutely perfect for me and yet be so out of reach? It was so confusing. I wanted to tell him to stop, that my emotions just couldn't take the hot and cold treatment. But that was apparently a very weak part of me because I couldn't bring myself to tell him to stop. Peter was ruining me. No earthly man would ever compare.

Peter looked into my eyes as he smiled down at me and briefly, it looked as though he'd let his guard down.

"What are we doing Peter?" I whispered.

I hated to ask it. I didn't want to break the spell. I didn't want to bring us back to reality, where Peter insisted on pushing me away. But time was a luxury that we didn't have and I felt like he owed me an explanation for his mercurial behavior. As if on cue, Peter's smile dissolved and his eyes lost their spark.

"Let's not do this now. I don't want you to lose your happy thoughts." Peter sighed and looked away from me.

Without another word, we left. The sunlight blinded me after the muted light of the cloud. We plummeted back to the cliff summit and I felt my hopes falling right along with us. I didn't need him to spell it out for me— his dismissal had been answer enough. But I had become very good at pushing down heartache over the last several years. It was a coping skill I wish I'd never had to master, but sometimes it proved useful. I pushed my feelings for Peter away into a small box in my mind and closed the lid. After swallowing past the lump in my throat, I refocused everything on the task at hand. After all, pirates awaited me.

CHAPTER XIV
PIRATES

I peered out from behind a haphazard pile of stones, laying flat on my belly with Peter by my side. I had no idea where the other boys were, but somehow, I could sense that they were close at hand.

Just as Peter had said, the Jolly Roger was anchored in the bay. A small dinghy, loaded with cargo, was being rowed out to the ship from a small shanty town nestled in the nook of the bay. I could make out two pirates on deck and one in the rigging. They were dressed in drab, unkempt garments, all with tricorn hats atop their heads. Yet more of my childhood fairytale, coming to life before my eyes.

"What is Hook up to now?" Peter speculated aloud.

"What do you mean?"

"Well, he's loading up the ship with supplies. He must be preparing for another voyage. Being that it's so close to May Day, I can only assume he has some nefarious plans to infiltrate the celebrations." Peter stared intently, taking in every detail.

"Where is the rest of the crew? I'm only counting three on deck and two loading the ship," Peter said absently, thinking aloud. I'd had no idea what to expect, so I found nothing out of place on the ship.

"I have to get closer, there's something off here. I need to find out what they're up to. Come on Gwen, we're just going to head closer to shore and see if we can't figure out where the rest of the crew's gone."

Peter whistled a bird call that was almost a perfect imitation. The boys responded one by one alerting us of their positions. They worked together seamlessly, for all their fighting, when it really mattered, they were all on point, executing their roles perfectly.

We flew from our cliff-top perch until we reached the tree line. Landing swiftly on the ground, we made our way down to the shore on foot. It was painstakingly slow as we moved from tree to tree, keeping ourselves hidden as we advanced. Peter was extra diligent, scanning every aspect of the surrounding forest. The trees began to thin out as we neared the water, and I could see up ahead that the trees ended altogether, giving way to a jagged, rocky shoreline.

The immense Jolly Roger was looming just past the trees, swaying gently with the tides. The three masts of the ship loomed, tall and ominous. It was so much bigger up close than I had realized. The ornate figurehead caught my attention. A beautiful woman, carved with long curling hair and bared breasts, graced the bow of the boat and it was stunning to look at.

Peter froze, drawing my attention from the ship. He looked over at me, holding a finger to his lips to keep me silent. I could hear a rustling ahead of us and when I dared peek from the tree we were hiding behind, I caught sight of a lone pirate about a hundred yards from us. He was crouched low and appeared to be creeping toward something.

I looked toward where he was stalking and saw a bright, red hued glow. A pixie was flitting about erratically, sparkling dust flying in all directions. She was carelessly drawing too much attention in this dangerous territory.

"Damn it, Lill! What the fuck are you doing?" Peter cursed through gritted teeth.

I saw two more pirates emerge from the forest. They were encircling her and she was too caught up in her tantrum to notice them creeping in on her. I could just make out her irate chiming as it carried along the breeze.

"What is she saying?" I asked.

"That we've abandoned her and that she doesn't care

what happens to her now." Peter's voice was a tight whisper, trying to keep hold of his frustrations.

He continued to watch, his brow furrowed, deep in concentration, straining to hear what she was saying.

"Fuck, Gwen. We need to get out of here now!"

As if on cue, utter chaos ensued the moment Peter finished his sentence. An explosion shook the ground in front of us, chunks of grass and dirt flying into the air around us. Peter shielded me with his own body as we were pelted with debris.

Everything seemed to be moving in slow motion. I looked to where the explosion had occurred and smoke rose from the scarred ground. It was also coming from the cannon ports on the Jolly Roger. Had they just fired a cannon at us? I passively watched, in my bewildered state, as pirates came running toward us from all directions, swords raised and mouths opened in battle cries that I couldn't hear. My ears were ringing in the aftermath, my hands shaking as the reality of the situation set in.

"Gwen!" Peter was shouting at me, but his words sounded muddled as if he was talking underwater. He shook my shoulders hard, and my senses came jolting back to me and my mind cleared. The scene around me came rushing back to reality. I stared back at Peter, his umber eyes appeared desperate with concern. He frantically ran his hands over me, checking for injuries.

"Are you hurt, Gwen? Damn it! Did you get hit?"

"I'm fine, Peter. I'm fine!" I yelled, my fear making me short with him. "Just get us out of here!"

The desperation in his eyes was replaced by determined resolve and he nodded at me, his face becoming stoic and his jaw set in a hard line. He pulled his sword and spun away from me, putting himself between me and the advancing pirates that had finally begun to reach us.

Peter was a relentless fighter. He gave no mercy as he ran through one pirate after another, their bodies landing at his feet. He was almost beautiful in this lethal dance, every move was intentional and well executed— no energy wasted. I looked to either side and I saw all of my boys in similar situations. Eben was closest to us, his face covered in blood, as he wielded his hatchet in one hand and a dagger in the other. He had a slight smirk on his face, like he was enjoying the fighting and the killing.

My fight or flight response was in full force and I was resisting the urge to turn and run. I wasn't sure what to do with myself and I started backing away from the carnage, my legs moving of their own volition. I don't know what possessed me to leave his side. He was fighting for me— to protect me— but the urge to run was overwhelming. I backed into what felt like a solid wall, and then big, strong arms wrapped around me. My cry of panic was cut off as a dirty hand clamped over my mouth. Strong hands dug into my skin painfully and all I could do was whimper. I tried in vain to throw him off, but he was a brute of a man and the more I struggled the tighter he gripped me.

"What have we here? A Lost Girl maybe?" His foul breath was hot on my neck.

He reached his hand up and grabbed my breast, squeezing so hard that I cried out, my scream muffled against his filthy hand. I'd never felt so helpless in my life. He began to back away from the fighting, pulling me toward the shore and away from my boys, who were too busy fighting off the onslaught of pirates to realize what had happened.

I continued to struggle, I couldn't just let him take me. Well, at least I wouldn't make it easy for him. The closer we got to the rocky beach, the more urgent the situation felt. If he got me to a boat, my chances of escaping would drop dramatically. I couldn't allow myself to think of what they might do to me once they had me aboard the ship. I had to act and I had to do it now.

I threw my head back toward him, and heard a sickening crunch as the back of my head smashed his nose. I was momentarily dazed from the sudden rush of pain that coursed through my head from the impact. I could feel a hot stream of his blood trickle down the back of my neck and soak into my clothes. His grip loosened briefly, enough that I could free one hand from his iron grip.

"You fucking bitch!" he bellowed. "You broke my nose! You think you're so fucking cute, I'll make you pay. I'll be taking it out of that pretty little hide of yours."

While he was threatening me, I used my free hand to work at maneuvering my dress up enough to reach my throwing knives belted to my upper thigh. I sighed deeply when I finally touched their cool metal, and I made a mental note to kiss Eben fiercely for providing me a way to protect myself.

I pulled one of the blades out of its sheath, slipping a finger through the ring at the base so I wouldn't drop it. I took a deep breath to clear my mind and focus on what I was about to do. I just needed to wait for the right moment so I didn't waste the opportunity. He spun me around to face him, grasping tightly around my upper arms. His weathered face was smudged with dirt and grime, and smeared with blood. Crooked, yellow teeth peeked out from an unkempt beard as he smirked at me, the stench of decay and liquor hot in my face. He let go of my arm with one hand and in the next moment I felt the impact, followed by a burning sting as he backhanded me, causing my head to whip to the side.

I pulled my wits together quickly because this was my moment. With my one arm now free, I plunged the blade upward into his abdomen, with as much force as I could muster. My blade penetrated just below the ribcage, puncturing his diaphragm. This time he screamed and let go of my arms, but as he fell he grabbed a hold of my locket, breaking the chain and taking it with him as he collapsed to his knees.

I stumbled backward and then I started to scramble my way back toward him. I needed to get my locket. It was my lifeline to my sister and I couldn't let him take it from me.

But the man was resilient, and even from his knees, with blood running down the front of his shirt, he managed to pull his sword and I stopped dead in my tracks. My rational mind screamed at me to run, this was my opportunity to escape, and as much as it shattered me to leave the locket behind, I had to go.

I turned on my heels and sprinted in the opposite direction. I was frantic and unsure of where I was going. When I turned to see if he was chasing after me, I tripped and landed hard on my hands and knees, scraping my palms on the jagged rocks. I looked up to get my bearings and looming on a stone ridge above me was the imposing figure of a man.

A pair of well-oiled boots stood before me, the sun glistening off their polished surface. He wore black breeches that were slightly too tight, his impressive masculinity easily visible through its constraints. He had a neatly trimmed, black coat that hung to his knees, covering a white linen top. A deep V exposed a hint of chest hair, and chains of gold and silver hung around his neck. One heavily jeweled hand rested on the pommel of a broad sword hanging from the belt at his waist. While the other was nothing more than a polished silver hook. The man before me could be none other than the notorious Captain James Hook.

I ventured a look at his face— I couldn't help myself. I was expecting a sinister looking old man, but that was not at all the reality. His face was surprisingly handsome, high cheekbones and a straight nose gave him a primal, masculine look. He had a strong chin, with a neatly trimmed goatee. The dark hair I'd been expecting was more of a dirty blonde, bleached from the salt and sun, and it fell in waves just past his shoulders.

I looked into his intense blue eyes, only to find him staring intently back at me as he brought his one hand up and ran it over his goatee. When our eyes met, I felt like I couldn't move. I felt an odd attraction to his dominating presence that I couldn't explain. He raised a brow as he looked me over, with a slight smirk crossing his full lips.

"Gwen!" Peter was beside me then, pulling me to my feet and instantly putting himself between me and Hook breaking the moment we'd shared. I felt flustered and shocked at my own response to him. Peter and Hook stared each other down for a tense moment.

"What have you brought back from beyond the veil for me this time Peter?" Hook's voice sounded deep and polished, his cadence slow and deliberate.

"She's not for you Hook." Peter was short, his voice clipped in anger.

"We'll see, Peter. We'll see."

Peter growled at him. I wondered if this would end in a fight, but while Peter was tense, Hook seemed amused and relaxed from his position above us. Without another word, Peter turned to me and swept me into his arms, holding me tight against him. I wrapped my arms around his neck and leaned my head against his chest. I felt my body relax now that Peter had me. I was safe.

Peter took flight with me securely in his arms, leaving Hook and the melee behind us. I peeked back at him one more time and found him laughing at our retreat.

"But Peter, what about the others? We need to go back. We have to help them!" I felt my heart clench at the idea of anything happening to my boys.

"They will be fine. Don't worry, they can handle themselves." He placated me with words he knew I wanted to hear.

"But my locket! They've got my mother's locket, Peter! We have to go back. I need that locket. I need to make sure my boys are okay." I started sobbing at this point. My mind was so overwhelmed with emotion that the tears just started to pour out of me.

"Everything is going to be fine, Gwen. Don't worry, we'll figure everything out once I get you safe." Peter's words sounded mechanical. He was masking his feelings, still telling me what he thought I needed to hear, while he dealt with his inner turmoil privately.

I didn't push him— I couldn't. I didn't have the strength. I could only turn my face into his chest, letting my emotions flow freely down my cheeks and onto his shirt.

CHAPTER XV
THE GROTTO

Peter set me down gently on a familiar beach, right outside the entrance to the grotto at the Mermaid Lagoon. The beach was deserted, not a mermaid in sight. Peter ushered me into the passageway, always keeping a hand on me as we made our way into the grotto.

"Are you hurt? Did he hurt you?" He sounded panicked as he asked, that desperate look returning to his eyes.

"No, I'm fine. Just shaken up a bit, but I'm okay."

"You have blood on your neck." He looked at the partially dried blood on my neck and walked around behind me, running his fingers in my hair, looking for injuries. I winced slightly when his fingers touched the tender spot on the back of my scalp where I'd struck the pirate.

"The blood isn't mine. I'm just bruised, I smashed his face with the back of my head and he bled all over me. I think I broke his nose," I admitted shyly and Peter chuckled a little.

"You were more of a handful than he expected," he said, sounding amused. But his amusement was short-lived. "I should have been there. I'm so sorry, I never meant for you to get hurt." His hand hovered over the marks forming on my breast. "Did he… did he touch you?" His question came out low and harsh, he couldn't even meet my eyes while he waited for me to answer.

"Not really, it was nothing. I'm going to be okay," I said with confidence as I tried to reassure him.

Aside from some bruises on my breast, I'd come out unscathed— at least physically. I wouldn't allow myself to think of the damage it may have done to me emotionally. I'd have time to sort through that after the shock of it dissipated. I knew it could have been so much worse and somehow I found comfort in that. Peter raked his hands through his hair and paced back and forth in the small cavern.

"I'll kill them all to a man," he seethed. I walked into his path and forced him to stop, placing my hands on either side of his face, bringing his eyes to meet mine.

"Peter, I'm here. I'm alright. It's over now."

"It was selfish of me to bring you to Neverland."

"No, I'm glad you brought me. My time here with the boys... with you... it's a gift."

"I don't know how you can say that. I've made so many mistakes. I should have known that Lill would compromise the whole mission. The idea that something could have happened to you out there... it's going to give me fucking nightmares. Everything that's happened is my fault." He broke away from me then, sitting down and hanging his head.

"You can't blame yourself for everything. Lill made her own choices. I don't think she meant to give up our location. She was probably just hurting and acting out. Do you know if she made it out okay?" I asked. I hated Lill for so many reasons, but I couldn't imagine the pain she must be in, to go and throw herself to the mercy of pirates.

"You really are too good for all of us. Lill has been nothing but awful to you and yet you still defend her." He shook his head a moment before continuing, "I don't know for sure if she got out, but the boys would never leave her behind."

"Is she the reason why you've pushed me away?" I asked quietly.

"Lill?" He sounded surprised at my question. "No. I care for Lill, she's my faerie, but that's as far as it goes. We're friends, not lovers."

"You're not lovers? So you haven't had sex with her?"

Peter looked visibly uncomfortable, reaching up to rub

the back of his neck before he answered. "Well, yes, we've had sex, but the only emotion involved was lust. It was simply satisfying a need— nothing more. Definitely not love. Is it not like that for you across the veil? Have you only had sex with men you love?" Now it was my turn to squirm.

"Well, no," I answered, embarrassed at my admission. Peter got up and came to me, his piercing brown eyes boring into me.

"Have you ever been in love, Gwen?"

"Umm… I'm, well I'm not really sure," I stumbled. But what did I really know of love? I knew love from my parents and sister. But Eros love was an elusive mystery to me. The only time I thought I was in love turned out to be a complete farce. "What about you?"

He didn't answer. He just stared at me. I was desperate to know what he was thinking, but I couldn't bring myself to ask.

"The idea that you could have died back there has put everything into perfect perspective for me. I've finally decided," he said, breaking the silence. He stood so close to me now that when I took a deep breath my breasts pressed into his chest. I swallowed and shook my head in response. He brushed my hair from my face, tucking it behind my ear and cupping my jaw. "I want you. I don't care anymore if you break me when you leave. I'd rather be a broken man who took his chance at real love rather than a foolish man that turned his back on it." Peter's words were soft, but spoken in earnest.

I could hear the resolve in his voice. I was shocked. I had been expecting him to further distance himself from me once he'd ensured I was unharmed. Of all the times the boys had told me what I wanted to hear, exactly when I needed to hear it, this one meant the most.

"I know I've made a complete mess of things, but not anymore. I'll take whatever you want to give me, in whatever time we have left, and that will have to suffice. I'll have to find the strength to hold it together until the end of eternity. Maybe we could meet there, in the end, and pick up where we left off."

I was awestruck by his words. My heart felt like it was doing somersaults in my chest. My mind was having trouble putting words to the feelings coursing through me: excitement, passion, joy, adoration… relief.

"So will you have me, Gwen?" Peter sounded hesitant, which was completely foreign to the cocky boy I was used to.

I paused for a moment, allowing everything to set in, unable to breathe. I closed my eyes and reached into the depths of my mind for that little box that contained all of the complicated feelings I had for Peter. I opened it up and let the flood of emotions pour over me.

"Peter, you've always been mine."

His mouth was on mine then, hard and needy. He crushed me to him, his hands roaming over my back. I responded in kind, weaving my fingers into his thick hair and holding him to me as our mouths explored one another.

217

Peter pulled away from me abruptly and I had a moment of panic—flashbacks from our first kiss rushed back to me. Had I pushed him too far, too soon? Had I been too forward in my kiss? I suddenly felt embarrassed at my eagerness. I had basically thrown myself at him once he'd started kissing me.

Peter walked to the far wall and pulled a satchel out from behind a crevice. I watched him with interest as he pulled a thick fur, from some unknown animal, and laid it down on the rocky surface. He pulled out a towel and a small package that contained the flowers I'd used for soap when I'd first arrived.

"I told you," he said as he peered over his shoulder at me, "I come here often when I need time to think. Sometimes I'm here for a while," he explained, answering my unspoken question.

"Come on, we need to get cleaned up. I don't want to be with you when I still have the filth of pirates on me. Will you join me?" he asked motioning toward the small turquoise pool at the center of the grotto.

I nodded and Peter approached me. Without asking, he started untying the laces of my corseted top. His hands were slow and deliberate, taking his time as if he was unveiling a treasure. He gently slid the corset and skirts off, the clothes landing in a puddle at my feet. He kissed my shoulder gently, and bit me softly, sending a shock to the base of my skull and I shivered involuntarily. He walked back around and kneeled at my feet, untying the laces of my boots, pulling them off and then slowly working each stocking down my leg and throwing them aside.

He gently unbelted my throwing knives and placed them with the rest of my clothes. He rubbed his hands softly where the leather belt had left indents on my thigh, and I shivered again— but not from the cold. My skin felt like it was on fire.

I was standing there, with Peter kneeling in front of me, in nothing but my peasant top, hanging just low enough to cover me. He stood up and made short work of his own clothes, kicking them to the side and standing, naked, in front of me. Small cuts, blood spatter and bruises covered his chest— remnants from his battle with the pirates. That, combined with his black tribal tattoos that curled up his arms and onto his chest, made him look dangerous and sexy.

He stood still, not saying a word, allowing me to take in every inch of his body. I couldn't help but notice he was aroused and I blushed fiercely, looking away and staring at my hands. I couldn't understand my own reactions. I was acting like a nervous, self conscious virgin. I'd seen him naked and I knew he'd seen me naked before too, but I was hesitant to take my shirt off now. It all felt more personal, just the two of us, with him staring intently at me.

Come on, Gwen! You can do this. You are working on being fearless... right? I thought, giving myself a mental pep talk. I sighed deeply and pulled my shirt up over my head, exposing my nakedness to him in all of my imperfect perfection. He looked me over, his eyes full of hunger. I looked away, unable to meet his gaze, covering my small chest with my arms, worried that he might be disappointed now that he got to see all of me up close.

"You… are absolutely stunning," he breathed. He stepped forward and gently grasped my hand, slowly unwrapping my arm that was banded around my chest. My vulnerability began to melt away with his words.

"Come, let's wash off the stain of this day," he said as he led me to the small pool. The tepid water enveloped me. I was eager to get the pirate's blood off of me.

"Turn around and I'll wash you." His voice was soft, but assertive and I was glad that he didn't seem as nervous as I was. His big hands smoothed one of the fragrant flowers over my skin. The air filled with that sweet pomegranate scent. Peter's hands felt slick as he worked up a lather on my back. His hands moved into my hair, washing out the blood that had matted there. I closed my eyes and moaned softly as he massaged my scalp. I'd never had a man wash my hair for me before. It felt amazing… and strangely erotic. The way he cared for me and protected me so fiercely had me undone. It was something I had never experienced and I wanted more. I wanted his hands all over me.

Once I was cleaned, I submerged into the water to rinse off. I felt like I needed that moment, surrounded by the buffer of water, to regain my composure. Peter's meticulous attentions had my heart racing and my sex throbbing with need. I stayed submerged until my lungs burned, but once I broke the surface, my mind was clear.

I wanted him. I wanted him more than I had ever wanted anyone else, my nervousness be damned. I wrapped my arms around his neck, entangling my fingers in his wet hair, and sealed my lips to his. I needed him to satisfy this need inside me that he had awoken. I had curbed my desires the entire time I'd been in Neverland, but I couldn't hold back any longer. I needed to be sated.

Peter scooped me up in his arms, my wet, naked body pressed against his. He kept his eyes locked on mine. He didn't need to say anything to convey his need. He placed me on the soft fur he'd laid out, his warm body covering mine as he kissed down my neck. He lazily trailed kisses between my breasts, teasing me before he finally brushed his lips, delicately over my hardened nipple.

I moaned at the sensation and arched up to press my nipple deeper into his mouth. He sucked hard, his hand copying the movements of his mouth with my other nipple, rolling it between his fingers and the sensation sent a warm rush of wetness between my thighs. He continued down, kissing and nipping as he crisscrossed my belly until he reached the peak of my sex.

He paused and looked up at me. "Do you want this Gwen? Because if you want me to stop, tell me now. If I go any further I'm not sure I'll be able to stop." Peter's voice was laden with need, but he waited, motionless, for me to give him permission.

"Yes. Please, Peter, I want this," I breathed, feeling needy and desperate for him.

He smiled wickedly before he flicked his tongue along my clit. A cry escaped my lips at the sudden rush of sensation and my back arched involuntarily as I shook my hips. His tongue was warm and soft. He alternated between slow lapping and teasing, to sucking and flicking his tongue along the center of my pleasure, until I was just on the brink of climax before he slowed down again. It was frustrating and mind blowing at the same time.

He slid a finger into my wetness, slowly working his way inside me. He hooked his finger, brushing my G spot before pulling out and I moaned. "Oh my god, Peter, I need you! I need something, please," I begged.

"You want me to make you cum?" Peter asked coyly.

I was writhing beneath him trying to get some sweet friction that would deliver me over the edge to that coveted orgasm. He banded his arms over my hips, pinning me in place so I couldn't move. He blew cool air on my sensitive sex and I whined.

"Yes!" I pleaded. I felt awash in sensation, the pent up sexual tension that had been mounting for days had reached its limit. Peter gave me a cocky smile, then plunged two fingers deep inside me and suckled on my clit, sending me over the edge.

I don't recall ever having an orgasm so consuming. My whole body tensed as the pleasure coursed through me in waves. I cried out his name, but I almost didn't recognize my own voice. Peter's fingers worked me through the entirety of my orgasm until I felt like a melted puddle in the furs beneath me. My breath came out panting in little mews as I reveled in the aftermath.

I looked up at Peter and he had a smug look on his face, obviously pleased with himself. He was kneeling between my legs, his hand now grasped his cock and he worked it up and down a few times, a small bead of pre-cum, glistening at the tip. I bit my lip as I watched. It was sexy as fuck and all I could think was that I wanted him buried inside me. He teased my opening with the tip of his cock, running through my wetness and lined himself up.

"Gwen, I know I can't keep you," he said slowly, his voice husky and low, "but in this moment, you are mine."

He slammed into me then, filling me completely. He paused there, fully sheathed inside me. The feel of him filling me was exquisite. He stared down into my eyes, his hand coming to stroke my face and he kissed me, gently. I don't think I'd ever felt so intimate with a man before, it was so much more than sex.

I felt connected to him, some cosmic connection that felt so right and I didn't want it to end. I started to grind myself against him, needing more friction. I knew I was on the brink of another mind shattering orgasm, and Peter began to move too, meeting me thrust for thrust.

"You feel so good, Gwen. I'm going to completely lose myself in you."

He curled his fingers into my hair, pulling gently and

thrusting into me, hard, and my orgasm shook my whole body. I clenched my eyes shut and I could see white points of light as the immense pleasure overwhelmed me. I could hear Peter cry out my name as he reached his own climax. I clamped down around him and we came together, sharing in that moment of sweet pleasure.

The grotto was silent, except for our ragged breathing. Peter's body was languid on top of mine. He stayed there a long moment, still inside of me, his weight was comforting and I never wanted him to move. I wanted to savor this moment, where I was utterly content and satisfied. I wanted to feel this way forever.

He pulled out of me and I groaned in protest as he flopped down beside me on the furs.

"Did I hurt you?" he asked, sounding concerned and I laughed.

"No, that was the complete antithesis of pain. I didn't want it to end," I said honestly. He smiled his typical, cocky smile at me.

"Well, in my defense, I've been fantasizing about this moment for quite some time, but even my fantasies couldn't prepare me for how good you felt. I'll do my best to hold out a little longer next time."

"This 'next time' you're talking about... how long do I have to wait for that?"

"Insatiable little thing aren't you?" Peter teased. "Don't worry, I'll be sure that you're good and sore before you leave."

He wrapped me in his arms and pulled me close, settling me next to him with my head on his chest where I could hear his heartbeat still racing. His words weren't lost on me though— 'before you leave.' That was the elephant in the room looming over this perfect moment. This was all temporary. I only had a limited time to indulge in my feelings for Peter. The number of times we could have each other was limited and it would be coming to an end soon. Just my fucking luck. I pushed those depressing thoughts from my mind and focused on Peter and his warm body beside me.

"Now can you tell me why you've been pushing me away this whole time?" I hoped that now Peter would be open with me about everything. He sighed deeply, his hand running absently through my hair and he kissed my forehead.

"I thought I was doing what was best for the Neverland... and I thought if I could just hold out and deny myself until you left it would have been easier for me to let you go. But I think that was a doomed cause the moment I decided to bring you back with me."

"The Neverland? I don't understand, why would us being together be bad for Neverland?" I shifted and rested my chin on my folded arms so I could look into his eyes.

"I'm not exactly sure how to explain, but I'll try. Neverland is deeply connected to those that live here, and there are some that have more of an effect than others. Tiger Lily, the Pixie Elders, and myself have deep-seated roots here. Our moods and actions have a direct impact on the health of the island.

When I brought Wendy back for the first time, she... well she changed me. I developed feelings for her that I'd never felt before. While she was here, everything flourished. But she couldn't stay. This wasn't the life she wanted and when she left, she took my boys... my brothers with her. She could offer them a life that I couldn't. She took my whole family with her the day she left and I wasn't prepared for how that would affect me."

He paused there, as though he was reliving the moment all over again in his mind.

"Their absence left a void inside that festered and grew, and because of it, Neverland began to die. I can't let that happen again. The people suffered and pirates began to take over everything. My selfishness created an imbalance that almost destroyed this place and as a consequence, Neverland stripped me of my youth and I began to age."

"I guess I never really gave much thought about how Wendy leaving had affected you. The stories she passed down described it as if you were simply on to the next adventure, quickly forgetting the details of your time together. Like nothing could break your carefree spirit."

Peter snorted at that.

"Well, I guess I did a good job at playing it off. I didn't want her to know. I wanted her to have the life she dreamed of and for Neverland to be nothing but a fond memory. But, I think Wendy overlooked one of my most crucial flaws."

"Flaws, are you telling me that Peter Pan has a flaw?" I feigned shock as I teased him. "What, pray tell, is the flaw you are talking about?"

"The fact that I'm only human." And there it was, the infamous Peter Pan, with all of the amazing things he'd seen and done, underneath it all, he was only human.

"I'm so sorry that Wendy did that to you," I said, anger blooming under the surface. How could she have done that to him, I thought to myself furiously. How could she not realize that she'd stripped him of his whole family?

"You don't have to apologize for Wendy. She did what she had to do. It was brave of her, really. She didn't let anyone or anything get in the way of the life she wanted. I admire her for that." He sounded reverent as he defended Wendy's actions.

"Well, I can still think that she was being a selfish bitch. She is my kin after all," I mumbled.

Peter laughed heartily at my response. It was such a nice sound to hear and I couldn't help but chuckle along with him.

"Do I detect a hint of jealousy?" he teased.

"Hmm… you'd like that, wouldn't you?"

I liked this teasing banter. It was so much better than the irritable brooding he'd been doing.

"So what now?"

"Now? Well I can think of a few things we could try," he said coyly. He flipped me on my back and started kissing along my neck.

"I meant with the boys, what are we going to tell the Lost Boys?" Peter groaned as though I'd touched on a subject he'd wanted to avoid completely.

"Nothing. Let's just stay here until after May Day," Peter mumbled as he buried his face in my neck.

"As tempting as that sounds, you brought me to Neverland for spring cleaning and epic adventures. Plus, I'd miss the others too much. I care about them," I answered honestly.

While Peter had pushed me away, the others had pulled me close. I couldn't set aside my feelings now that Peter had finally gotten around to declaring his intentions.

"I'll tell them that we're together— end of story. I'll make sure they leave you alone. I'm the captain. Once I give the order, it's final."

"Peter, stop it! I'm not some edict to be followed and I don't want them to leave me alone." I started the sentence fiery but ended it low and hesitant. I didn't want to push Peter away.

"So what exactly are you saying Gwen?"

Peter sat up then as the conversation became more tense and I sat up too. I kept my gaze on my fidgeting hands as I thought of how to ask for what I wanted. Why was it always so difficult to simply state aloud what you want? Life would be so much easier if we could just be honest with each other instead of over analyzing the strings attached.

"You remember when we played Trust or Faith, and Eben asked if you'd be willing to share me?" My own voice sounded so frail to me. I wanted to be confident, but I felt like I might be opening Pandora's box.

"Fuck..." Peter got to his feet then, pulling a hand through his disheveled hair. "It's my own damn fault for pushing you away. I pushed you right into their arms. What the fuck did I expect? I could see how they felt about you. They were coming after you with everything they had. I knew this was going to happen and it's my own fault."

Peter was rambling as he paced back and forth. The fact that he was totally naked while he did so, was more than distracting, and I had to force myself to concentrate. He seemed to be in an argument with himself rather than responding to me.

"Just because I have feelings for them, doesn't diminish my feelings for you. I'm not sure how it's all going to work, but I can't deny that I want them," I explained, desperate to get my point across.

Peter turned and stared at me in all his naked glory. I straightened my back and lifted my head slightly in my resolve.

"I know, I'm confusing and what I'm asking is totally fucked up. I get it. But deep down, it's what I want and I'm asking you to try."

I felt braver than before, now that my mind was made up. This was what I wanted and I had to be firm in my convictions or I would be forced to give up one or all of my boys. I'd had to compromise my happiness so many times to accommodate others, but this was my time. This was my special gift that I was giving to myself, to have my every fantasy, before I returned to my reality. I was determined to make Neverland my dream come true. Peter let out a deep sigh and appeared slightly deflated. "Honestly, Gwen, I knew this was a possibility. And like I said before, I don't care anymore. I just want you. Would I prefer to keep you all to myself? Fuck yeah! Who wouldn't want you all to themselves? But the Lost Boys are my family, we already share everything, and if that's what you want, then I'm all in. I told you, I'd take whatever you're willing to give me and we'll figure out the rest as we go."

"Really, you mean it?" I asked, sounding skeptical.

"They aren't good enough for you, by any means and I can't promise you that I won't be jealous as fuck when you're with them, but yeah, I mean it."

I squealed, jumping to my feet and wrapping my arms around his neck. I squeezed him tight and then pulled his face to mine, kissing him desperately.

The nervous anticipation that I'd bottled up while I'd waited for his response poured out of me in a passionate kiss and Peter responded in kind. His hands cupped my naked ass and pulled me up in his arms, my legs wrapping around his middle. He backed me up against the wall of the cavern, my heated skin chilled against the cool rock. His hands tangled hard in my hair as he kissed me and my whole body responded to his possessiveness.

He held me up with one hand while using the other to position himself and wasted no time before he impaled me against the wall. I threw my head back as he filled me and let out a deep moan. This time it wasn't sweet and innocent. Peter thrust into me hard and furious. Claiming me with every thrust of his hips. He grunted as he pounded into me, our bodies moving in sync with each other, his hardness hitting all the right spots in this position, each thrust driving me closer.

"I want you to remember me. Inside you, right now. How good I make you feel when I'm fucking you. Remember this when you see the other boys again." His voice was heady as he spoke the words and it ignited a fire inside me.

He fucked me with such an abandon that it brought me to the brink and I spilled over into an all consuming orgasm. I cried out his name and raked my nails along his back as I came. My sex clenched tight around him until he reached his own climax, spilling his hot seed inside me as he shuddered. He rested his forehead against my shoulder as he caught his breath.

"I love it when you say my name when you get off. It's so fucking hot," he panted as he held me in place— still inside me as we returned to reality. I laughed at his comment. That same feeling of contentment washed over me in our satiated bliss. I'm not sure it's possible to be fucked into happiness, but I think that was as close as it gets.

"You keep fucking me like that and I'll keep calling your name when I cum," I said coyly.

Peter carried me back to the furs and laid me down. I

was utterly spent. The encounter with the pirates this morning seemed like a lifetime ago. So much had happened since then and yet, the sun was just now overhead. Bright streams of sunlight poured in through the opening in the cavern's ceiling, warming the patch of fur that I laid on. Peter laid behind me, pulling me into him, spooning his warm body around me.

"Get some rest my beautiful girl. We'll talk some more when you wake up," Peter whispered in my ear as I drifted off into a deep sleep. I dreamt of my other boys, desperately hoping they were safe.

CHAPTER XVI
LUSH

"Gwen, love. Wake up. It'll be getting dark soon." Peter ran his fingers down my arm, causing my flesh to come alive. "We should head back to camp."

I moaned in protest as I begrudgingly woke from my bliss. I rolled to my back and stretched my arms over my head. Peter was propped up on his elbow watching me with adoration in his eyes. He reached over and tucked a stray piece of hair behind my ear. Causing a smile to creep across my face.

"You're even more beautiful when you sleep." He

smiled. "I want nothing more than to stay here with you, naked, but," he sighed, "the boys will be worried."

My moment of sweet bliss quickly shifted focus to the boys. "You're right, we should get back." I sat up quickly as the reality of the situation set in. "What if the boys need help? We…"

We still didn't know if they were able to evade the pirates. What if the unthinkable had happened? I was so consumed in my own selfish desires that I had pushed them from my mind. What if? Worry began to consume my thoughts.

"The Lost Boys are capable of taking care of themselves," Peter interrupted. "Pirates are no match for us. It's you they'll be worried about." He gently placed a kiss on my forehead before hopping up and tossing my clothes at me.

We made our way back to camp, stopping off at Peter's place to clean up. We still hadn't made contact with the boys. Although Peter continued to assure me they would be alright, I wouldn't be able to relax until I saw them with my own eyes.

"I'll let the boys know we made it back in one piece." He dragged his hand through his mussed hair, his face heavy in thought. "I'm gonna go out for a walk after I speak to them. I need to be alone for a bit."

"But we just got back." My heart stopped. "Peter, is everything okay?" Was he having second thoughts about sharing me? Had I asked too much from him?

"I'm just not ready to see the boys fawning over you." His brow furrowed. "I agreed to share you with them. That doesn't mean I have to like it." He shook his head as if trying to clear the thought. "Head down to the fire pit when you're done. I'm sure you'll find your boys there." Peter grabbed my hand and pulled me into a hug—my face clearly not hiding my concern. He cupped my jaw in his hands. His dark eyes, tainted with decades of painful choices, gazed longingly at me. "I told you, I'd take whatever you're willing to give me. I meant it. I won't be gone long. Being away from you pains me more than you know." He leaned in and kissed me slow and passionately. Claiming me for his own, reminding me of his talents, before he walked out the door. Leaving me with my thoughts. Alone again.

I wanted to get down to my boys as quickly as possible, to ease my psyche. My mind was running amuck. And unlike Peter, I wasn't enjoying the alone time.

At first glance Peter's home appeared simple, yet cozy. A table and a pair of chairs, a sink in the corner. A bookshelf with various trinkets and books. A mussed bed, next to it a small nightstand.

And there it was. Not hidden, not on display, yet readily

accessible. Nestled into a bowl on the nightstand, was the infamous thimble. Wendy's kiss. After all these years, he still kept it close. It was still shining. Not tarnished at all. He obviously handled it frequently.

I felt a tightness form in my chest. Jealousy and anger began to cloud my mind. She had caused him such heartache – taking his family away from him and forcing him to choose between a life not meant for him and her affections. Yet here was the proof that his love had never waned. Was it love or was it obsession? It couldn't have been real love or she never would have abandoned him. Lill's spiteful words echoed in my mind. 'You're nothing but a stand in for a long dead Wendy.'

I tried to shake the thoughts from my mind. Wendy was no longer a threat, she had passed many years ago. I wasn't a stand in. Right? I tried to convince myself. It probably brought him comfort, all those years without her. Was our family heirloom not just that? A treasured memento. At least for Wendy it was. The acorn was Peter's kiss— the exact equivalent to Peter's thimble.

My hand absently reached for the gilded acorn. My locket! I had forgotten that I'd lost it in the fight. My heart began to pound heavy in my chest. How could I allow myself to forget? I had to get it back, but how?

Focus, Gwen!

Get dressed and find your boys. You can worry about Peter and your locket later.

In a basket at the foot of the bed I found one of Peter's

shirts. If I had to wash him from my body I at least wanted something of his touching my skin. Shrouding myself in that delectable earthy, cinnamon scent of his. It clung to my curves reminding my senses of how we had spent the afternoon. My body was alive with the memory. A smile formed at the corner of my mouth. He didn't have afternoons like *that* with Wendy— at least that I'm sure of.

"GWEN!" Ryder called rushing to me. His hands instantly inspected me for injuries. "Are you alright? We've been going crazy with worry." He wrapped me in a bear hug. "I'm so sorry we weren't there, Hen."

"I'm fine. Peter kept me safe. Tell me you all made it back safely."

Tripp was just behind Ryder. "Peter told us what happened. We never should have let you get that close to Hook." He dropped his head in shame. "I'm sorry Gwen. We left you in danger. It's unforgivable." He pulled me into his arms stroking my hair. "I won't let it happen again."

I looked toward the fire pit searching for Eben, and my heart stopped. "Where is Eben?"

"He was talking with Pan last I saw him. He's fine. We're all fine."

I let out a sigh of relief. My boys were safe.

"Come on. Let's get you fed." Ryder grabbed my hand and walked me to the table.

Tripp handed me a cup filled with mead. "You must be starving. Eat."

I was famished. The day had completely gotten away from me. I shamelessly stuffed my face while my boys watched contentedly. The food here in Neverland, though simple, had yet to disappoint.

"So what did you think of Hook?" Ryder asked, breaking the silence.

"Honestly?" I paused, taking a sip. I wanted to choose my words carefully. Hook was down right sexy. He was nothing like I'd imagined. He looked more like a rock star than a pirate, and I was alarmed by my attraction. "He was not what I was expecting. He was… more alluring than what I pictured in my mind. I always thought of him like the cliché pirate. Tricorn hat, frilly ruffles under the neck. Don't get me wrong, he was seriously intimidating."

"He's trouble Gwen." I heard Eben's voice behind me and jumped up from the table.

"Eben!" I threw my arms around him, burying my face in his neck.

He pulled away to look me in the eyes. "True evil is always alluring. To quote Shakespeare 'The Devil hath power, to assume a pleasing shape.' Don't be fooled by his appearance, Gwen. Hook is dangerous, and you would be wise to remember that."

"Thank you for teaching me to defend myself." I pulled

him into me and kissed him sweetly. "If it wasn't for your knives, I would have been in trouble."

"You had to use your knives?" His brow furrowed as his jaw clenched. "I'm sorry we weren't there. It won't happen again," he said, echoing his brothers.

We sat around the fire reflecting on the day. It was getting dark and the faeries had begun to gather in the lanterns hanging above, creating a beautiful, glowing atmosphere. I hadn't noticed until Tripp pointed it out, that the faeries were dancing quite sensually as if on display. They charged the air with a sexual energy, unlike anything I had ever experienced before. The faeries here in Neverland dripped with eroticism. They were not the innocent little things I was told about as a child. It was no wonder my boys had been physical with them. They were bewitching. My mind started to wander... just how many of them had they been with? I was driving myself mad with jealousy.

"We spoke with Peter," Eben said, breaking me from my insecure thoughts. "He told us we have his permission to pursue you. That he agreed to share."

"True, we agreed to..." I hesitated before I said the word "share." It was foreign to me, this idea to share. I had heard of polyamorous relationships, I just never thought I'd find myself involved in one. Who was I kidding? I never imagined I'd be in Neverland with Peter fucking Pan and his Lost Boys either. But here I was, loving every moment of it. Honestly, I couldn't wait to see what was next.

"One big fucking family!" Ryder exclaimed. A huge smile on his face.

Everyone laughed, dispelling the awkwardness we were all feeling.

"Ryder, why don't you regale us with a story about May Day," Eben suggested.

"What kind of story were you thinking?" Ryder asked with a bit of mischief behind his voice.

"Tell her why we celebrate May Day." He looked at me and bit his lip suggestively. "Tell her about the nymphs and the satyrs."

"I don't remember hearing anything about nymphs or satyrs in Grams stories?"

Tripp shook his head in frustration. "You know how storytelling goes. Things get lost in translation. The native Neverlanders are nymphs and satyrs. They are the Divine."

"If we're gonna tell stories of May Day, then we should do it properly. It is after all the time of year for Lush Tea." Ryder turned to look at Tripp as if seeking approval. "What do ya say Tripp? Fancy some Lush?"

"Lush, *yes*! That's a great idea," Eben replied a little too excitedly. "I'll get a kettle."

Tripp contemplated for a moment. "Pan will be pissed he missed out, but, it is spring cleaning… I'm in."

"Okay, I'll bite, what is Lush?" I asked, as Tripp walked away.

"Lush Tea is generally used during May Day rituals. It helps you to... connect," explained Ryder. "It allows you to feel things a bit more intensely."

"It makes you feel amazing— everything is amplified," Eben added, raising his brows.

"Wait, is this a drug?" I asked, my anxiety starting to ruffle its feathers. I'd never done more than a little weed and alcohol. "What exactly am I 'connecting' to? Is this going to get me high?"

"Technically, yes. It's a ceremonial tea that will intoxicate you," Tripp interjected carrying a wooden box and a large blanket. "We drink it on special occasions. But I won't lie to you, it's also used in ceremony to enhance sex. It makes you feel... nice." He lifted the intricately carved top to show me what looked like shimmering loose leaf tea. "You don't have to drink it if you don't want to. And just because it can enhance sex, doesn't mean it has to happen. You are safe here with us. I can promise you that."

"Enhances sex huh?" My mind was buzzing with the possibilities. My boys and a sex enhancing tea, mixed with the sexually charged faeries dancing above our heads seemed like a heady combination. The idea of letting go and succumbing to my primal needs was intoxicating on its own.

"Lush is all love, Gwen. No need to be scared," Ryder assured me.

Eben looked at me with a devilish grin. "What do you say Gwen? 'Be always searching for new sensations. Be afraid of nothing.'"

"Did you just quote Oscar Wilde?" Be still my literature loving heart. First Shakespeare and now he's quoting The Picture Of Dorian Gray. How apropos.

"Don't look so surprised. I like to read," he grumbled.

"I think boys who read are sexy." I gave him a flirtatious smile before returning my thoughts to the idea of taking an unknown sex enhancing substance with temptation surrounding me. I pondered just a moment before deciding I was going to go all in. Eben was right, no more fear. "I'm here and I feel safe with you all. Let's do it!" Maybe this would be the push we needed to quench my carnal thirst. The sexual tension between us was palpable. After the dreams I had last night, these boys had my libido on fire, and I was about to combust.

The boys crowed with excitement as I tried to swallow my growing anxiety.

"This is going to be great! Your first time is always the best," Eben said as he paced in front of the fire, watching the kettle impatiently.

Ryder spread the blanket out in front of the fire while Tripp began preparing the tea. He sat down and patted the ground implying I should sit down next to him. Eben promptly joined us as Tripp finished out the circle.

"May the fae bless this tea and infuse it with love and

abundance," Tripp said as he handed the cup to Ryder. After taking a large sip Ryder turned to me.

"Are you sure?" he asked. I nodded yes, before my nerves could stop me. "May the fae, bless this tea and infuse it with love and abundance," he repeated.

My hands were shaking a bit as I reached out for the cup. My mind was made up. I was going to do this. Nerves and all. I brought the cup up to my face. Steam curled up from the hot shimmering liquid, filling my senses with a warm aroma that reminded me of root beer. I hesitated a moment before taking a large gulp. Ryder looked at me with approval and smiled. It was my turn to pass the cup. I turned to Eben, his dark eyes staring into the depths of my soul. "May the fae, bless this tea and infuse it with love and abundance." He took the cup and pulled two huge gulps before turning to Tripp.

"May the fae bless this tea and infuse it with love and abundance." Tripp took his sip and gently placed the cup on the ground.

"As an offering to the faeries, we leave a bit in the cup. If we are lucky they will come to drink with us."

"Am I supposed to feel something?" I asked.

"It takes a bit for the effects to kick in. Try and relax, just go with it," Tripp tried to reassure me.

"Shall we get to our story?" asked Ryder, always eager to entertain. "May Day is a celebration of fertility." He waggled his brows. "We celebrate the union of the nymphs and satyrs, ensuring Neverland continues to grow."

"Basically sex— we are celebrating sex," Eben simplified.

Ryder gave a nod. "He's not wrong. Here in Neverland the nymphs and satyrs are closely connected to the land. They believe, without the celebration of May Day, the land will slowly die off and simply cease to exist."

"Without fucking Neverland dies," Eben interrupted. "At least that's what the fae tell us."

"Wait, what?... I'm confused," I said. "How does sex have anything to do with the land?"

"Well, we know that Peter is inexplicably connected to Neverland. His moods down right alter the weather here. In fact when Peter is gone, Neverland, for lack of a better term, 'sleeps.' But Peter didn't create Neverland. It was born of divine parents. The story goes kinda like this: Neverland is the result of the first satyr and nymph's copulation. They say you can actually see the cycle with the changing seasons. It was your typical boy meets girl, with a touch of Divinity added in the mix. In the spring everything is fresh and new," —he looked directly at me and raised his brow—"clean, if you will."

"Spring cleaning," I said, nodding my head.

"Exactly! So it's spring time, and a sexy little nymph is catching the eye of our virile satyr. He spends this time courting her. Tempting her with his raw masculinity. About halfway between spring and summer, she decides to give in to her desires and give herself to him completely. They share a moment of passion and, *boom*! In the fall she gives

246

birth. This was the moment Neverland was born. The nymphs and satyrs who are here in Neverland now are the Native people of the land. They *are* the land. The Natives believe that their unions 'feed' the land. That they are the embodiment of the originals. If they don't fuck, the land won't be fertilized. Without fertilized land Neverland as we know it will age, shrivel up, and die. As for how Peter fits into the story, no one quite knows for sure. When it comes to Neverland, you just gotta go with it," Ryder concluded.

"Here's to fucking! May Neverland never die!" Eben shouted as he stood up and ripped his shirt off.

The boys followed suit, crowing excitedly as they dropped their shirts to the ground. I couldn't help but stare. My eyes feasted on their chiseled muscles, flexing and glistening in the firelight, surrounding me in temptation.

"Enjoying the view, Hen?" Ryder asked with a cocky smile on his face.

"Maybe?" I responded flirtatiously, as a smile crept into the corner of my mouth.

Tripp offered a hand and pulled me up into an embrace. "If anyone gets to be too much for you, you tell me. Understand?" he whispered in my ear, making me feel safe. I nodded and assured him I would. He grabbed my face, making eye contact.

"Do not hesitate."

"Promise," I said as I felt someone come up behind me, electrifying my skin— effectively turning me into a Lost Boys sandwich.

"I have something for you," Eben spoke into my ear.

I turned around and pressed my back into Tripp's muscular frame. His hands dropped to my waist, keeping me in his embrace. Eben's face took me by surprise, as I had a moment of déjà vu. Much like my dream, he had smeared ash across his eyes like a mask. Cranking up the volume of his bad boy vibe. Without hesitation, he gently placed his thumbs on the bridge of my nose and swiped a line of ash under my eyes and across my cheek bones— leaving a black line across my face.

"Damn, Gwen. You look good enough to eat." He pulled my face to his and claimed my mouth with his own. My hands found his bare chest, warm and firm. I became acutely aware of Tripp behind me. His hands skimmed up my sides until he was caressing the skin under my breasts. His lips found the gentle curve where my neck met my back and shoulders. Kisses turned to biting and licking. So many sensations unlike anything I had ever felt before. I gave into the pleasure, kissing Eben deeper. Two boys were definitely better than one. The tea hadn't even begun to kick in, and already, my mind was whirling.

"You like being caught between the two of us, don't you?" Tripp whispered in my ear. My inner thighs were instantly wet with desire— his own arousal pressing into my ass. I shamelessly moaned as Eben kissed his way down my neck.

"Well, well, well... that's a sight I won't soon forget. I walk away for one minute." Ryders voice brought us back to the moment, breaking the spell. His face was also painted with a black mask-like swath. "I thought we were gonna share? Come on, I brought my drums."

"Sorry, bro. She's hard to resist," Eben replied, winking and biting his lip as he pulled away. He grabbed my hand and pulled me back to the blanket. "Tripp, join our tribe. Mark your face. We're like Lord Of The fucking Flies here!" He chuckled and looked at me from the corner of his eye to see if I caught his literature reference. It was adorable to see him trying to impress me with his literary prowess.

Ryder and Eben both grabbed a drum and started to play— filling the air with a tribal pulsing. As I watched the flames from the bonfire dance, I began to realize I was feeling fucked up, and the sensation was climbing higher. My senses were becoming heightened. I turned to look at the boys. Were they feeling it too? They seemed completely entranced by the drumming. Not a care in the world. I took a large breath to try and relax. I too, began to get lost in the rhythm. The crackling of the burning wood, the beating of the drums, the smell of the smoke billowing through the air — it was hypnotic. I started to feel as though I was one with the music. One with the land. The tea had taken hold.

My mind completely focused on the sound, the tribal energy coursing through my body. I couldn't sit still any longer. The music and flames were calling out to me. I got up and started to move my body in dance. I had no inhibitions, no shame. I just needed to move my body. With my arms up to the sky, I started to move like I was, myself, a flickering flame. My hips grinding back and forth finding the beat of the drums.

I felt amazing. Not a care in the world. There were no thoughts other than what I was physically feeling at that very moment. I wanted to feel the air on my skin, needed to feel the heat from the fire. I could feel my sexuality driving my movement.

Before I could rationalize my thoughts, I grabbed my shirt and pulled it off over my head. Completely exposing my naked body, and I didn't care. I had no fear. No thoughts of shame. I felt alive, truly alive, for the first time in ages. I could feel everything. I closed my eyes, enhancing my other senses. The drums sent vibrations through my body. The wind and heat tickled my skin with their warm fingers. My nipples were taught with need, feeling desperate to be touched. Desire consumed me.

I felt hands, not my own, gliding up my thighs. I looked down to see Tripp naked on his knees. His hands on my thighs. His eyes locked on mine. I could see his need, his desire almost painful in his expression.

"You are perfect in every way. Let me worship at your temple."

I pulled him up and kissed him hard. My aching nipples grazing his naked chest sending electric pulses through my body. "Worship me," I begged, as he lifted me up and carried me back to the blanket and laid me down. He slowly spread my legs and started to kiss my inner thighs. I could hear his excitement in his hitched breath. Biting and licking, causing me to whimper with need. He spread my lips and began to tease me with his tongue, sending a rush of pleasure straight to my core. I closed my eyes and arched my back with desire. I could feel hands on my nipples, teasing and pinching, adding to the mounting tension. Tripp slid a finger into my wetness causing me to moan, and then a second gently stretched me. His tongue teased my clit while I shamelessly ground my hips, seeking more pressure. Eben and Ryder started to suck and bite at my nipples, sending me straight over the edge. I began to climax, my legs quivering with pleasure. My toes curled as the waves washed over me. My body reeled with electricity, lost in bliss.

Eben traded places with Tripp as he positioned himself between my legs. He wrapped his hands around my back and pulled me up into his embrace. I sat in his lap, my legs wrapped around his torso. His massive cock, hard, glistening with excitement— waiting to be satiated. His black rimmed eyes looked at me for permission.

"Will you have me?" he asked.

I grabbed him, firm in my hand. "Yes!" I raised myself up, and then slowly impaled myself on him, causing us both to gasp. His cock was huge, causing a sensation of tightness that wavered between pleasure and pain. I could feel him filling me entirely as I slowly rode him up and down. I never understood pleasure from pain until now, until this moment. This pain was exquisite, and I needed more. I grabbed a fist full of hair on the back of his head and claimed his mouth, kissing him as though he were oxygen and I was suffocating.

His hands gripped my ass, guiding my movements. Pleasure mounted as I started pumping faster, my clit rubbing against his mons giving me the friction I was so desperately seeking. I threw my head back, leaned into Eben's arms, and rode out my orgasm crying out in pleasure— pulling Eben into the throes with me. In one fluid movement I was on my back again. Eben lifted my legs into the air as he thrust through his own climax, groaning with pleasure.

Ryder wasted no time. He gently rolled me over onto my belly and lifted my hips, pulling me on to my hands and knees, exposing my tender flesh to the cool air. I could feel the wetness dripping from my cunt, sliding down my thighs. Greedy for more, I was one with the pleasure. Desire and hunger took over my mind. There was no fear, no shame. Just need and pleasure.

"Say yes, Hen," he asked, all the while staring at my exposed sex, spread and glistening.

"Yes," I mewed, pushing back up against him, needing to be touched. The head of his cock dipped into my opening ever so slightly. His hand wrapped around my body and his fingers toyed with my clit as he pushed in. My breath escaped in a sigh of contentment. His cock fulfilling my need. His hips pounded into me, like a well oiled piston. I arched my back, as I pushed against him, trying to take him deeper into my core. My muscles gripped his cock, as the tension began to build again. His fingers were weaving a spell over my clit and I was taken over by the pleasure, crying out— lost in the moment. Losing all control, my body was no longer my own. A slave to the orgasm. Ryder pushed me forward dropping me to my belly, I arched my back lifting my hips as he pumped harder, lost in his own rhythmic pleasure. My muscles contracted, draining his cock.

"Gwen," he groaned as he found his release, and playfully bit my shoulder.

I rolled over onto my back and found Tripp watching, with hunger in his eyes. His hands on his shaft stroking himself. I got up and walked over to him and dropped to my knees. I looked up at him, the way he had with me, only a few moments ago. My hands rested on his muscular thighs and his magnificent cock was only inches from my face.

"I want to taste you." I looked into his eyes, seeking his permission. I wet my lips and bit my bottom lip.

"I've been saving it just for you," he replied with cocky confidence.

I started slowly, bathing him with my tongue. Taking my time to explore his manhood. His length— the veins caging his girth in a glorious display. His own salty excitement dripped from the tip. This is what I was missing. I felt an insatiable hunger take over. I took his length into my mouth causing him to throw his head back and moan. His hands fisted in my hair letting me know he liked what I was doing. I could feel Eben and Ryders cum dripping down my thighs. I wanted Tripps. I wanted to taste his desire. I needed to taste it. I looked up at Tripp, he was watching me devour his cock. His mouth gaping, his breathing growing ragged. We locked eyes, sending Tripp over the edge. His orgasm pumping into my mouth, hot and deliciously salty. I swallowed every drop before pulling away. Savoring his taste. He pulled me to my feet and kissed me fiercely.

"You are divine, Gwen. My goddess, and I will worship you for all eternity." He pulled me down, back to the blanket. I laid my head in his lap. His hand stroked my hair as I melted into the sensation, happy and sated.

Eben grabbed my feet and began to trace his fingers over my legs, as though he were trying to memorize every curve. Ryder gently placed his head on my belly, gazing up at the stars. We relished in the warmth of the fire, four becoming one, connected now in a way that would never untangle. A profound hedonistic experience that would change my life. Forever. The effects of the tea were starting to relax its grip on my mind. Ryder was right— Lush was all love. Tonight I felt cherished, worshipped. For once, I wasn't worried about the future. My thoughts were purely here and now. Happiness. My eyes began to grow heavy. Completely content and shrouded in exhaustion, I drifted off to sleep tangled in the arms of my boys.

CHAPTER XVII
MAY DAY

"Gwen."

I heard my name being called, pulling me from the depths of my dream world, and my eyes fluttered open. Peter's umber eyes were staring back at me. He was crouched beside me and ran his knuckles along my chin. I smiled reflexively at him. My soul was happy to see him, but my mind was still clouded with sleep and it took me a moment to realize where I was.

My naked limbs were still entangled with my sleeping boys. My head still pillowed on Tripp, Ryder's arms encircled my waist, while Eben's cheek rested on my thigh, his arms intertwined with my legs. I looked back at Peter and his expression looked pained, but he smiled at me nonetheless.

"Peter... I can explain."

"No, you don't have to explain. I said I was okay with it and I've had some time to wrap my head around everything, so I'm good. I just wanted to wake you up, we have a lot to do today. It's May Day."

May Day? It was May Day? How was it here already? My mind was reeling and my heart started racing. I'd had no time, it had all passed too quickly. It occurred to me that I'd never asked when May Day actually was. I'd subconsciously put it to some distant time in the future that we would eventually get to, but I guess I'd been blocking the idea of it's arrival altogether.

"But Peter, I'm not ready... I didn't realize..."

I began to sit up, a flush of anxiety blooming from my chest and coursing through my body, leaving a tingling in my fingers. My boys all began to stir at my movement.

"Shhh, Gwen. It's fine, you don't have to worry. Just because it's May Day, doesn't mean you have to leave just yet. You know you can stay as long as you want."

My initial inclination was, yes! I want to stay, now that everything was so perfect. I wanted time to explore all of them and bask in the glory of my little harem. I couldn't, for the life of me, figure out why I'd needed to go back in the first place.

Have you ever walked into a room with the full intention of doing or getting something, and the moment you arrive, you've completely forgotten what you were there for? You know you had a reason, but that reason has slipped your grasp and it's now lingering just off the reaches of your mind. That's the confused feeling I had as I racked my brain, desperate to put a reason to my need to leave Neverland behind and return to my world. I'd heard the stories about how Neverland made one forget their prior life across the veil, but it was incredibly unnerving now that it was obviously happening to me.

I grasped at my throat for something and came up empty... a necklace. A necklace should be there and I knew, without a doubt, it had to do with my reason. I needed that necklace and I now felt more naked than ever without it.

"Are you alright Gwen? You look... concerned," Peter asked.

"I'm fine, I'm just missing a necklace? Yes! I lost it yesterday with the pirates..."

That was it! My locket. I'd lost my mother's locket. The more I focused, the more it came back to me, like a fog clearing. The locket was my life line to someone important. I grasped on to the thought, even if I didn't know all the details, my emotions told me that this was important. I had to go back.

"I'm sorry about your locket. Maybe one of the boys could go back and see if they can find it at the battle site," Peter suggested.

"Yes, please. It's important to me. I can't leave without it."

"Pan, will you leave Hen alone? We're trying to sleep over here," Ryder mumbled as he nuzzled into my belly.

"Sorry Ry, it's time to rise and shine. We've got shit to do for May Day." My head lifted as Tripp yawned deeply and then he ran his fingers softly in my hair.

"Good morning, my goddess. I hope you slept well," Tripp said, his voice still raspy with sleep. Peter grasped my hand and started to help me to my feet but Eben's arms tightened around my legs.

"Wilt thou be gone? It is not yet near day." My heart melted as he quoted Romeo and Juliet to me. I mean isn't it every girl's fantasy to have Shakespeare recited to them?

"I have more care to stay, than will to go," I quoted Romeo back to him and he looked up at me, his dark eyes full of satisfaction and he smiled wickedly at me before he nipped my leg with his teeth.

"I could stay here all day, but Pan's right, we have a lot to do today. I promise, we'll have time to spend together later."

"Round two, yes please." Ryder was so cheeky. "Pan, you missed the Lush last night, it was epic."

"Fuck off Ry, you don't have to rub it in," Peter groaned.

"No but you may have to rub it off later just thinking about it," Ryder quipped and Peter punched him in the shoulder and all the boys chuckled. They all seemed at ease with the whole situation and I was thrilled.

"Come on, Gwen. I've got some breakfast for you and I've asked the nymphs to help you get ready for the celebration tonight."

MIRA AND FAUNA arrived shortly after breakfast. They carried baskets of brilliant flowers on either hip and laid them at Peter's feet as if they were some kind of offering. The nymphs were so beautiful that they almost didn't seem real.

Mira, who Peter explained, was an ocean nymph, had a pristine complexion of milky white skin, with hair that was so pale that it was almost silver. It hung in shimmery strands over her gauzy blue dress that was so sheer it left little to the imagination.

Fauna, a forest nymph, was her opposite. Her hair was fiery red and curled in perfectly tight ringlets. A smattering of freckles graced her nose and cheeks. She had a dress that appeared to be fashioned out of skeleton leaves, patches of her skin visible through the veining.

They both greeted my boys warmly, kissing each of them on either cheek. I felt instantly on guard and I couldn't help but wonder if they had slept with either of them. But the boys were only cordial and polite, nothing more. And the nymphs themselves were so warm and friendly that I found it difficult to hate them just because of my own insecurities.

The pair brought me to a waterfall basin. There were several turquoise pools, where a group of nymph's were gathering, bathing and laughing communally.

"This is where all the fae women come to bathe and purify ourselves before tonight's festivities, so we can be clean as we bring fertility to Neverland. You too must be purified if you intend on celebrating with the Lost Boys," Mira instructed.

"Come, I'm sure the others are eager to finally see the human girl that's captured Peter's attention. They are all disappointed that he's been spoken for tonight," Fauna said bluntly. I had to remind myself that their idea of polite conversation was probably very different from mine.

They had no sense of modesty either and quickly stripped me of my makeshift dress, yet another of the Lost Boys shirts, leaving me awkwardly trying to cover myself. When I looked around, I realized that all of the fae women had stopped to stare at me and they all whispered quietly amongst themselves.

"I didn't know Peter liked small breasts," Fauna commented. Her tone wasn't rude or malicious, but more envious than anything. I instantly flushed, feeling more self conscious in front of these beautiful nymphs than I had in front of the boys.

"Take it from me Fauna— small breasts age better. Peter is finally looking toward the future." An older woman retorted as she joined us and promptly shooed the other nymphs away. She was long limbed and elegant, graceful in her movements. Her hair, that was a silver blue, was combed perfectly into a chignon. I could see the depths of her beauty even in her advanced age.

"I'm Amara. Welcome. I'm glad you could join us for May Day."

"Thank you. I'm glad to be here, I think," I said hesitantly and she laughed.

"Never mind the girls. They are young, and they were just babes the last time a human woman was in Neverland. Our ways are slightly different from yours, they just aren't sure what to make of you. Come and I'll show you what you need to do to get yourself ready. I'll help with your hair and paint your face. If you are to be Peter's tonight, then you will need to be exquisite."

With Amara's help, every inch of my body was scrubbed clean until my skin was pink. I was washed with fragrant flowers and scented oils were rubbed into my skin until I shimmered and glowed. My hair was brushed and smoothed until it was dry and then Amara fashioned my locks into a loose and flowing braid, white and peach flowers woven into a crown around my head.

I felt utterly amazing and beautiful until I pulled the boys borrowed shirt back on. I felt like I was wearing a sack compared to the delicate clothes the nymphs were wearing.

The outfit that Peter had given me, the only outfit that was actually my own, had been covered in pirates blood and I hadn't had a chance to clean it yet. Amara stared at me and shook her head.

"Well that just won't do. Peter holds a place of prominence in Neverland, so whoever is with Peter needs to be perfect. We can't have you showing up in... well, that," she said disdainfully as she gestured at my clothes. She crossed her arms over her chest and rested her chin in her hand, looking deep in thought.

"I think I can make this work," Amara said as she pulled a peach colored flower, that looked like a peony, out of her hair.

"What do you mean?" I asked, confused at how a flower would somehow help with my wardrobe issues.

"You see, I'm a mountain nymph. I have certain gifts from the Neverland. This flower grows in the mountainous landscape of my home and I can manipulate it to my will," Amara explained as she focused on the flower in her hand. Her palms began to glow, faintly at first and then brighter, the light engulfing the flower. I watched in shocked interest as the flower began to transform. As she held the flower it elongated and flowed down toward the ground.

"Yes, this will do nicely with your complexion," she exclaimed. She looked over the garment that had transformed from the flower she had been holding only moments before. The dress was simple— a sleeveless, sweetheart neckline that gave way to a layered skirt, each section like a ruffled petal. The tips of each 'petal' were saturated in the peach coloring and faded out to a soft cream.

"That is the most beautiful dress I've ever seen," I gasped as I looked at the delicate garment she held.

"Let's get you out of those rags. If I'm correct, this should fit you perfectly."

"This is for me? It's really too nice, I can't accept it," I said, feeling overwhelmed by the gesture.

"You're a daughter of Wendy. Once upon a time, she was sweet to me. I owe it to her. And besides, you are Peter's chosen. Trust me, you want to be perfect tonight."

"Thank you. I'll have to find some way to make it up to you."

"Forget it child, this is nothing. Let's get you dressed. Mira and Fauna are due to have you back shortly."

I pulled off Tripp's old shirt that I was wearing, taking a moment to inhale and saturate my senses in his woodsy scent of pine and sandalwood before setting it aside and stepping into the dress Amara had created for me. She helped me to tighten the laces in the back, pulling the dress in tight around me. As she had said, it fit perfectly. The corseted top fit snugly, accentuating my tiny waist and it pushed up my small breasts into a shelf of cleavage. The petaled skirt flared out from my hips and cascaded all the way to the ground. The fit was so natural, the dress was simple, but feminine, the true embodiment of a flower.

I stood in front of the still pools we had bathed in and

stared at my reflection. I had never felt so beautiful before, as if the dress and the way my hair was fashioned accentuated my own natural beauty.

Amara finished off the look by painting geometric symbols on my face, shoulders and décolletage, with a shimmering white paint.

"These are symbols for fertility," she explained.

"They don't, like, increase your chances of getting pregnant or anything like that do they?" I asked, momentarily worried that maybe my IUD would somehow become ineffective against some fae magic painted on my face.

"The fertility we are talking about is the fertility of the land and not the womb," she chuckled a little as she explained, as if teaching a child. "Now you must go and get back to the camp, Peter will be anxiously awaiting your return." She held me at a distance and looked me over approvingly, giving me a warm, motherly smile. "You will outshine everyone tonight my dear," she cooed and pulled me in for a hug.

"Just a bit of warning" —she whispered in my ear as she embraced me— "beautiful things in Neverland aren't always what they seem. A beautiful exterior can harbor some of the darkest intentions," she cautioned. She pulled away with a smile as if she had only been sharing pleasantries.

It was a similar sentiment to what Tripp had said to me when he had warned me about mermaids. It was a concerning thought, because I had yet to see one creature in

Neverland that wasn't beautiful. But I guess if she was taking the time to warn me specifically, I needed to be on guard tonight.

"Thank you for everything. Will I see you at the festivities tonight?"

"Possibly. But I get the feeling you will have many that will be vying for your attention. If I heard correctly, you plan to satisfy not only Peter, but all of his Lost Boys as well, and that is no small feat." She gave me a knowing smile as I blushed. "But I think it's only fitting for a daughter of Wendy to be Queen of the Lost Boys."

CHAPTER XVIII
A GIFT

Mira and Fauna led me back to camp, leaving me at the outskirts and promising to find me later at the celebration. I walked alone into the camp. Pixies flitted around above my head, carrying flowers to and fro. The ground below was littered with fallen petals, leaving a colorful carpet for me to walk on as I made my way toward the center of the camp.

I couldn't wait to see Peter and the boys. This could potentially be my last day with them and I felt my anxiety grow with each passing moment that we were apart. As I entered the center of the camp, the boys were waiting for me. They stood in a semi circle, all with their hands clasped in front of them, dressed in their finest.

The boys wore form fitting, linen jackets in black that hung just below their waist and criss crossed over a gray undershirt. They were cinched together with thick, ornately woven, leather belts that were more for esthetic, than for holding the plethora of weapons they typically carried. They had tall, black leather boots and their torn pants were replaced with tight, dress breeches. Peter stood out from the group, unlike the others, his jacket was hunter green and he carried an ornate dress sword at his hip. They had obviously spent time preparing, not a smudge of dirt anywhere and each had slicked and styled their hair. Even Ryder's blonde mop had been tamed and he looked much older in that moment.

As soon as I entered the clearing, all eyes were on me. Eben smirked at me, his eyes hungry. Tripp smiled one of his million dollar smiles and Ryder's jaw fell open as he stared as if I'd completely entranced him. Peter stood stoic, ever the leader, not showing any obvious emotion, but overall he looked pleased. As per my usual, I blushed fiercely with all of their attention directed at me. No one spoke as we all took each other in for a long moment.

"Well damn, aren't any of you going to say something?" I asked, the prolonged silence driving me crazy. Peter walked toward me and bowed before me, grasping my hand in his and placing a lingering kiss there as he stared up at me with his piercing umber eyes.

"You are the most beautiful creature I have ever seen," he said as he straightened to his full height, still holding my hand in his. "Will you do me the honor of coming to the May Day festival with me?"

"Isn't that the whole reason I'm here?"

Peter grunted and smiled at my response. "Well yes, but I wanted you to be mine—" He looked down at his hands for a moment and then glanced over his shoulders at his Lost Boys standing behind him. "I wanted you to be ours tonight, and everything that goes along with that," he corrected his original statement to include the rest of the Lost Boys, even though it looked as though it pained him to do so.

"Absolutely. I wouldn't want to be anywhere else than with the four of you." I smiled back at Peter and made it a point to look at each one of my boys as well.

"Alright! Let's get the party started! I've got some spring cleaning brew for us to share before we head to the village for the main show. Oh and Gwen, you look fucking edible!" Ryder said excitedly, now that it seemed we'd gotten the formalities out of the way. Ryder brushed a tender kiss on my lips before heading off to get us drinks.

"Ever my goddess, Gwen. You blow me away with your beauty," Tripp breathed into my ear as he pulled me into a hug. "I think everyone, male and female, will be envious of us tonight."

I rolled my eyes at this.

"What? I'm not joking, you are perfection. You still aren't seeing yourself clearly, but I'll keep working on it."

"Thank you, Tripp. You clean up nicely too. I think the nymphs all wanted to drown me earlier so they could stake their claims on all of you."

Tripp laughed. "I think you've broken me, because I don't think anyone will ever compare to you." His laugh had died out and he was staring at me seriously now, making the point that he'd meant every word he'd just said.

Eben interrupted us before I could respond.

"Gwen, can I talk to you for a minute?" He had a concerned look on his face and it was obvious that something was weighing on his mind. "Alone?" he said as he glanced at Tripp.

"Yeah, of course," I answered as he grabbed my hand and pulled me out of the central clearing, away from the others.

"Do you remember the other day, when we met Lill to get faerie dust?" he asked as he stared at me, his eyes looking darker than usual.

"Yes," I said hesitantly, starting to worry about what he planned to tell me.

"Well in exchange for the faerie dust... I'm now expected to... well I'm expected to sleep with her." He rushed through his admission and I had to take a moment for my brain to catch up. Was he saying what I think he was saying?

"What do you mean, you're expected to have sex with her? I was there, there was no mention of sex for faerie dust in that conversation. I think I would have remembered that!" I lashed out, feeling my emotions getting the better of me.

"When I agreed to take her to the May Day celebration, it was also agreeing to the sex that makes up that celebration. I'm sorry, Gwen. At the time, I didn't realize that I would feel this way about you now."

"Oh, really? So our first kiss didn't mean anything to you? Because the way you kissed me that day said otherwise." I couldn't keep my voice from wavering slightly. The idea of him, my Eben, with her, was turning my stomach and I felt panicked over something that hadn't even happened yet. He sighed and hung his head, as if I'd pointed out something he didn't want to talk about.

"Okay, yeah, maybe I was feeling things for you then, but I didn't want to." He seemed to get angry then, pressing his full lips into a hard line, the muscles in his jaw taught. "I agreed to go with Lill to prove to myself that I didn't feel anything for you besides lust. That sex was sex and it didn't matter who it was with." I pulled back from him, as though his words had burned me.

"And do you still feel that way?" I asked, even though I wasn't sure I wanted to know his answer.

"Gwen, I've had sex with her before, you know that. It doesn't mean anything," he pleaded with me.

"Yes it fucking does. It means everything!" I yelled at

him. "It means you are getting your pleasure from someone other than me. That I have to think about you, getting off on the way *she* makes you feel, even though you're mine."

I needed to get a handle on my emotions, it was making my filter disappear and I was saying things to Eben that I should be keeping to myself. I couldn't hide my jealousy. But he *was* mine and the sense of possession overwhelmed my rational thinking.

His expression softened as he looked at me. "Don't you get your pleasure from more than just me?" he asked quietly. And there it was, plain as day. I was a fucking hypocrite.

"But Lill hates me," I replied half heartedly. I had been trying to rationalize it to myself this whole time and really there wasn't much else I could come up with.

Eben snorted a laugh. "Yeah well, sometimes I hate the other Lost Boys too."

"So are you asking me to choose?" I asked hesitantly. I wasn't sure what I'd do if he pushed me to choose between them. I'm not really sure that I could.

"I'm not asking you to choose. What I really want to do is take you away from all of this and make you mine. I've never felt that way before, about anyone… ever. But I know you wouldn't be completely happy and your happiness means everything. So whatever you want me to do, I'll do it."

"I sure as hell don't want you with Lill, under any circumstances. But what does that mean for the bargain you struck? It's not like you can give back the faerie dust."

"She won't be happy about it. I don't think you want to be anywhere near her when I tell her. And… I'll owe her a debt," Eben explained.

"At least that's something I can live with." I felt relief wash over me now that I didn't have to think of Eben with Lill.

"Seeing that you've laid your claim on me, I have no other choice. I'm yours after all." He smiled coyly at me, pulling me toward him and kissing up my neck, effectively wiping thoughts of Lill from my mind and filling it with hunger for what the night had in store for me and all my boys.

"By the way, I need you to wear these tonight," he said as he held out the rolled bundle that contained my throwing knives.

"Do you really think I'll need them?" I asked, feeling panic wash over me as a flashback from the last time I'd used them, raced through my head.

"No, I don't think you'll need them. I just think you can never be too prepared. Hook's been planning something, we just don't know what yet. Plus, you look extra sexy with them on, so win win." He smirked as he tried to make light of the situation. I rolled my eyes at him exaggeratedly, but ultimately, I couldn't keep the smile off of my face.

"I'll wear them, not because you asked me to, but because I like having them close. You did clean them off right?" I asked, thinking of the bloodied blade that I'd stabbed the pirates with. Now it was Eben's turn to roll his eyes at me.

"Come on, up with the skirts and let me get these on you," he commanded.

"I can do it myself, you know."

"Oh, I know you can." He smiled a wicked smile at me and I blushed.

Eben crouched before me and I complied. I pulled my skirts up, resting my foot on his knee and he belted it into place. His fingers moved up my inner thigh, pushing my skirts higher and he bent his head to peek at my exposed sex — still no goddamn knickers! I pushed him back and he stumbled a bit.

"Hey, you can't fault me for looking. You're so fucking beautiful. There isn't a man alive that could resist," he said in his defense.

"I'm sure you'll get ample opportunity later to indulge yourself. Now let's get back to the rest of the boys. I'm ready to get this night started."

"SHALL WE DRINK TO NEVERLAND?" Ryder asked as he filled our cups with mead.

"Nah," Peter said. "I say we drink to Gwen, who is the

object of our idolatry tonight. She shall bless this May Day with love and abundance." Peter raised his cup.

"Hear hear!" Eben seconded the toast and we all clinked our cups together.

I felt the mead warm me all the way to my belly, leaving the warmth pooling there. I couldn't keep a smile off of my face, I was elated to be here, with all of my boys. In this moment, I had everything I wanted and it was perfect. I pushed all other thoughts from my head, and focused on the here and now.

"We have a gift for you," Peter said.

"A gift? You didn't have to get me anything, just being here in Neverland is all the gift I need."

The idea of them getting me a gift was uncomfortable. I had nothing to give them in return and I cursed at myself for not thinking of getting something for them. All I had to offer was myself. Even though I had never felt so beautiful before, I still didn't feel worthy of these amazing men.

Peter dismissed my comment with a roll of his eyes and a shake of his head. He presented me with a small, wooden box. The box itself was beautiful. The contrasting wood grain was exotic and the surface had been sanded to a buttery softness. I opened the lid to find a necklace nestled on sweet smelling grasses. It was an acorn, perfectly symmetrical, its red chestnut color was polished and shining. Delicate leaves in gold filigree scrolled along the cap of the acorn and created a hoop for the golden chain. I was stunned at the gift. I lifted my hand and fingered the necklace.

"I know it's not your mother's locket, but I thought it was appropriate that I give you a 'kiss' of your own," Peter said sincerely.

"Peter, it's so beautiful! Thank you, thank all of you. I love it!" I gasped and I felt tears prick my eyes and threaten to leak out. Peter reached out and pulled the necklace from the box.

"Turn around and let me put it on for you."

I obliged and turned around, pulling my braid to the side, exposing my back to him. With the barest touch, he clasped the necklace in place and I had a moment of deja vu.

"It looks beautiful on you, just like it did on mum."

A familiar feminine voice echoed the words in my mind. I couldn't place a name with the voice and it was infuriating.

"Did anyone have any luck finding my mother's locket?" I asked, knowing that if only I had that locket, I would be able to remember.

"I'm sorry, Gwen. I went back to look for it and I couldn't find it anywhere," Tripp admitted, obviously disappointed with his failure.

"I hoped this would maybe somehow make up for it. You can start over with this necklace," Peter said in his attempt to comfort me.

I shook my head and pushed the thoughts from my

mind. Tomorrow I would focus and figure everything out. Tonight was all about me and my boys.

We were interrupted by a procession of faeries. They were a glowing hoard that encircled us in soft, warm light with trails of glitter falling from their wings. Four picturesque pixies approached us and hovered in front of Peter— two males and two females. One pair that was fair and one pair that was dark.

"They are the Pixie Elders," Tripp whispered into my ear. I'm not sure if 'elder' was an appropriate word because there wasn't anything about them that was old. Peter bowed slightly toward them and they returned in kind. The sweet sound of bells filled the air as they talked to Peter in a language I still couldn't understand.

"We're ready," Peter answered. The four pixie elders turned and flew out of the camp and the rest of the group began to follow behind. I noticed Lill flit up to Eben and land on his shoulder. She gave me a menacing look before she focused her attention back on Eben.

"Pan, I'll catch up with you. I just need a private minute with Lill," Eben said. Peter nodded at Eben and then reached for my hand.

"It's time to go, Gwen. The celebration is waiting for us," Peter said as he wrapped my arm around his and we followed after the glowing light of the faeries.

CHAPTER XIX
THE LAKE OF SPIRITS

Faerie after faerie approached me as we marched in a formal procession to the May Day celebration, and presented me with an array of exotic flowers. I quickly accumulated a large bouquet.

"Why are they giving me flowers?" I asked Peter quietly.

"Because you're with me. They're offerings. They are hoping for a fruitful May Day," Peter explained and he winked at me briefly.

Was he implying that they were giving me flowers in hopes that I would have a lot of sex with Peter? I started having visions of what this 'celebration' might look like. Was I walking into an orgy? This all seemed so foreign to me but if I'd learned anything about Neverland, it was to just go with it.

I could tell that we were close when I heard the steady thrumming of drum beats. We entered a village, where the small houses rose from the forest floor and appeared to be a part of the enchanted landscape that surrounded us. Flowers decorated every inch of the village. Crowds of nymphs and satyrs lined the path we followed, all of them straining forward, eager to catch a glimpse of us.

I had grown accustomed to the nymphs after the day I'd spent preparing, but I was intrigued by the satyrs. I wasn't sure what to expect. The nymphs had been so beautiful. I was wondering how their half man half goat counterparts would in any way compare to their beauty, but I was so wrong.

The satyrs, each one of them, were gorgeous. They had strikingly handsome faces with beautifully sculpted, masculine bodies. Their muscled torsos were covered in golden dust, giving them a gilded look. Black horns curled under their thick hair and I found myself curious to touch them. They were dressed in nothing more than loin cloths. Their muscular legs were covered in a shimmering coat of fur and they had polished black cloven hooves rather than feet.

I felt like I had walked into a Greek myth. I was Persephone, goddess of fertility, being brought to the

Underworld to be seduced by Hades. As much as I was curious about them, they were curious about me too, as I felt all eyes on me.

Peter stopped as we reached a dais at the end of the path. The most beautiful woman I had ever seen stood from her throne and greeted us. Her clothes barely covered her warm caramel skin that was ornately decorated in tribal style tattoos. She was toned, but still voluptuous, with a perfect hourglass figure. Her body was painted in similar geometric symbols that Amara had painted on me earlier.

She wore a unique headdress. Its centerpiece was a small, horned skull of an animal, accentuated with flowers and feathers. Her dark hair was woven into perfect fashioned braids that hung over her ample breasts. She was surrounded by satyrs and nymphs that were lounging on cushions strewn along the dais.

"Peter Pan, welcome to May Day. May you prosper in love and abundance," the woman said. Her raspy voice was full of formality. Peter gave her the slightest hint of a bow.

"Tiger Lily, may you prosper in love and abundance," Peter recited the greeting.

So this was Tiger Lily. She had been a pivotal part of the 'fairytales' that Wendy had passed down to us. I reminded myself that she was a princess in her own right and she too, held a place of prominence in Neverland. She held herself in a way that exuded confidence and demanded respect. Honestly, she was intimidating as fuck.

"Might I have a word in confidence with you Peter?" Tiger Lily asked.

I felt my temper flare at being ignored. She'd completely disregarded me, as though I wasn't standing right beside Peter. It seemed all the more offensive after the formal way she'd greeted him. She was obviously no stranger to decorum. Peter looked at me, his brows furrowed with indecision.

"Don't worry, Pan. Me and Ry will keep an eye on her," Tripp confirmed and Peter nodded.

"I'll be just a moment," Peter assured me as he turned to Tiger Lily. "Lead the way."

The two headed off together and disappeared into one of the larger dwellings.

Alone.

I felt a prick of jealousy flare inside of me. Peter wouldn't do anything with her while I waited patiently outside for him, would he? She was so beautiful, and sex in Neverland didn't seem to have the same emotional meanings attached to it as it did back home. Arrg, why was my subconscious trying to sow the seeds of doubt!

"Hen, don't sweat it. Tiger Lily ain't got nothing on you. Let me distract you with some food. May Day is known for its feast! Plus, you're going to need the energy for what we've got planned for you tonight!" Ryder insinuated as he pulled me in beside him and planted a kiss in the crook of my neck.

"Ryder, have I ever told you how much I love you?" I

told him, teasingly. He always had a way of making me smile, no matter how I was feeling and I adored him for it.

"Damn! I knew May Day was going to be fucking amazing!' Ryder exclaimed. "Did you hear that Neverland? She fucking loves me!" Ryder shouted at the top of his lungs and picked me up, spinning me around in his arms. I laughed at his antics.

"I love you too, Hen. The only difference is that I really mean it. You're still making up your mind, but that's okay. I can wait and you know for damn sure, I'll do everything I can to make you mean it," he said. The sincerity was clear in his voice and I stared at him, taken aback.

How did they all seem to know me better than I knew myself? I had thought I was in love before and I had gotten burned. Now I was petrified to admit to myself that I might be falling in love with them— all of them. I knew this was utterly ridiculous, since I had only spent a few days with them. My rational mind tried to tell me that love at first sight was only a romantic notion. But when he spoke like that, I found it hard to deny the feelings that I knew were growing inside me.

The spread of food for May Day was unlike anything I'd seen before. Food of all kinds stretched out on table after table, like some medieval feast. Even if I tried only one of everything, I would have been full half way through. Ryder enjoyed feeding me little tidbits of food— much to the chagrin of all the nymphs that seemed to congregate around us, desperately hoping for some attention from Ryder and

Tripp. The boys were polite and sweet, as per their usual character, but they never shifted their main focus from me and I was literally beaming from their ministrations.

I also enjoyed the attentions of several of the exotically sexy satyrs. I was approached any time Tripp and Ryder were distracted. They would either present me with a flower or recite some beautiful poetry. The flirty, sexual tension was thick in the air and my libido was in hyperdrive.

"Ryder, there you are! I know you've been hiding from me," a high-pitched voice called out, drawing our attention to a petite nymph that was making her way toward us.

"Fuck," Ryder muttered under his breath.

"This ought to be good." Tripp chuckled to himself. The dark brunette approached Ryder, twisting her short curls in her finger and batting her lashes at him.

Obviously, there was history here, and instead of being jealous, I found it rather amusing. I was curious to see how Ryder would handle it.

"Daphne! Hey, how are ya?" Ryder asked, trying to be casual, but looking seriously uncomfortable as he tried to rake his fingers through his hair, but finding it slicked into place.

"Don't 'hey, how are ya' to me. You are trying to avoid me, so you can have your fun with the new girl, and I'm here to remind you of the promises you made to me last year."

"Promises?" Ryder laughed awkwardly. "I don't recall making any promises."

"Oh let me refresh your memory, something about how you planned on shooting your 'fertility' all over my face!"

I snorted a laugh when she said this, it was definitely something Ryder would say and I was dying!

"Okay, let's go talk about this... over here." Ryder looked desperate to get her to stop talking in front of me.

"Sorry, Hen. Don't hate me! Let me just clear things up with Daphne, I'll be right back." The pained look on Ryder's face was precious.

"Good luck with that," I said and I kissed him quickly before he turned to go. "Oh and Ryder," I called to him, "hurry back to me."

His smile brightened his whole face and he blew me a kiss before chasing after Daphne.

"And just like that, I have you all to myself," Tripp gloated. I got the distinct impression that Daphne finding Ryder hadn't been a coincidence after all.

"Did you have something to do with that?"

"Maybe. I told you, you've ruined me. There is no depravity I won't stoop to if it means I get to have you all to myself," Tripp said, and he sounded so pleased with himself.

"Come on, I have something I want to show you."

I perked up, excited at the thought of a mini adventure with Tripp.

He led me out of the main village and into the surrounding forest, down a well worn path. The trees opened up to reveal a pristine lake, nestled in between the dense forest and sheer cliffs of a craggy mountain. The water was clear and I could see multi-colored pebbles lining the bottom.

"This is The Lake of Spirits," Tripp explained.

"The Lake of Spirits? Why do they call it that?" I questioned, the name sounding rather ominous.

"Let me show you."

He grabbed my hand and pulled me from the trail. He led me through a bramble of branches to a secluded sandy beach at the lakes edge. He walked up to the water and jumped a short distance to a large stone jutting up from the water's surface, just past the shoreline. He looked back at me, reaching his hand out, beckoning me to follow.

"Come on, Gwen. Trust me. I won't let you fall in."

"I trust you," I replied, grasping his hand without a second thought. He pulled me to him, my feet landing softly on the rock in front of him. He continued to pull me until I was pressed against his firm chest and his strong arms encircled me.

"The Lake of Spirits," he whispered, nuzzling into the hair behind my ear, "has the power to show you a glimpse of your inner spirit. Or more accurately, the energy fields that your inner spirit projects," Tripp explained.

"Like an aura?" I asked.

"Something like that. I've told you before, that you just don't see yourself clearly and I get the feeling that no matter how hard I try and explain, you won't fully believe me. So I figured I'd show you," Tripp said. He spun me around until my back was pressed firmly against him, his arms wrapped tight around my waist.

"See for yourself," he whispered softly in my ear. I stared down at our reflection in the calm water.

The surface was so smooth, it looked like glass. The reflection of Tripp and I was perfect, as if looking into a mirror. Only… not really. A warm glow of pink surrounded my body in a halo. The mist of color swirled and eddied around my form, looking alive. Tripp's reflection illuminated in a bright yellow, glowing around him like sunshine. With his arms still tight around me, our two distinct colors swirled around each other.

"That's amazing! I've never seen anything like this. What do the colors mean?" I asked, entranced by our glowing reflection.

"The pink, which is a rare color, means that you are gentle in nature, that you exude love to everyone you come in contact with. In times of crisis, you help to heal those around you," Tripp whispered into my ear. His warm breath tickled my neck and I felt goosebumps raise on my arm.

Something about his statement jostled my memories. I was needed… to help heal someone. I shook my head slightly, dismissing the thought. I wasn't going to let my nagging memories ruin this night. Tomorrow would be here all too soon and I'd have time then to figure it all out.

"So what does the yellow say about you?" I asked, trying to refocus on the moment. This moment, where I was in the arms of this beautiful man, being completely swept off my feet.

"I think the Lake of Spirits might be a little off when it comes to me. It's supposed to mean that I'm confident, and that I inspire others, and that I spread joy to those around me."

"Actually, I think that is spot on," I said. Tripp turned me around to face him and looked into my eyes. His moss green eyes were vibrant and full of emotion.

"I've done a lot of things I'm not proud of. Things that if you knew, might change your opinion of me. Pan was right when he said that we're not good enough for you."

"Tripp, maybe I was meant to help you see yourself more clearly, too. All of those things that you've done, they have turned you into the man you are now. A man that I am falling in love with." That last part came out in a whisper, and part of me was hoping he wouldn't hear it.

Tripp narrowed his eyes at me, his brow pulling together for a moment. The next thing I knew, he was sweeping me up in his arms. I let out a little cry of surprise. "What are you doing?"

"I've claimed your mouth already, and now I want to bury myself in that sweet little pussy of yours."

I was shocked into speechlessness by his words, but my body reacted as a rush of need washed over me, and wetness slicked my sex at the idea of Tripp inside me. He was always surprising me with his prowess. He was so responsible and strait-laced, that he always caught me off guard when he was so forward when it came to anything sexual.

He carried me back to shore in his arms and placed me on the sandy beach. He walked around behind me and ever so slowly, started loosening the tight laces of my dress. His big hands gently slid the dress over my thighs and off of my body, draping it over a nearby tree branch. He walked back to me slowly, staring at my nakedness with a sly smirk on his face. He knelt before me again, his big hands gliding up the back of my legs and cupping my bare ass. He held me in place and grazed his nose over my exposed sex, the barely there sensation, making me suck in a quick breath. His warm green eyes met mine as he dipped his tongue in to taste me. I threw my head back as I moaned.

Tripp stopped his teasing. "Look at me, Gwen. I want to see the pleasure in your eyes," Tripp commanded.

I looked back down at him, biting my lip, feeling more exposed as he watched me. He sucked at my clit, flicking his tongue over the center of my pleasure. I felt my legs begin to tremble and I fisted my hands into his thick hair to help balance myself. I felt my pleasure begin to peak and I pulled his face away.

"I want to cum with you inside me," I panted.

He looked up at me, with one of his killer smiles. He tried to stand but I pushed him backward until he was lying on his back. I wanted to be in charge. I unfastened his belt and pushed aside his clothes to expose his hard chest, he was so beautifully sculpted. I couldn't help but run my hands hungrily over his olive skin.

I made my way to his breeches, untying the laces holding them together and freed his massive length. I worked my hand up and down his cock a couple of times, and watched with satisfaction as his eyes rolled back in pleasure and a moan escaped his lips. I had planned on drawing it out, making it last, but I was feeling too needy to wait.

I straddled over him, using one hand to tease my clit with the head of his cock. I positioned him at my opening and stared down at him, seeking those intense green eyes. When his gaze met mine, I impaled myself on him, fully sheathing his length in my wetness. We both cried out in unison, my toes curling in the sand.

He grabbed my hips, pulling me up and down, riding his cock, his strong arms flexing as he dug his fingers into me. I arched my back, seeking just the right spot where the head of his cock rubbed my G-spot and I worked it, in and out, pushing myself further until my orgasm exploded through me, sending shockwaves of pleasure coursing through my body.

"That is the sexiest thing I've ever seen."

Startled, I turned to find Ryder with his cock in his hands, working himself as he watched Tripp and I fucking. The idea that he'd been watching us, turned me on in an unexpected way. Seeing him stroke himself only fueled my desire for him. I beckoned him to come over to us.

I wondered how far they'd allow this to go. I wanted them both, at the same time, but would they want that too?

I never thought it was something that I would want. I'd had sex, I'd had dirty, raunchy, pull my hair sex— but this was new territory for me. Two men at once? Bloody hell! What the fuck was I thinking? I'm not sure my mind was processing rational thought in that moment. I was enslaved to my desires.

Ryder stopped in front of me and I grabbed his hard shaft in my hand, copying the movement he had just been doing. Tripp watched intently, still grinding his hips as he fucked me slowly, taking in the scene. I slipped the tip of his cock into my mouth and sucked hard. He hissed with praise as I worked him with my mouth, still stroking him with my hand.

"I want you inside me too Ryder," I moaned, giving in fully to my primal desires.

Ryder's eyebrows shot up briefly, but he wasted no time questioning me. He walked behind me and pushed me forward until I was leaning against Tripp's chest. I had a moment of panic, I had no idea what to expect, could I handle both of them or would it be too much?

This was my last chance to change my mind but, damn, my need for the both of them overruled my fears. He caressed a cheek and then gave it a small slap. The sting, sending a shock of pleasure through me. I felt him behind me, rubbing the head of his cock, still slicked in my spit, against my sensitive opening. Ever so gently he worked his way inside me, taking his time to stretch me slowly, until I was filled with two of my boys. Ryder, now the first Lost Boy to claim my ass.

He leaned forward, and grabbed my breast, playing with my nipple, while I took a moment to adjust to the both of them. Ryder began his slow movements, in and out, and I could feel the two of them inside, separated by a small section of overly sensitive skin. Ryder's movements pushed me forward, rocking me on Tripp's cock and I could hear them both, breathing hard, trying to keep to the slow pace, all of us enjoying the gradual build up of pleasure.

I kissed Tripp deeply, raking my fingers through his hair, feeling utterly lost in the onslaught of sensation. With the two of them inside me, they hit all of my sweet spots and before I knew it, my climax snuck up on me, shaking me to the core, my whole body tensing around my boys.

"Fuck!" Ryder seethed, followed by a mumbled line of obscenities and Tripp let out a throaty moan as my orgasm brought on their own climax, filling me completely.

None of us spoke, we just reveled in the aftermath of our pleasures. Ryder was draped over my back and I was resting completely on Tripp. I really liked this Lost Boy sandwich!

"Holy hell. You are fucking amazing, Hen. Sorry, wish I had some epic words to describe it, but my mind is a puddle in my skull after that," Ryder said, still catching his breath.

He pulled out of me slowly and sprawled out on the sand. I cradled Tripp's face in my hands and kissed him softly before I rolled off of him, laying between them, as I regained my composure.

"We should probably make our way back to the village before Pan sends out a search party for us," Tripp said with a sigh.

"Or maybe he's still having his private conference with her majesty," I said sarcastically. I propped myself up on my elbows, feeling my jealousy over Tiger Lily, rearing its ugly head. "Do you think Peter's had sex with her?"

"Do you really want me to answer that?" Tripp responded.

"Aww Hen, don't worry. I like Tiger Lily, don't get me wrong, but she couldn't hold a candle to you. Did you see how many fae she gathered for her harem this year? She is trying to make a show of it, but she's threatened by you." Ryder said, making me smile as always.

"Do you mean that she plans to have sex with all of them?" I asked, thinking of all the nymphs and satyrs that had been on display around her throne.

"She is a fae princess, so it's her responsibility to ensure that she brings fertility to Neverland," Tripp explained.

"Well damn, she's got some serious stamina. I'm happy I only have the four of you to please," I mused aloud and the boys laughed.

"Trust me Hen, you're going to need some stamina. We're just getting started."

CHAPTER XX
DECEPTION

We emerged from the forest as the sun began to sink in the horizon and twilight set in. I quickly spotted Peter and Eben deep in conversation— neither of them looked pleased.

"It's about time you finally joined us. Gwen's been worrying about you guys. Tripp and I had to distract her," Ryder said smugly, smiling ear to ear.

Peter and Eben looked up at us, looking a little shocked as they took us in. It was as if we had the words 'just fucked' tattooed across our foreheads, and I blushed in embarrassment.

"You assholes started without us! I can't fucking believe it," Eben complained, throwing his hands up in irritation.

"I've recently become very fond of assholes," Ryder said dreamily and I promptly elbowed him in the ribs. My face must have gone from a delicate blush to a dark crimson.

"Unbelievable!" Eben said. "That's it, I get dibs on Gwen the rest of the night."

"Get in line, Eben," Peter taunted and grabbed my hand, pulling me into him and kissing me passionately, as though we'd been apart for days.

"Peter," Tiger Lily's sultry voice interrupted our kiss. "The festivities are about to begin. Your presence is required."

"Yes, thank you, Tiger Lily. But first, I didn't get the chance to introduce you to my girl," Peter said, smiling at me and I felt giddy when he called me his girl.

Tiger Lily smiled condescendingly at Peter but then cleared her face of all emotion as she turned to me.

"I am Tiger Lily, Fae Princess of the Ninth Realm, descendant of the Divine." She stated her line of titles with pride mixed with some obvious intimidation.

"Gwendolyn Mary Darling Carlisle... of London, England. But you can call me Gwen," I said, patronizingly.

"May you be blessed with love and abundance," she said, as if she had tried to take the higher ground. I took a deep breath, and tried to calm my inner bitch, who really wanted to shove that 'love and abundance' up her ass. I would not allow her to ruin this night for me, because really she meant nothing to me.

"And same to you," I managed to say with some semblance of politeness.

She gave me a half smile and headed back to her dais, her hips swaying exaggeratedly and I rolled my eyes. Damn, it was like walking into a lion's den. I had to try and keep the attentions of four gorgeous men, all the while being surrounded by beautiful women, who would fuck them all in a heartbeat. I lifted my chin, grabbed Peter's hand and followed behind her, holding my head high, royalty in my own right, as the Queen of the Lost Boys.

We settled down on a pallet of soft blankets that had been setup beside Tiger Lily's dais. Tiger Lily set herself up in her throne and all those who were part of her harem crowded in around her. We sat in silence, as the village was cleared of all children. Once they were all tucked away for the night, and only the adults remained, the entertainment began.

The drum beat that had been the background noise for the entire evening, picked up, and was accompanied by the melodic notes of a flute. A symphony of voices joined in the harmony, singing in a language I'd never heard before. The twilight had given way to full night. The village was now illuminated by the flickering of fires and torches.

A procession of nymphs, draped in heavy white robes, each carrying a small torch, paraded into a clearing toward the center of the village, where an actual May Pole had been erected. It was a good twenty feet tall, wrapped in brilliant linens and decorated with clusters of flowers. The nymphs aligned in a circle around the maypole and stood silent with their heads bowed. A flurry of pixies joined the circle, adding a soft glow, like fireflies, to the flickering torchlight.

A hushed silence fell over the gathering, even the music had ceased. All that could be heard was the sound of the crackling fire. The anticipation was thick in the air, everyone's attention stuck on the figures. All at once they began to hum. Low at first, barely noticeable, but slowly raised in pitch. They began chanting unfamiliar words again. The tone of their voices was enchanting, mesmerizing even. They all raised their arms and began to sway back and forth, moving in perfect unison. Many of those in the crowd began to sway along with the chanting as they all became entranced by the scene. The group began to dance around the maypole with their torches still in hand, light from the flames ghosting behind them as they picked up speed, moving fluidly along with the music.

My attention was pulled from the entrancing sight when I felt Eben's hand caress my leg, tracing small circles on my skin as he worked his way up my thigh. I glanced over at him, and he wasn't watching the dancing nymph's. He was staring at me with dark eyes, the orange flicker of firelight reflecting back at me. He leaned in and started kissing up my neck as his hand moved further up, grazing over my belted throwing knives and encouraging me to spread my legs to give him further access to me.

"It's so damn hot that you're armed. Maybe I'll have you leave these on while I fuck you," he said. Then he ran his talented fingers over the delicate skin around my knife belt.

I peered around us, feeling self conscious that someone might be watching us. I looked over at Tiger Lily, and my eyes widened in shock. As she sat on her throne, a satyr was kneeled between her legs, eating her out right in the open! But it wasn't just her, everyone on the dais was engaged in some sexual act. I had thought I'd prepared myself for this, but I was shocked by the reality of it, and a little intrigued at the orgy that was taking place before me.

Eben bit my neck, drawing my attention back to him, still caressing my thigh. Well… when in Neverland. I spread myself open to him. Closing my eyes, I shut everything else out but the sensual caress of my lover and the pulsating music, pretending it was only the two of us. His fingers grazed along my wet folds. I was dripping with my own arousal, and the remnants of Tripp's release from our earlier tryst. Everything was so sensitive, I had to curb the urge to moan out loud, and instead, I sucked in a breath through clenched teeth. I couldn't help but squirm under his gentle touch. Eben laughed softly in my ear, pleased with himself at the response he was getting from me.

"Do you like that?" his husky voice whispered in my ear and I nodded. "I didn't hear you Gwen," he said and his fingers stopped abruptly, leaving me desperate to feel his touch again.

"Yes, it's amazing," I breathed, my words coming out in a pant.

"Do you want me to make you cum like this?" he asked as his fingers began again, working my clit in earnest.

Before I could answer him, a blood curdling scream pierced through my lust clouded mind. I jumped in surprise and my eyes flew open. Even Eben pulled away from me and had his hand grasped around his dagger instantly. Everyone was immediately tense, gazing around, bewildered.

Another scream broke the hushed chatter and confusion. My boys were on their feet now, each with a weapon in hand. Several satyr's emerged from darkened edges of the village at a dead run.

"Pirates! The pirates have breached our sentries and are heading this way!" The first satyr to reach us explained between labored breaths, keeling over with his hands on his knees as he tried to catch his breath. Tiger Lily and Peter looked at each other with solemn expressions.

"I thought you said the borders were secure?" Peter seethed at Tiger Lily, his dark eyes glared at her.

"It was secure. I had some of my best men out there," she countered.

The village had begun to fall into chaos as everyone began to scatter from the village center, seeking refuge from the coming onslaught. More screams made in pain reached us, an ominous warning for what was coming for us.

"What are you going to do Peter? You are Neverland's protector. It is your responsibility to meet this challenge," Tiger Lily commanded imperiously.

She looked between me and Peter, as if she needed to remind him of his responsibilities. Peter straightened to his full height and he cloaked any emotions. His stoic mask replaced his anger as he prepared himself for battle and he barked out his orders.

"Ryder, Tripp, each of you take a contingent of satyrs and fan out. You all know these woods, use it to your advantage. Be the shadow they don't see coming. Turn those mother fuckers around and drive them from the mainland. I want them scurrying back to their ship like the rats they are." Tripp and Ryder nodded. "Eben... man I need you to stay behind..."

"Are you fucking serious?" Eben growled before Peter could finish.

"Yes! I am dead serious," Peter bellowed. He reached for Eben, grasping the back of his neck and pulled him until they were nose to nose. "I need you to stay with Gwen. You're my best fighter. I need you to protect her if we fail. We all need you to protect her. You understand don't you?"

Peter asked, his tone was stern. Eben's jaw clenched and then released.

"Of course. You know I'll protect her with my last breath," Eben responded.

"I will protect her as well, Peter. You don't have to worry about her. But you must hurry or they will be in the village, raping our women and pillaging our goods," Tiger Lily added.

Peter nodded and turned to me. He pulled me in and kissed me, fierce and deep and far too short for my liking.

"Stay with Tiger Lily. Eben will keep you safe," Peter commanded and I just nodded. Both Tripp and Ryder kissed me a passionate, parting kiss and they started to head off into the darkness.

"Wait!" I called, feeling overwhelmed at the speed in which everything was happening. "Come back to me in one piece... because my heart can't take it if you don't."

"You know that means she loves us," Ryder said as he winked at Tripp and they left, fading into the darkness.

"COME WITH ME. We will wait this out in my home. It is the most fortified place in the whole village," Tiger Lily said as she beckoned me to where she and Peter had gone off earlier to speak privately. She held the door open for me and ushered me inside. Eben tried to follow behind, but she held her arm across the door, stopping him from entering.

"You may not enter. You know the rules. No unaccompanied male is allowed in my dwelling. You are neither my mate or in a position of power. You may guard the door." She was harsh with him, and it pissed me right the fuck off at how she spoke to him, as if he was beneath her.

"If he's not coming in, then neither am I," I shot back at her.

"No, she's right. You'll be safer waiting in there. I'll keep guard outside," he assured me. He then kissed me chastely before turning his back, scanning the hubbub of the village as everyone tried to flee from the oncoming danger.

Tiger Lily closed the door behind us, shutting us in to the earthen home. It was dimly lit with candles, the recesses of the home cloaked in dark shadows. A smoldering fire was at the center of the home, surrounded by brightly colored cushions on the floor.

"Sit," Tiger Lily commanded as she walked over to a large shelf cluttered with books and artifacts.

"You don't get to order me around," I retorted sharply.

She glanced over her shoulder at me, looked me over and sneered. "Suit yourself. Stand for all I care." She shrugged and started pilfering through the shelves obviously looking for something.

"What is your problem with me? Are you jealous that Peter chose me?"

"Gwen, jealousy is not a notion that I entertain. I am here to help you, even if you can't see it yet."

"Help me? I don't need your help."

"Tell me, what are you going to do now that spring cleaning is coming to an end?" she inquired, effectively changing the conversation and I wasn't sure I liked the direction she was taking.

"I'm, well, I have to go back to my world," I stumbled in my response. This was a sore spot that I did not want to discuss with her.

"So you are going to crush Peter's heart, just like Wendy did all those years ago?" she accused.

"No, it's not like that. Peter knew from the beginning that I meant to leave. I've always been honest with him. And I am not taking the Lost Boys with me when I leave, like she did," I insisted, trying to separate myself from Wendy and the mistakes she had made with Peter.

"But you let him fall for you. You did your best to change his mind when he tried to push you away," she stated plainly. How the fuck did she know that!?

"I don't see how any of this is your business."

"Oh but it is my business. Peter Pan has become vital to Neverland. My people depend on me to keep them safe, and Peter plays a key role in that."

I scowled at her, but I had no response.

"It's not your fault, really," she continued. "I thought Peter was done bringing Wendy's back from beyond the veil, but for some reason, he cannot help himself. And this time, I fear he will not be able to do right by you."

"What do you mean?"

"You must believe me when I tell you, Peter doesn't intend to bring you back across the veil. You are effectively his prisoner now. Only you won't even know it because your memories are fading."

"You're lying! Peter knows I have to go back. He would never do that to me!" I was seething, my voice raised in irritation at her preposterous claims.

"Do you even remember why you have to go back?" she asked, poignantly, and I clenched my jaw tight. I hated that she seemed to know so much about me. I started to feel incredibly vulnerable in this conversation.

"No, you don't. And I bet Peter hasn't tried to remind you either. He's counting on the fact that you will forget. Unfortunately, the memories that tie you to your world are diminishing faster, because you love him."

"I don't believe you."

"I have proof. Come here, let me show you."

I walked over to her hesitantly, not sure I wanted to see what 'proof' she thought she had, and my mind was spinning at the accusations she was laying at Peter's feet.

"Peter has always had a pixie. A fae counterpart that assists him in his responsibilities to Neverland. Each one of them keeps a journal and they report to me."

"You're spying on him?"

"Gwen, I told you, I am the protector of my people. They are my first responsibility. There is nothing I wouldn't do for them. Peter is not of this world, he is not fae, but he has somehow become ingrained in Neverland. I must always be sure that he keeps Neverland's best interests first and foremost."

She led me to a small table and laid out a miniature book that was about the size of my thumb.

"This is the journal of Tinkerbell. Remember, Gwen, I am trying to help you."

She delicately opened the book and placed a glass stone on top of the page she flipped to. The stone acted as a magnifying glass so I could read the tiny writing.

It's been several moons since Peter has brought the Wendy lady to live in Neverland. I am no longer in his favor, as he prefers her to everyone else. I am worried about this obsession he is developing for her. I think we need to find a way to get her back across the veil as soon as possible. I fear that if Peter becomes more attached, it will lead him down a dark path.

I pulled in a breath as my earlier fears came rushing back to me. That thimble, he'd kept her kiss all these years later. Tinkerbell's journal only reignited my fears.

"That doesn't mean anything. So he had a crush on Wendy and Tinkerbell was jealous." I dismissed her proof and pushed the miniature journal away. I didn't want her to see my own convictions waning.

"There is more." She flipped to another page and pushed it back in front of me.

The Wendy lady is finally gone and she's left nothing but destruction in her wake.

Peter tried to sabotage her return. He promised the Wendy lady and the Lost Boys that he would return them across the veil. All the while, he'd instructed me to go on ahead and bar the window to keep the Wendy lady out. He wanted her to believe that she had been forgotten. His obsession has become so consuming that he conspired to keep her for himself by tricking her into returning to Neverland with him to live forever. But it was all a lie. By the hand of the Divine, his plans were foiled by the Darling mother and he was forced to leave the Wendy lady behind. Peter has deteriorated since she left and Neverland suffers. The sun hides behind clouds, storms rage, pirates are taking over our fae forces. His obsession with her has destroyed him and we all suffer. We can never let this happen again.

I was stunned in disbelief. Had Peter's love for Wendy mutated into a dark obsession? Was I just a stand in for a long dead Wendy, as Lill had said? Could I trust Tiger Lily? Could I trust Tinkerbell's words? I was so confused, so conflicted.

"This can't be true," I mumbled half to myself.

I heard a scratch and a sputter and a single match lit the dark recess of the house, shedding an eerie glow on the face of a man. I was stunned to find the viciously handsome features of Captain James Hook, appearing as if out of nowhere, in the back corner of Tiger Lily's home. He pulled a hit from a silver contraption that held two cigars, the tips flaring a brilliant red, and a small swirl of smoke billowed up from his mouth as he exhaled.

He sat casually in a chair, his boots propped up. I stumbled backward, and Tiger Lily moved quickly to me, grabbing a hold of me and placing a hand over my mouth. I felt the tip of a blade press against my lower back.

"Don't scream and don't even think of pulling those knives you have hidden under your dress. He is here upon my request, just hear us out. We are both here to help you," Tiger Lily whispered in my ear. "I'm going to take my hand away, but if you even think of doing something stupid, I will gut you right here and blame it on the pirates."

I felt myself tremble as my heart pounded in my chest. I couldn't seem to think clearly. What the fuck was happening?

"You bitch," I hissed at her.

"You read the journal. I can't let it happen again. I'm sorry Gwen, but you have to go. We both want you to return home, I'm just making sure it happens."

"You don't care about your people. They are getting slaughtered as we speak and you let it happen," I spat at her.

"It's about the greater good," she said coldly.

"You'll never get me out of here. Eben won't let you take me."

I heard the legs of the chair scrape across the ground

and heavy boots hit the floor as a sinister laugh escaped Hook's mouth.

"Gwen, darling. I hate to be the one to break your heart, but the Lost Boys are in on this plan as well."

"I don't trust a damn thing you have to say."

"If I were you, I wouldn't trust me either. But don't take it from me, just open the door and see for yourself. Eben has abandoned you. This was the plan all along," he drawled as he rolled his cigar holder in his one hand.

I stalked to the door and neither of them tried to stop me. I knew Eben— the real Eben. He wouldn't leave me at Hook's mercy. I threw the door open and my heart sank. Eben was gone. Aside from a few villagers scurrying around, there was no sign of him anywhere.

I sank to my knees, completely shattered. No... no! I was having a hard time coming to terms with what my eyes confirmed to be real. It felt like my heart was breaking in my chest and I felt like I couldn't breathe. How could I have been so naive? They had been playing me this whole time. Tiger Lily knelt beside me and tried to comfort me.

"Get the fuck away from me. Don't fucking touch me!" I barked at her as I sprang to my feet, holding my head high. I wouldn't allow her to see me in a moment of weakness. I couldn't allow the tears to fall, and it took an immense effort to hold them back.

"See, my dear, I knew you could be reasonable," Hook said in his gravelly voice.

"What do you plan to do with me now?" I asked,

steeling myself to cover the fact that I felt like I was dying inside. Eben's betrayal was like a hot knife in my chest.

"I will of course be escorting you beyond the veil and returning you to your sister. Michaela is her name, correct?"

Memories came flooding back to me. It was like the moment before death when your life flashes before your eyes. Michaela! I had forgotten my beautiful sister— my beautiful, sick sister. Her angelic face flashed in my mind's eye. She was my reason. Why I had always planned to return home. As hard as I tried to stay strong, tears escaped, unbidden, from my eyes.

How could I have been so foolish? So selfish? I was so ashamed. But this was my punishment, for some unknown atrocities that I'd committed against the universe. That's the only way I could rationalize everything that had happened to me. I was on some cosmic shit list and I would be paying the price for the rest of my miserable life.

"Yes, I need to get back to my sister."

"Ahh I see. Now you remember."

"You need to leave before Peter returns. He will fight to the death for her. His obsession has rotted inside him like a wormed apple."

"As much as I'd love to engage in such a fight with my worthy opponent, we must be off with the tides if we plan to make haste across the veil. Tiger Lily, it has been a pleasure to serve you," he said formally and bowed to her.

"You need to finish your end of the bargain. Make it look real."

"Smee! See that Princess Tiger Lily gets a proper beating and try not to enjoy it too much," Hook barked his orders as if commanding a dog.

A large man emerged from the shadows, a thick salt and pepper beard hung down to his chest. The firelight glinted off of his bald scalp. He stalked toward Tiger Lily and without hesitation backhanded her with so much force that she fell to the ground. He proceeded to kick her small form, landing blow after blow. She didn't make a sound as she took the brutal beating.

"Stop it! Make him stop! He's going to kill her!" I screamed as I pleaded with Hook.

I had no idea why I felt the need to defend her? This bitch had utterly crushed my soul only moments before and yet I couldn't bear to see them beat her so ruthlessly. He looked down at me with hungry eyes, as if the violence had aroused him, and I found myself shrinking back from him.

"Alright Smee, we're done here. Get our pretty little cargo ready to sail," he commanded. Smee turned from Tiger Lily's writhing form, bloodied on the ground and focused his attention on me. I began to back away from him, but in a few long strides, he grasped my upper arm viciously and spun me around. He pulled my hands behind my back and started to bind my wrists.

"What the fuck are you doing?" I asked Hook.

"Perception, darling," he said as he approached me—getting in my personal space. He used his cold, metal hook to lift my chin up so that I could see into his eyes. "The perception is that you are now my prisoner. I think we shall keep it that way." He snickered and then turned for the door.

Smee promptly lifted me up and slung me over his shoulder like a sack of potatoes and followed after Hook— a dog following its master. And we disappeared into the inky blackness of the Neverland night.

CHAPTER XXI
CAPTAIN JAMES HOOK

S mee had taken me directly to the captain's quarters. He had stripped me of my knives and left me bound and shaken. How did this happen? How could my boys be in on this? How could Eben leave me to be taken? None of this was making any sense. Yet, was it in my face the whole time? Had I chosen to ignore the red flags? Peter, himself, had tried to warn me. How could I have been so naive? I felt foolish and heartbroken.

The Jolly Roger was exactly how I had imagined — straight from the story books. The room was rich in intricately carved wood. Dramatic candelabras lit the room in a flickering glow of candlelight. Crimson drapes hung heavy, like a canopy over a large four post bed. At the center of the room sat a large table, covered in scrolls. A single candle sat melting on top of a wax covered skull that served as a centerpiece of sorts. There was a large window at the far end of the room and I could see the moonlight reflecting off the rippled sea.

Was I really about to head back home? Was my time here in Neverland over? I wriggled in my ropes hoping to loosen them, only causing them to grow tighter.

A door opened catching my attention, and in walked my deceptively handsome captor. He appeared to be middle aged. Time had added a patina to his face, enhancing his masculine features. I wondered if, like Peter, time had stopped for him. His hair fell in salty waves at his shoulders. He wore leather pants that left little to the imagination. A deep V neck shirt topped with a leather vest. A sash around his waist. He was adorned with heavy jewelry. Large skull rings sat on his tattooed fingers, while his hook seemed to glisten in the candle light, as if he had just finished polishing it. I remained silent, nothing but the sound of his boots hitting the floor as he walked over to me. I was frozen in fear. My nerves were getting the best of me. I took a large breath and reminded myself of the rules of Neverland.

Just go with it.

"A beguiling thing you are, Gwen. Your beauty outshines your predecessor." I blushed at his compliment.

"Are you going to untie me now?" I asked, a little attitude in my voice. I was trying to keep my composure as he slowly circled, inspecting me. He had no reason to untie me. I was at his mercy.

"I quite enjoy the look of you bound in ropes," his voice was deep and seductive. "Such a shame to waste a beautiful binding." He paused and I heard him pull in a large breath, savoring my scent from behind. "We'll have time to play later," he whispered in my ear. He cut the ropes from my hands and they dropped to the floor in a thud.

I spun around to face him, rubbing my wrists where the ropes had bitten into my skin. He was sex incarnate. A beautifully packaged poison tempting you to take a taste of its sweet death. Time to play later? The words echoed in my head.

"Come, have a seat." He motioned to the table in the center of the room. "Join me for a drink."

I made my way to the table, but before I could sit down, I heard chains. Chains dragging across the floor. There, chained to the wall and muzzled like a rabid dog, was the crocodile. I remembered Ryder telling me that Hook had kept the beast to do his bidding. I never imagined he'd have it chained in his private quarters. The thing was huge and menacing. It hissed at me as I made eye contact.

"Ignore her," he said as he waved his hand dismissively. "She wouldn't dare act without my command. That crocodile is my bitch."

"The way Wendy tells it, you're the croc's bitch."

Hook slammed his fist on the table, causing me to flinch. Rage washed over his face. I'm not certain, but I think I saw his eyes flash red. I don't know why I said it. I wanted to show him that I was brave, that I wasn't afraid of him. The truth, however, was that I was afraid. I was afraid that I found him alluring. That his darkness intrigued me. He was hot as hell and my body responded to his presence more than I cared to admit.

"Wendy was an immature little girl who didn't know her heart from her head. I never understood Pan's obsession with her. Aside from her alluring innocence, she was nothing but a nuisance." He poured two glasses of rum while mumbling under his breath, "Traitorous bitch."

He slid a glass over to me and I stared at it waiting for him to take the first sip. If I remembered correctly, Hook had a penchant for poison. I wasn't going to take any chances with this man. I had no idea who to believe at this point. Hook and Tiger Lily could be double crossing me. He took his glass in hand and swirled it before taking a large swig. "It's not poison, sweetheart. Just rum. Drink," he demanded.

Without thought, I did what I was told. The rum was sweetly spiced— a pleasant surprise. I took a second sip enjoying the warming sensation washing over my body. I wanted nothing more than to numb my feelings. I wanted to escape the negative thoughts clouding my mind. The "what ifs" threatening to ruin my connection with my boys and tainting my memories. I needed to keep a level head. I was in the private quarters of the notorious Captain Hook. Like it or not, I was in danger. Getting drunk here, with him, would be a mistake. Tears filled my eyes and threatened to spill down my cheeks. My heart was overwhelmed with feelings.

"Spilling tears over a boy... really? You know you are nothing but a replacement for a long lived obsession. A rare beauty like you deserves better than that."

Hook was right. I did deserve better than that. I reached for the acorn Peter had given me— my heart searching for redemption.

"Surely I'm more than just a replacement. We shared..." I trailed off not wanting to share my private memories with Hook. I looked down at my glass and took another sip. A little buzz wouldn't hurt. I needed to drown out my thoughts.

"That boy has been obsessed with the girls in your family since he first laid eyes on Wendy. He tried to keep her for his own, like a goddamned pet, and he was trying to do the same with you. You should be grateful we stepped in when we did."

"Keep me like a pet? Like you keep the crocodile?"

"That crocodile is lucky to be alive. I keep her as a reminder of what I can do to those who dare defy me. She ate a piece of me, and someday, when I see fit, I'll eat a piece of her. Let me ask you something," he said, changing the subject back to me. "When Peter brought you here to Neverland, did he even offer you a choice? Or did he just bring you here, taking advantage of an intoxicated girl?"

How had he known I was drunk that night? I tried to think back to the night Peter came to my room. Did he ask? My memory was murky. I couldn't quite remember the details. I remembered him coming to my room and mentioning spring cleaning. I remembered waking up in Neverland, disoriented. I shook my head no, as I tried to wrap my brain around what Hook was implying. "I don't remember being given a choice." Fuck, Hook was painting a very different picture of the Peter I thought I knew. I looked up at him, and for a moment I thought I saw compassion in his kohl rimmed, forget-me-not blue eyes.

"Was that" —he nodded at my necklace— "supposed to be a replacement for this?" he asked as he grabbed one of the chains from his neck and pulled out my locket.

"My locket!"

"What did he give you? A simple acorn? No pictures? Peter knew you would forget about your sister without the real thing. An acorn, in place of a kiss. How childish." He laughed. My smile quickly disappeared at Hooks words. "Your boys didn't look very hard for it. My bosun found it lying on the ground. Let me do the honor of returning it to you." He then removed my locket from his neck as he stood up. The cold metal of his Hook grazed my skin as he pulled my hair to the side, sending a shiver down my spine. He gently draped the chain around my neck, and without difficulty, clasped it in place.

I immediately opened it. There she was—my anchor— my Michaela. I ran my fingers across the engraved words '*To die will be an awfully big adventure.*' Everything came flooding back. Mic was sick, and alone. How could I forget my sister? The guilt became consuming. I took another sip, disgusted with myself.

"So, Gwen. Tell me. What's it like to sacrifice your life, your happiness... simply to care for a loved one? Better yet, tell me what it feels like to finally be selfish for once." His words hit me hard, like a blade piercing my heart.

"She's my sister. I would give my life for hers. She didn't ask for the hand she was dealt, and neither did I." I hung my head in shame. "Yes. I've been selfish since coming to Neverland," I said it quietly, as if doing so would make it sting less. Hook reached across the table and lifted my chin. His eyes held me hostage in their stare.

"There is no shame in caring for yourself. Though it may feel like it, the world does not rest on your shoulders, my dear." His thumb gently caressed my jaw, before he leaned back into his chair. He was right. Mic would have encouraged me to lose myself in the moment. But it was time to go back.

" I didn't choose to come here. I played the cards I was dealt. And yes, I've enjoyed it. I took advantage of my situation. For once in my life I did what I wanted," I said with conviction. I didn't regret the choices I'd made. Given the opportunity, I'd make them again.

Hook smiled. I could tell he was pleased with my response.

"I find your selfishness quite captivating. You have tasted freedom, and yet you are ready to go back to your pitiful, selfless life." He shook his head. "Your loyalty to your loved one is admirable."

"Have we left?" I asked abruptly, breaking the tension between us. "Are we headed back across the veil?" I felt desperate to get home now.

"We left port as soon as we boarded. I've given my crew orders to sail straight on till morning." He paused for a moment, "I assumed you wanted to get back to your Mic as soon as possible. You've been here what, a few days? Your dear sister could be dead by now."

"What! Why would she be dead?"

"You do know, that time here in Neverland, moves differently than you're used to?"

"No! How different?" I demanded. How did he know I called her Mic? I found it unnerving that he knew so many personal details about me. I took another sip finishing off my glass.

"Peter never told you? You see love, I told you he was trying to keep you here." He poured us both another round.

"How long? How long have I been gone?"

"It's hard to say exactly. Maybe weeks, maybe months." He raised his shoulders in a shrug.

I dropped my head in my hands. I'd been so selfish. Wishing my time here would never end. Why didn't Peter tell me time was moving differently? Maybe Hook and Tiger Lily were right. What if Peter had been trying to keep me here? What if I was just an obsession? A replacement. I'd been so selfishly obsessed with the attention from my boys that I'd forgotten about my dying sister. What had I done?

The rum was going straight to my head. My logic was unraveling rapidly. So much for staying sober. I drained my glass, slammed it on the table and walked over to the window.

I looked out at the sea, moonlight bouncing off the caps in a shimmering dance. The sky was clear and filled with stars. I tried to memorize the beauty that was Neverland. I'd likely never see it again. My memories could be just that. I could choose to remember the amazing moments. I could forget about the betrayal, right? I wrapped my arms around myself, wanting to feel some comfort. Somewhere out there was my sister. I only hoped I hadn't been gone too long.

I felt him approach my back. His heady scent invaded my senses— musky leather mixed with salt from the sea.

"We live on a placid island of ignorance in the midst of black seas of infinity, and it was not meant that we should voyage far." He quoted H.P. Lovecraft and it could not have been more appropriate.

"Give me the opportunity to at least say goodbye. Let me write them a letter?" I asked. I had to at least find some closure for myself. Some way to let them go.

"Maybe we can work a trade." He dragged his hook

down the back of my arm sending a shiver down my spine. "Do I make you nervous?"

My breath hitched, afraid to answer. I could feel the heat from his body against my bare shoulders.

"Answer me, Gwen." His voice was stern and commanding. "Do you fear me?"

"No," I lied. "Should I?"

He leaned in closer. I could feel his breath on my ear. "Does fear... excite you? Does it turn you on to know that at any moment I could gut you like a pig with one quick rip of my hook?" My mind should be screaming to pull away, but my body was coursing with rum and excitement. "Allow me the pleasure," he purred as he leaned in and kissed my neck as I tilted my head to the side, closing my eyes, allowing him more access, "of distracting you." His hand wrapped around my waist. "Let *me* fill your thoughts. Let me make your last moments here in Neverland pleasurable."

I turned around to face him and we locked eyes. He looked at me like a wolf stalking prey. My body was alive with electricity. Was I really going to let Hook seduce me? Would I live to regret it? "I—"

"Shhhh," he quieted me. "There is no shame in giving in to pleasure."

I took a step back and found the edge of the window frame. He stepped closer, stroking my cheek with the back of his hook. The cold metal, dangerous and strangely erotic. He pressed his body against mine, pinning me against the wall. "What about my boys?" I asked, dropping my head.

My boys— I had to give them the benefit of the doubt. I wasn't ready to believe everything Hook and Tiger Lily had said. I owed them at least that much.

"What about your boys?" Hook snarled, obviously irritated by my hesitation. "They left you for dead. Aren't you tired of playing with boys?" His voice softened as his lips grazed my ear. "Let me show you what a man can offer you."

My heart began to pound in my chest. He lifted my chin with his hook and kissed me hard, his tongue claiming my mouth with a mastery I'd never known. Igniting a fire within my traitorous body.

"Give yourself to me freely, and I promise you, I'll get them your letter."

I tried to stall "I... I, " my breath hitched as his hook slid up my inner thigh and pressed against my core.

"I can smell your desire. You want this as much as I do."

His words only turned me on more. My body was no longer in my control. My head was spinning with rum. I had tasted his poison, and I wanted more. My legs spread, a wordless agreement to his offer. He growled, giving me a devilish grin as he lifted my dress and grabbed my thighs— wrapping them around his waist. The cold metal of his hook was a constant reminder of the danger I was inviting in.

We kissed again— hard and fast, like animals in heat as he carried me back to the table sweeping it clear. Glass shattered as it hit the floor. He laid me back, lifting my dress and placing my feet on the edge of the table, spreading my legs wide and exposing my glistening sex. He dragged the sharp point of his hook down my thigh, leaving a red welt in its wake. I trembled with both fear and excitement. I felt the cold, hard metal slide down my slit and I moaned shamelessly at the unfamiliar sensation. He took his time coating his hook with my excitement and made eye contact with me as he slowly licked it clean.

"You taste like sin, and I will have more."

He dropped down and began bathing me with his tongue. Taking his time and savoring every moment. I lost myself in the pleasure, gripping my knees and pulling my legs back, giving him better access. He inserted a finger and I cried out for more. "Greedy little thing you are," he said as he added a second and focused his attention to my throbbing clit. His tongue made quick work of me, drawing me to the edge.

"You're gonna make me cum!" I cried out, as he brought forth a mind shattering orgasm.

"I'm not done with you yet, beautiful. Stand up," he ordered.

I stood up and he turned me around. I felt his hand grip the top of my dress and in one violent swoop, his hook cut through my corset laces, dropping my dress to the floor, leaving me naked.

"Turn around. I want to look at you." I spun around, his eyes examining my body while he bit at his lip. "A truly magnificent specimen you are." He pulled open a drawer at the center of the table and pulled out more rope. "Place your hands together in front of your breasts."

I shook my head no.

"I'm not—" I paused, trying to choose my words carefully. I had never been tied up before and the idea of allowing Hook, a dangerous man, to bind me, made me quite nervous. It also seemed to be turning me on in unexpected ways.

"If I wanted you dead, you'd be dead. Quit playing coy. It's clear you are enjoying yourself. Your pussy is dripping down your thighs."

I didn't have to look down to know he was right. My body was ripe with desire. I had given in to temptation. I had tasted darkness and I liked it. "Put your hands up," he said sternly, and I obeyed. Hook wrapped the rope around my wrists twice and back over through the middle knotting them.

He wasted no time pulling me forward, leading me to the foot of the four post bed. About three quarters of the way up, embedded in the post, was a hook. His bed had been made for this. I wondered how many women had been here before? He placed my bound wrists over the hook and I grabbed hold of the post. His hook pulled at my hip, bending me over as he caressed my ass.

SMACK!

I jumped at the sensation of his slap. The sound startled me. I moaned as the sting set in. His hand rubbed the now sensitive skin.

SMACK!

I yelped this time as the sting became warmth. Hook stripped down to his leather pants, and his body did not disappoint. His chest was strong and defined. Tattoos scattered across his body. His abs led my eyes to his deep V cuts. A delicate trail of dark hair, dipping below his low slung pants.

SMACK!

I moaned as he slapped my ass again, bringing back the sting. He untied his pants and pulled out his cock. Reaching between my legs, finding my clit, he covered his hand in my wetness before gripping his cock and stroking himself, while admiring my now pink ass. He positioned himself at my opening and slowly pushed in. My body gave no resistance. I moaned as he began to fuck me harder. The force of his thrusts pushed me forward into the post. He bent his body over mine as his hand explored my breasts. Rolling my nipple in his calloused fingers.

Making his way down my body, he found my aching clit and made quick work of my orgasm. I cried out as It rushed out of me, violently. My body gripped his from within. I felt his rhythm change as he found his own pleasure. His body again, folding over mine as he finished. He gently lifted my arms down from the hook and released the binding.

"Lay down on the bed." He licked his lips. "I will have you in my mouth."

I crawled onto the bed and laid down, spread eagle, while Hook crawled up between my legs, his eyes never leaving mine. Using his hook and his hand he held my legs apart while he ravished my body once more with his tongue. Electric fire rushed through my body. I arched my back and cried out as his skilled tongue brought out yet another earth shattering orgasm. Hook stood up and dragged his hand down his face, wiping our cum from his beard.

"Now I know why Peter wanted to keep you for himself." He tossed his shirt at me, before walking over to the window and staring out at the sea.

Peter. Why did he have to mention Peter? I had, for a moment, been distracted. Selfishly pushing Peter to the back of my mind. I just wanted to get home and try to move on. I just wanted to get back to Mic. I slid his shirt on and joined him at the window.

"Hook?" He looked at me.

"Please, call me James."

"James, can I write that letter now?" I whispered, worried he might go back on his word.

He sighed, still looking out at the darkness.

"I never thought I would find someone who could rival my hedonistic ways." I looked at him with confusion. "You were willing to make the ultimate sacrifice, albeit against your knowledge, for pleasure, to indulge your selfish desires. To live the life you could have only imagined." He sounded almost reverent as he spoke. I dropped my head in shame.

"It's not too late." He lifted my chin with his hand. "Sail with me. Together we could rule all of Neverland. Queen of the Lost Boys. HA! I'll make you Queen of the Pirates. We'll spend our days seeking pleasure in all its forms." I couldn't believe what he was offering. Become his queen? I just wanted to get back home.

"I need to get back to my sister." I stared at him silently, as I watched the hope in his melancholy eyes turn dark. His entire demeanor shifted.

"I was hoping you would change your mind. But my word is my bond. I told you I would get them a letter. In the drawer at the table you will find paper and a quill. Do as you wish."

"Thank you."

"You should get some rest. You have a busy morning." And with that he left the room.

I busied myself with my goodbye letter. Allowing myself one last cry. Finding closure in my words and sealing my memories away for a time, when thinking of them wouldn't cause my heart to break.

THE DOOR BARGED OPEN, waking me from a dreamless sleep. The crocodile hissed and pulled at its chains quickly reminding me of its presence.

"Enough!" Hook spat back at the croc. He came toward me with a handful of clothes and dropped them on the bed.

"Get dressed and meet me on deck. Make haste. We've reached the veil."

I took a moment to let it sink in. We have reached the veil. I was almost home. Hook had brought me a pair of tight fitting pants and a V neck shirt, much like the one he had been wearing. I quickly dressed and made my way through the door.

Hook stood at the mast in the center of the ship while his crew scurried about. Standing by his side was an imposing man. His muscled arms were heavily tattooed, and the scowl on his bearded face gave me the impression he would rather be somewhere else.

"My love, this is Lucius. He will be your escort through the veil."

"Wait, what? I thought *you* were bringing me across the veil."

"This is the end of the line for me, my love. Faerie dust does not agree with me, and furthermore, a captain never leaves his ship."

"Madam." Lucius bowed his head and kissed my hand. "I am Lucius, 7th Son of Artos, Prince of the Second Realm. It will be my honor to escort you home," he said with distaste in his voice.

Hook chuckled under his breath. "A hefty title for the runt of the litter." The runt of the litter? This guy was huge. What an odd thing to say.

"Pleasure to meet you, Gwendolyn Mary Darling Carlisle, of London, England."

Hook stepped forward, brushing Lucius off to the side. He wrapped his hook around my waist and whispered in my ear. "Are you sure you don't want to spend eternity sailing the universe as my Queen?"

"I can't," was all I could say.

"As you wish." He pulled back, releasing me from his embrace. "Lucius, it's time. Take the girl home. Smee! The faerie dust."

Smee appeared, as if out of nowhere, carrying a small lantern and presented it to Hook. He popped the latch and reached in, pulling out a small pixie. She dangled from his hook by her bound wrists, her eyes downcast. I stared at Hook in shock.

"Don't fret, my love. Like you, she enjoys being tied up. She has but to fly away, whenever she so chooses. You know, pixies are naughty creatures." He smirked at me and raised an eyebrow. I watched as he spanked her behind and a trail of faerie dust fell into Lucius's outstretched hand. I was appalled, intrigued and aroused all at the same time. I knew then that Hook had brought to life a part of me that I might never be able to hide.

"Can I have my knives back now?" I asked, not even giving him the pleasure of a response to the display he'd just put on.

I squirmed under his intense scrutiny. I knew he could easily deny me, and what recourse would I have? But I desperately wanted my knives back. Not even for their protection, but as a memento of my time in Neverland.

They had been Eben's at one time and somehow, I felt like being able to hold them in my hands would bring me closer to him— to all of them.

Hook nodded at Smee. Like the dog he was, he pulled out the small bundle of knives, and shoved them into my chest so hard that I had to take a step back to keep my balance.

"Thanks," I said sarcastically at Smee. "I guess this is goodbye then. Thanks for everything, James Hook."

"It's been my *pleasure*." He accentuated the word pleasure and I felt a chill run down my spine. He bowed to me. "Gwendolyn Mary Darling Carlisle."

Our goodbye felt overly formal after what had happened between us. I mean I had just been naked in his wicked arms only a few hours ago. From enemies, to lovers, to strangers in a matter of moments. I guess I shouldn't have expected anything different. He had offered me a quid pro quo and I had accepted. I had used my body to get something I needed, and I'd liked it. What kind of woman did that make me?

Lucius grabbed my hand and led me to the edge of the ship. "It will be night time once we cross over. You better keep your shit together." He held out his hand and blew a cloud of faerie dust in my face.

CHAPTER XXII
THROUGH THE VEIL

Lucius and I lifted gracefully from the deck of the Jolly Roger. I'd had to compartmentalize my mind to handle everything I was feeling and still hold onto a happy thought in order to make flight possible. Lucius was not shy with his displeasure when it took several attempts for me to come up with a happy thought. With his pissy attitude, I had to wonder what the hell his happy thought was.

"I'm fucking working on it!" I snapped at him. "I don't have a lot of shit to be happy about at the moment. Give me a goddamn break."

He had thrown his hands up in frustration and paced back and forth on the deck while he waited for me. I wondered what Hook had on the prince, because I was damn sure he hadn't signed up for the task of returning me home.

It was bittersweet as I watched the Jolly Roger fade into the distance, becoming nothing more than a fleck of sand on the great expanse of the ocean below. I had come to terms with leaving, at least that's what I was telling myself. But now that it was actually happening... it felt almost unbearable.

My traitorous heart pined for my Lost Boys and for Peter. Even though they had betrayed me, I couldn't just flip a switch and turn off my feelings. I knew in my heart of hearts that, for a moment, I had loved them and it was like rubbing salt in exposed wounds. My depression was accompanied by an avalanche of guilt. Guilt over leaving my sister, guilt over my own selfishness, guilt that I'd had sex with Hook, the very arch nemesis of the boys I'd thought I was in love with only yesterday.

The universe's plan to destroy me was almost complete. I had envisioned myself returning home, carrying the memories of my true loves. Memories that I could pull out during desperate times, to relive the joy they'd brought me. Instead I was left with a gaping hole where my heart had once been. I only had tainted memories to bring back with me. My spirit felt tired. How much could one person take?

I wondered how much of what Hook had told me was

the truth, because my gut instinct told me I couldn't completely trust everything he'd said. Of course my libido was fanning herself just thinking of the insanely hot sex I'd had with him, and it was telling my gut to shut the fuck up! I guess the only thing I had to bring back with me was some seriously amazing sexual encounters.

I'm not sure if that was a good thing or not, seeing as now, all I had to satisfy myself was operated by double A batteries. No earthly man would ever compare. I needed to write men off altogether after this experience. If only I could just turn myself into a lesbian. If only it worked that way.

As we sailed through clouds in what should have been a most thrilling and spectacular adventure across the veil, my mind drifted to the letter I had left for Peter and the boys. Would Hook make good on his promise and deliver it to them? It was kind of pointless to ponder the idea, because I would never know the outcome and thinking about it seemed like a useless act of futility. But I hoped that he would. I decided to believe that he would, so that I could give myself at least a little bit of closure.

I was able to say my piece in that letter. I had poured my love, anger and sadness into that letter. I looked for that small box inside my mind and spent a long time mentally placing all of my feelings for all of my boys, and even some feelings for Hook that I'd tried to deny, and placed them securely in that box. And then I put chains and locks on it and then welded that fucker closed. I threw that damned thing into the dark recesses of my mind. It was the only coping mechanism I had to keep myself sane.

Distraction was key right now. I began to focus on Mic. My mind was much clearer as we left Neverland behind and I could now easily pull details of my former life. What condition would she be in when I got home? We had never been away from each other for any length of time. For me, it had only been a few days. But if Hook was to be believed, then it could have been months for Mic.

I tried desperately not to feel guilty about it, because I'd had no clue. Fucking Peter! That was probably the thing I was the most angry about. A part of me knew deep down that I might have decided to stay regardless of the change in time, but I wish I had known. He should have told me, given me the chance to decide for myself.

I began to establish some life changing plans that I would act on as soon as I got back to London. First things first. I needed to sell that damn house. I couldn't live there without it bringing back memories. I couldn't bear to face those memories on a daily basis. The house was worth a fortune, even in its dilapidated condition. I would sell it and move somewhere far away and take Mic with me. We would find the best cancer specialists in the world and I would figure everything out. I needed a fresh start.

The planning gave my mind a purpose finally and I felt the first wave of relief wash over me. It felt good to feel like I might actually have some control over my life. I mean really, I was in a tailspin and plummeting to the ground, on the brink of complete catastrophe, but that little bit of control kept me going.

As I was consumed by my planning, I hardly noticed as the scenery changed around me, leaving the open seas behind and giving way to the hustle and bustle of the city. The bright lights of Big Ben were like a beacon, guiding me home and my heart leapt in my throat. I couldn't wait to see Mic now. We were so close and the anticipation coursed through me. If anyone could help me make sense of the last few days, it would be her.

Would she even believe me or would she be calling me a shrink straight away? No... she would believe me. She was always my cheerleader— always on my side. She would be the only person I would ever be able to tell. I had to start getting some kind of story together to cover my ass for my long absence, but that could wait.

Lucius led the way and it struck me as odd that he knew exactly which way to go without even asking me or consulting a map. Should anything really surprise me anymore after all the magical crazy shit I'd seen over the last few days?

My heart squeezed in my chest when my family home came into view. It felt as though an entire lifetime had passed since I'd left. It was still my childhood home, but the house seemed to have a whole new meaning now. This had been Wendy Darling's home— where the love story had started between her and Peter. I knew I couldn't live here anymore. My childhood memories were now replaced by the tormenting thoughts of Peter and my Lost Boys. If it wasn't for Michaela, I'm not sure if I would have ever returned.

Lucius stopped and hovered in front of the window where it had all begun. I slowly came up behind him, excited to be home but anxious for what I might find there. I absently grasped at my necklaces for reassurance. The acorn kiss from Peter was now joined by my mother's locket and the paired necklaces somehow kept me grounded.

I glanced at Lucius before looking in the window myself, studying him for some cues at what I might find there. His eyes flashed for a moment, looking animalistic in the moonlight. Then his typical pissed off scowl seemed to soften, and his face looked almost peaceful as he gazed through my window. I couldn't hold back any longer and looked for myself. Michaela laid sleeping on my bed. Her frail form was curled around my pillow. Her head was wrapped in a scarf to cover her bald scalp and she wore comfy sweatpants that hung from her bones. She looked so much worse than the last time I'd seen her.

Hook had been right. Goddamn it, the one time I desperately wanted to be lied to by a man. Why did it have to be this, that he had been honest with me about? I watched as a young woman I'd never seen before came into the room. She was dressed in white nursing scrubs and carried a water glass with a small cup full of pills.

"Who is that? What is she doing to her?" Lucius

grumbled, his whole body tensed as he watched the woman walk over to Mic in the bed.

"It's fine, I think she's a home health nurse," I said, trying to calm him down, but feeling instantly concerned myself. She placed the pills on the bedside table and pulled the blankets over Mic before dimming the lights and closing the door.

"Thanks for getting me home. I think I can take it from here," I said, trying to get rid of him, so I could have my reunion with my sister. I didn't want an audience to watch us ugly cry over our time apart.

"Who is she?" he asked, still not taking his eyes from Mic.

"She's my sister," I answered, staring blankly at him. I couldn't for the life of me understand why he was showing so much interest.

"She's so beautiful. What's her name?"

I shot him a peculiar look. Michaela was absolutely stunning, but her illness had taken its toll on her body, leaving a shell of the woman she once was. "Her name is Michaela, and she's sick, so just back down over there buddy," I chided. Was it something about this house, this window and the women that lived here that attracted supernatural men?

"What's wrong with her?" he asked, looking at me with desperation.

"Listen Lu, whatever you're thinking right now— she is off limits. She is too frail to deal with the likes of you. So just put that right out of your mind. I appreciate that you brought me home, but I need you to leave now. Go report back to Hook that I've returned safely and hopefully he'll let you off on whatever it is that you owe him." I was a little more harsh with him than I intended, but I needed to get him to leave. He scowled at me and I think I most definitely hit a nerve with my comments.

"Tell her that I asked about her and I'll go."

"Yeah, yeah," I said as I brushed him off.

"No, promise me you'll tell her," he said sternly, grabbing my arm in an iron grip.

I was speechless for a moment, not sure what to make of his unusual behavior. But I didn't need to deal with crazy, fucked up men right now. I'd had enough of that already. So I decided to placate him, knowing he wouldn't leave until I agreed.

"Yes, I promise I will tell her. Now will you please go."

"For what it's worth, love makes you do some irrational, fucked up shit. That's true even for Peter and his Lost Boys."

I scoffed at him as he turned and left, taking one last longing look at Mic before he disappeared into the night. What the fuck had he meant by that? Who was he to speak about love? I'd bet my life that this asshole had never experienced love before. Ugh! I hated the ridiculous way that men made you analyze everything. I didn't need his cryptic words now. It was worth absolutely jack shit to me. Fuck that! I needed to focus on Mic. She needed me, she needed all of my attention right now.

I opened the window, thrilled to find that it wasn't locked shut. I rushed to her bedside and knelt slowly beside the bed, not wanting to startle her. I knew I had only been gone for a few days, but now that I was here with Mic, the days apart really did feel like months. I gently placed my hand over hers and took her skeletal hand into mine, rubbing my thumb over her cold fingers. Her sunken eyes twitched and fluttered open. She blinked several times as she came awake. Her head tilted to the side as she pursed her lips, her eyes staring straight at me. She opened her mouth as if to speak but nothing came out. Her brows pulled together as she took a cleansing breath.

"Am I dead?" Her eyes widened. "Oh god! Are you dead, Gwen?" Mic's voice was full of emotion. But she was more concerned about me being dead than over herself being dead.

"No, you're not dead and you're not dreaming. I'm here. I'm back."

The words rushed out and it was hard for me to keep the emotion out of them as my voice trembled. She stared at me inquisitively for a moment, running her hands up my arms and cupping my cheeks as if needing to feel my solid form for herself to believe that I was real.

"It's really you? You're really here, I can't believe it!" she cried and then pulled me in for a hug. Her small frame heaved in sobs and my own emotions came pouring out of me as well. I could no longer hold the tears back. We cried in each other's arms for a long time, not speaking. No words could express what the tears could.

She finally pulled away from me, looking at me with her red swollen eyes. "Are you okay, Gwen? Where have you been?"

I took a deep sigh as I prepared myself for how the hell I was going to explain all of this.

"Let me put on some tea. It's a long story."

I woke up early the next morning and started preparing a proper English breakfast. Mic had lost so much weight since I'd been gone that I needed to fatten her up. We had been up half the night as I'd laid out the whole story for her. She had listened in rapt interest, hanging on my every word. And just as I had expected, she had believed every word of it, not even a hint of disbelief on her face. It had been cathartic to finally share my story with someone I knew I could trust. It was like a weight had been lifted off of my shoulders. I actually felt optimistic, which was a surprise. I even put on some music and danced around the kitchen as I cooked.

Mic joined me as I was finishing up the meal. I settled her in Dad's old chair with blankets and a cup of her favorite tea.

"So, I was thinking... We should probably look into selling this old house. I think we could get a great price on it. I'm going to do some research after breakfast to see what cancer specialist we can get you in with." I started spewing out the plans that I had been concocting, needing to give myself some purpose.

"Gwen, stop," her stark tone pulled me up short.

"You need to go back."

"What? What the hell are you talking about? I just got back. I'm not going anywhere. I'm here to take care of you until you get better, then we can enroll in university and—"

"No, Gwen, no! Are you looking at me?" she shouted at me and stood from her chair, her weak form swaying with the gravity of her emotions. "Are you even seeing me right now? I am dying, right before your eyes, right now and you cannot ignore it anymore!" She was so angry and I didn't know what to say.

"I am not taking any more treatments. There is nothing left to try. The doctors say I have a few more months if I'm lucky. I'm on Hospice now. You can't deny it anymore, sweetie," her tone softened as tears began to fall down my cheeks.

"I don't believe it."

"It doesn't matter if you believe it or not, you can't change it. But what you can change is what you're going to do moving forward, and I think you need to go back."

"You obviously weren't listening when I told you that they betrayed me! Peter wanted to keep me as a pet, and the others just wanted to use me before they sent me back!"

"I was listening and I was watching you relive your time with them. You love them, and it sounded like they loved you, too. Did you ever think that maybe you let your fears taint your rational thinking? You never gave them a chance to explain everything. You just left."

Her body wavered again and she had to catch herself on the arm of the chair. I rushed over to her and helped her back into the chair. I kneeled in front of her and placed my arms over her legs.

"I needed to come back here to be with you. My place is here with you, so it was pointless to go back and hash it out with them. It was only a fantasy that couldn't last, there was no need to prolong it."

"You know, you deserve to be happy. It's alright to let yourself be happy. Seems like you started to be in Neverland, but you got in your own way. I have my path and I've accepted that. Now you need to follow your heart. You have to find a way to go back."

EPILOGUE
-PETER-

I couldn't control the anger that had consumed my soul. It surged through me as I destroyed the arms cellar that had once been my home with Wendy. The darkness, that lay in the deepest depths of my soul, had stirred and was growing in my chest. This was the consequence I'd been so afraid of— the consequence for allowing myself to love her.

Now, I was blind to the rage. I wasn't thinking rationally. I could only process the emotions of losing Gwen and it manifested into utter violence. My hands bled from the destruction I'd caused but I didn't care. The pain was actually a welcome feeling. The place was a mess, weapons strewn upon the floor, shelving tipped over. Tripp and Ry had stood stoic, the dim flickering light of the torches casting dark shadows on their forlorn faces. They had watched in silence as I had fallen into complete madness.

Eben dropped in through one of the stumps and I froze, the only movement coming from my heavy breathing. This is who I'd been waiting for. My muscles flexed and I charged at him, throwing him against the cavernous wall. My bloodied hand wrapped around his throat and I had to reign in my anger, lest I break his neck right now. Eben let me pin him against the wall, the fight in him completely gone. His hands wrapped around my forearm as I increased the pressure I had around his throat.

"You betrayed me, Eben," I snarled, my voice sounding feral and the resounding thunder outside reiterated my anger.

"I never betrayed you, Peter."

"Fuck that. You left her! I put her protection in your hands and you let her get taken by the enemy. You betrayed me," I accused as I stared into his dark eyes. My hand tightened around his throat. I knew I was cutting off his air and yet he did nothing to stop me.

"Peter!" Tripp yelled at me. "Let him say his truth," he commanded, growing a pair of balls for the first time and challenging me.

He was in my face then and Ryder was right behind him, the two of them asserting their intention to stop me if I meant to kill Eben right here and now. I pulled back, giving Eben a chance to speak. If I was going to get Gwen back, I needed to know what happened. Eben pulled in a few ragged breaths after I released him.

"Alright, tell me why. Why the fuck did you leave her?"

"Lill… Lill came to me." He coughed and sputtered for a moment before continuing. "She told me Silas was injured. I owed her a debt. She couldn't bring him back to the village on her own. She called in her debt and asked me to bring him back. I thought Gwen would be safe with Tiger Lily for the short time it took me to bring him back to the village," he confessed. There wasn't much conviction in his voice. It was obvious that he regretted his decision and I laughed.

"I don't give a shit what your excuse is, you never should have trusted that someone else would protect her."

"Oh, so now you don't trust Tiger Lily?"

"Well, thanks to you, I don't fucking trust anyone!"

"You think I didn't want to protect her? I fucking love her too, Peter! Don't you dare think you're the only one of us who loves her," Eben seethed.

He had no clue what she meant to me. He'd left her to help save one of Lill's many sexual partners. Did he think that was a good enough excuse for leaving her unprotected? She was my world and I would be damned if I was going to let her go now. I wouldn't leave her to the depravity of what Hook had in store for her. She was mine and I would get her back. I had to get to the bottom of this. I needed to know what happened last night.

"Where is Lill now? Where is Silas? I need to talk to them."

"Silas was gravely injured. He hasn't woken yet and I don't know where Lill is."

"We need to go after Hook. This cannot stand. We need to get her back. Eben, you need to—"

We were interrupted when a bruised and battered Tiger Lily appeared from one of the various tree trunk entrances. She was hunched over, favoring her right side, her face swollen and covered in bruises. She was drenched from the downpour outside. The enormity of my emotions had brought a damned monsoon upon Neverland and gave no indication it would be letting up anytime soon.

The Pixie Elders were right behind her, followed by Nico, the eldest of the prince brothers and leader of the beasts. The entire Neverland Council was present, which almost never happened

"Peter, we must talk about this daughter of Wendy issue," Tiger Lily said. "Your... err, distractions have come to the Council's attention and must be addressed."

"Addressed? You let Hook take my girl! There is nothing to be discussed besides your incompetence," I spat at her, not even trying to hide my irritation.

"Peter, this has gone beyond just you and me. Regardless of what you think, I did my best to protect her. She wanted to leave with the pirates. She betrayed us all. I know you don't want to hear this but it must be said."

"You're a lying bitch! Gwen would never side with Hook." My filter had completely disappeared. I couldn't be reasonable, even with Tiger Lily,. I knew Gwen and she would never betray us. There was something terribly off here.

"Peter!" the Pixie Elders tinkled their condemnation at me. "You must control yourself and look upon the evidence rationally. Tiger Lily, who is an esteemed member of this Council, has given testimony to the contrary. You must consider this over and above your personal feelings."

"Agreed," Nico seconded. That bastard never showed up unless it was dire circumstances. How the fuck was Gwen's abduction dire circumstances to the Neverland beasts?

"I don't give a fuck about what you have to say. I'm going after her."

"We need to vote on this," Tiger Lily said.

"Vote? There is nothing to vote on. She is a prisoner of Hook. We have to save her."

"Not so fast, Peter," the Pixie Elders said in unison. "Tiger Lily was present when she was taken. You can see with your own eyes that she has been beaten. She confirmed that this daughter of Wendy went willingly with the pirates. She was destined to return beyond the veil after May Day anyway, so the expected outcome has been achieved. We must consider the facts and come to a vote."

"A vote! You have to be fucking kidding me!"

"This is no laughing matter, Peter. You are obviously too emotionally attached to make sound judgement, but we will allow you to cast a vote anyway. So, who votes in favor to rescue the daughter of Wendy?" Tiger Lily began the formal vote for the Neverland Council.

I rushed to be the first to cast my vote. "I vote yea," I stated matter of factly, hoping to set the tone for how the rest of the Council would vote.

"I vote nay," Nico stated firmly.

"We also vote nay," the Pixie Elders said in unison.

"What the fuck!" Ryder interrupted, his emotions getting the better of him. "Are you seriously going to leave her in Hooks hands? You know what terrible things he might do to her!"

"Pan, get your man under control. He has no voice on this Council and if he wishes to remain present, then he will hold his tongue," Nico said in disdain.

I placed my hand on Ryder's chest as he made a go at Nico.

"But, Pan, we're talking about Hen. You love her," Ryder pleaded. As if he needed to remind me of the gravity of the situation.

"Love? *Ha*! What does Peter Pan know of love? His own mother didn't even love him," Tiger Lily seethed. "This is nothing more than a boyish obsession, but it ends here. No more Wendy's! The only love you should ever know is the love of duty. *Your* duty is as a pillar of Neverland. End of story!" she proclaimed, standing righteous in her comments.

"Let me handle this, Ry," I said firmly, trying my best to reign in my explosive temper. Her words cut deep into my soul, but now wasn't the time to start a war of words with her. Ryder finally backed down, but I could see the tension on his face. His jaw was clenched and his fists were balled at his sides.

The tie vote came to Tiger Lily. I looked, imploringly, at her. Tiger Lily had always been my friend and I needed her support now more than ever. But her callous comments festered in my brain. Had I ever seen this side of her? Had I ever really seen her clearly?

"Peter, I cannot condone this type of behavior. We all must keep Neverland's best interest at heart and this daughter of Wendy has tainted your mind. I have to vote nay." Tiger Lily effectively destroyed any friendship I'd thought we'd had. Every fucking person I knew was betraying me. I couldn't trust anyone.

"The Neverland Council has ruled. There shall be no rescue of the daughter of Wendy, for she has chosen her own path. So shall it be," the Pixie Elders proclaimed.

"So shall it be!" Tiger Lily and Nico, said in unison. Effectively solidifying the will of the Neverland Council.

"And if I refuse to follow this edict?"

"We have voted and if you go against the Council we will throw the entire weight of fae magic against you and your Lost Boys. We will not tolerate a defector within our midst," Tiger Lily said coldly. It was as if I didn't know her at all. As though we hadn't been friends— hadn't been intimate with each other.

"Do you understand, Peter?" Tiger Lily asked, straightening to her full height. Despite her pain she was showing a display of power, trying to reign me in before the Council dissolved.

"I understand that I have given everything to Neverland and now her Council has betrayed me."

"The Council has spoken, Peter. You will abide or you will force our hand. It is that simple. We will be watching," the Pixie Elders said and it was a dismissal. There would be no further discussion and the Council began to disperse into the storm that continued to rage outside.

I knew that I could never abide by their decree. I needed a plan. I would pull in every favor owed to me. I would not stop until I had Gwen safe by my side.

"Alright boys," I said once we were officially alone. "I'm drawing a line in the sand. Either you're with me or you're not. I'm giving you an out. If you're not with me, then get the fuck out."

TO BE CONTINUED. . .

The Neverland Chronicles

-Prequel-

-Volume I-

-Volume II-

-Volume III-

TSKinleyBooks.com

ABOUT THE AUTHOR

T. S. Kinley is a passion project created by two sisters with a shared obsession and vision. We came together with the dream of creating something beautiful, imaginative, and yes... SEXY. *Once Upon a Time...* it all began with sisterly gossip about erotica and romance novels. Our conversations quickly became fantasies about our own desires to author such work. We would muse how some day in a utopian future, our fantasy would become reality. Ultimately we decided rather than wait for the future to find us, we would create utopia ourselves. Using our love of books, natural gift of creativity, and some savvy study on publishing itself, the concept for our very first book was born. We started off as a Cosmetologist and an RN, and quickly developed into a dynamic writing team with a style that lends a unique perspective to our books.

If you haven't signed up already, please subscribe to the T.S. Kinley newsletter.

Receive exclusive sneak peeks on new releases, contests and other spicy content.

Visit www.TSKinleyBooks.com and sign up today!

Follow T.S. Kinley on social media. Let's be friends! Check out our Instagram, Facebook, Pinterest, and Tic Tok pages and get insights into the beautifully, complicated mind of not one, but two authors! You have questions, something you are dying to know about the amazing characters we've created? Join us online, we love to engage with our readers!

AUTHOR

Made in the USA
Monee, IL
21 April 2025

16130818R00218